PRAISE FOR *DEADLINE*

"A thrilling whodunit! I found myself turning p
to its highly satisfying and humdinger of an en
storytelling and razor-sharp dialogue will make you yearn for more—and the good news is you can immediately satisfy that craving by diving into his sequel, *Dangerous Inspiration*."

Gina Vild
Author of *The Two Most Important Days,
How to Find your Purpose and Live a Happier, Healthier Life*

"I loved this book! Detective Ronan Mezini uniquely perceives the world through crossed sensory pathways. The novel blends a gripping mystery with deep explorations of justice and truth, culminating in an enticing ending that left me longing for more."

Louise Carter
Communications Executive, Sydney, Australia

"A masterwork: The type of mystery that makes headlines—with a detective so hard-boiled you can almost taste his thoughts."

Scott Duke Kominers
Sarofim-Rock Professor, Harvard Business School

"Greg Stone has a talent for bringing to life the characters of his beloved Boston, and one is quickly drawn into the world of journalists and detectives who push forward this fast-paced novel. Detective Manzini is a smart and entertaining narrator, and the story—built around a series of unsolved murders—grips you and keeps you reading. Stone, a former Boston journalist, has a talent for the everyday details and language that take a reader into his world."

Carlos Alvarenga
Author of *The Rules of Persuasion*

"*Deadline on Arrival*, Greg Stone's new detective thriller, is a page turner that had me reading it non-stop from start to finish. Stone smoothly develops his plot, sense of place and vivid characters. Stylishly written with all the twists and turns of a master of the genre."

Sonia Goldenberg
Documentary filmmaker and *New York Times* columnist

PRAISE FOR *DANGEROUS INSPIRATION*

"Imagine a bunch of strangers, a secret which binds them, then follow the colours of perception and you'll have the sort of *Dangerous Inspiration* Agatha Christie would have created."

Andrea Purgatori
Journalist and author of *Four Little Oysters*

"*Dangerous Inspiration* is a 'whodunit' that draws its roots from a different era, but takes place firmly in today's world. In fact, it's a lot like its wry and amusing protagonist. This book is smart, but not pedantic. It is observant, but it doesn't drown you in details. And it works just as well with a beer as it does with a nice cup of tea. But don't think that means that you'll be putting it down."

Steve Schlozman, MD
Author of *The Zombie Autopsies*

"Gripping from the outset … a good old whodunnit!"

Jenna Ward
Professor at Coventry University
and Director of the Art of Management & Organization

"Ronan Mezini is a hard-boiled ex-detective who likes philosophy, Shakespeare, good red wine and complicated women. He's trying to write a book at an artist's retreat in Vermont but gets caught up in a series of murders committed during a wild storm. Mezini likes to talk to himself, and his often hilarious soliloquies keep this whodunit moving from beginning to end."

F. James Pensiero
Deputy Managing Editor (Retired), *The Wall Street Journal*

"Avid mystery buffs (like myself) will instantly recognize the familiar (and beloved) tropes of *Dangerous Inspiration*, a classic homage to Christie and her ilk: a group of strangers summoned to an isolated location, their psychological unveiling during the ensuing mayhem, and the final denouement which reveals all. Within this construct, and with many winks to it throughout, Greg Stone has created a memorable group of quirky characters. Events quickly unfold in this action packed story with twists and turns leading to an unexpected resolution. I thoroughly enjoyed it!"

Ina Saltz
Professor Emeritus, The City College of New York
Author and Content Creator, LinkedIn Learning

DEADLINE ON ARRIVAL

THE PREQUEL TO *DANGEROUS INSPIRATION*

A Ronan Mezini Mystery

GREG STONE

copyright © 2024 by Greg Stone

All rights reserved.

No part of this book may be reproduced or transmitted in any form or by any means, electronic or mechanical, except for the purpose of review and/or reference, without explicit permission in writing from the publisher.

Cover artwork design copyright © 2024 by Design by Definition
daniellefine.com.com

Published by Paper Angel Press
paperangelpress.com

ISBN 978-1-962538-91-6 (Trade Paperback)

10 9 8 7 6 5 4 3 2 1

FIRST EDITION

To Mary, Lauren, and Jack, with all my love

Cast of Characters

Ronan Mezini, a literate homicide detective gifted with synesthesia

Staff at *The Boston Observer*:

    Ollie Burns, a tenacious investigative reporter

    Amy Stout, an equally persistent police reporter

    Jan Watkins, Ollie's boss, a wounded editor

    Anika Mehta, an entertainment reporter who thinks she's in show biz herself

    Kenny Moran, a rather "inventive" columnist

    Paul Green, the hardnosed Managing Editor

    Elias Olson, a sarcastic tech guru

    Oscar Sosa, a comical sports editor

    Nico Lyons, an intellectual business editor

    Caleb Baird, a former book reviewer

Ollie's Aunt Jessica

Mezini's Aunt Eleanor

Troy Carr, Amy's boyfriend, the consummate PR counselor

Liam Terrell, an investor from Fast Accurate Complete Truth

Aldous Denby, a private equity investor from Persephone

Josh Salinas, an anti-media activist

Brent Garner, an SEC attorney and Mezini's old friend

Michael Cronin, Cambridge Police Chief

Dr. Jack Grimes, an expert on serial killers

Johnny Garlowe, Mezini's former partner on the homicide beat

Prologue

I HAVE ALWAYS HAD a complicated relationship with my so-called life. For all of my thirty years, I have had a condition called synesthesia, which makes the senses cross over. (That's a tough word, I know. It's pronounced sin-es-THEE-zia.) In some ways I can "see" sounds with my eyes. For instance, when I hear an annoying person speak, his voice might appear to me as a red, jagged ray of light. On the other hand, a smooth Mozart melody looks like an inviting, blue river. Sometimes I experience words as flavors, or numbers as various colors.

It's like living in a movie with special effects all day long, kind of a multimedia mélange. I was pretty moody as a kid. Once word got around about my, uh, differences, my classmates mocked me and often treated me like a freak.

As you might guess, I had trouble in school. By the way, I grew up in the northern part of Cambridge in Massachusetts, close to Harvard on the map, but in other respects as far away as Mozambique. I was always a voracious reader, but I'd often brood in my own private realm with architecture of my own creation. In math class, thanks to my synesthesia, I would readily see equations in swirling graphics in front of me, but coming up with the correct answer to a simple algebra problem was practically impossible. If I had gone to the school nurse, she would have probably had me committed as psychotic.

One day in fourth grade a teacher named George Christo asked me to explain the Declaration of Independence, and I said it reminded me of a ham sandwich with spicy dressing. Displaying the sadism that was prevalent at the time in parochial schools, he taunted me. "Do you realize that you're a flake?" he said. His words were doubly scary because he was built like a linebacker.

When the kids laughed, Christo just stood there smiling. And so it came to pass that "Flake" became my nickname.

One day three older kids cornered me in the hallway. "Hey, weirdo," one of them said. "What color are these fists? Do they look purple to you?" Then he backhanded me across the face. I wriggled free and tried to elbow him under his chin. That just made him angry. All three of them punched me in the gut, in the eyes, everywhere. I almost blacked out.

Oddly, it was Christo who rescued me. He threw the kids on the floor and told them to get up and wait for him in his office. I don't know if he congratulated them or punished them. After this, he suddenly had greater respect for me. "At least you tried to fight back, Flake Boy," he said.

An English teacher in high school, kind old Richard Baker, was the only one who understood me. He encouraged me to use my "visions," as he called them, for inspiration. "You're a born writer," he'd say. I try to keep his words in mind to nullify the thousands of insults from other adults and kids who called me weird, crazy, or just plain stupid. Unfortunately, college was never part of my vocabulary. I just assumed that I'd never be able to stop brooding long enough to study in a disciplined way.

Writing has always been especially tough for me. Bear in mind that you can create just about every piece of music from 88 keys on the piano, and that's hard enough. But writing is another challenge altogether. The English language has some 170,000 words, though most people use only 10,000 to 40,000 of them in their lifetimes. The choices are overwhelming. It doesn't take much to turn genius into drivel.

I should have mentioned that my name is Ronan Mezini, known as "Mez" to my friends. I'm a homicide detective in Cambridge, Massachusetts.

My family may have been uneducated, but they were brilliant. My dad's family was Albanian and Italian, and my mom's was Irish. There were no college grads in the house though there were plenty of books. As you'll notice, I pepper my remarks with a lot of cultural references. I'm not showing off. It's just the way I think. Like Lincoln, I educated myself simply by reading. Books never insulted me, unlike many people I knew.

I think of my synesthesia as a gift rather than a disorder, sort of a low-level superpower. I'm in good company. Many famous people, living and dead, have had the condition, among them Marilyn Monroe, Einstein, Van Gogh, Beyoncé, Stevie Wonder, and Billy Joel. Even Beethoven, whose music has kept me sane in many ways. He said that the key of D minor was orange and B minor was black. In a strange way, I can see what he meant.

Even with my, uh, eccentric mind, I promise to be a reliable narrator. I may be subjective—aren't we all?—but I swear I'm accurate. All the information you're about to read came from characters I came to know quite well as a detective.

Nothing I had experienced before could have prepared me for this situation.

As Henry James might have said, we'll turn the screw one more time as we start a bizarre and inexplicable story.

1

BLOOD AND PRESSURE

Present Day, May

IT WAS LATE AFTERNOON in the newsroom at *The Boston Observer*, the city's leading newspaper. Sitting at her desk in the investigative unit's office, Ollie Burns heard a forceful knock on her closed door. "Come see me," editor Paul Green shouted, as he walked away. His strident voice trailed behind him. She could see him receding through the small glass window in her door.

Ollie sighed, logged out of her computer and closed the door—standard procedure at the I-Desk to foil prying eyes. As she crossed the newsroom to Paul's office, she reacted to the curious glances of her coworkers in their cubicles with an eye roll. Though the number of writers and editors had dwindled because of the downturn in the journalism business, she still felt the impact of the stares from the remaining thirty or so colleagues.

It was 4:00 PM and reporters were frantically typing, struggling to generate accurate copy with enough flair to hold the readers' interest. Many of them were mumbling to themselves, trying to craft their stories out loud. It's a challenge to write creatively while staying within the four walls of the facts. Not an easy task, yet reporters do it several times a day.

It was a safe bet that Paul Green would be belligerent, and probably for no reason, Ollie thought. She reminded herself that her team had won two Pulitzers in recent years. One for a series on sexual assaults by high school guidance counselors, and another about accidents with assault rifles at gun shows—one causing the death of a child.

Ollie was about 5' 9", with long limbs. She was all vertical lines, yet her face was as round as an apple. That, coupled with ginger hair and freckles radiated innocence, an impression undercut by expressionless blue eyes.

Though most of the reporters at *The Observer* avoided Paul, Ollie enjoyed jousting with him. He ruled by intimidation, and she respected that, to a point. As deadlines approached and tensions rose, his immediate reaction was to yell. At high volume. In between sneezes, that is. He was allergic to just about everything—dust, pollen, mold—and he had never heard of the elbow cough. He snorted into his palm instead and constantly sniffled. He always kept an abundant supply of tissues in his pockets, just in case.

He claimed he was willing to listen. But whenever reporters suggested a new idea or had the audacity to disagree with him, he'd shut them down immediately. He was a Republican in a liberal business and prided himself on trying to keep the news neutral, at least within the margins of his very subjective notion of objectivity.

Paul's favorite expressions were "C'mawn," meant as a motivator, or "How can you hate life?" on the rare occasions when he was satisfied. He had been, in his day, a good police reporter. It had been a long time since he ventured out onto the street to *create* a story from scratch. It was much easier to stay inside, bark at the staff, and scare everyone into submission.

What is it now? Ollie wondered, as she headed to his office. Her recent story about sleazy money managers brought in more comments than a supermarket selling rotten turkeys at Thanksgiving. *What does he expect? A daily blockbuster? That jerk never did an investigative piece in his life. Ease up, girl,* she said to herself. *You're overheating.*

"You rang?" Ollie asked flippantly as she stood at the threshold of Paul's office, which had a glass wall overlooking the newsroom.

"Close the door and sit down," he commanded.

"Aye, aye, Chief," she said as she complied.

"Don't call me Chief. Burns, do you have any idea why I called you in?"

"To offer me a raise and an extra two weeks of vacation?"

"Not funny. I want to discuss my *expectations*. Do you know what distinguishes an I-Desk story from a normal one?"

"Something you like to read," she joked with a calculated sneer. *Jousting was the best policy with a wild animal*, she thought.

"Uncovering substantial wrongdoing. That's what makes the I-Desk special." He repeated, "Uncovering substantial wrongdoing. That's what wins awards."

"And haven't we done that?" Ollie asked, in as neutral a manner as possible.

"Singles, doubles, no home runs, lately." He thrust his chin forward, as he always did whenever he fell into his default mode as a bully.

Ollie wasn't having it. "Are you kidding me? What about the article about the corrupt brokers? Remember that guy who said, 'You have to churn and burn to earn?' He and his team were buying and selling stocks left and right on behalf of the clients, just to generate commissions—"

"That story affected very few people, and only rich ones at that. I want something that hits everybody."

Ollie just stared at him, the best way to counter his aggression. She even tilted her head back so her chin would stick out, mimicking his posture.

"Why the fuck are you staring at me, Burns? Do you think that's going to calm me down?"

She got up and started to walk out.

"Sit down," he yelled. Then, realizing he had gone too far, he added, "Please."

Again, she complied and sat down stiffly. "Don't bark at me like a rabid dog, Paul."

"I'm saying," he said with enforced calm, "that the I-Desk is famous for sledgehammer stories. And you're supposed to be the most aggressive reporter on the team. Just make sure the next story will be the main topic of conversation all around the city."

Deadline on Arrival

"That's like telling a chef to make the most delicious meal ever. Why are you talking to *me* about this, anyway? Why not Jan?" She was referring to her boss, Jan Watkins. "This is what I'd call a 'skip-level' review."

"I'll speak to her too, don't worry," he said as she turned away.

Walking back to her desk, Ollie could feel anger simmering, rattling the lid of her control. Thanks to the new "open" design in the newsroom, which the staff hated, the partitions on the cubicles were just 18 inches higher than the desks. Not much visual privacy, and even less noise protection. *No doubt this was some consultant's idea, designed to encourage collaboration*, she thought.

Knowing that all eyes and ears were upon her, Ollie turned around, and went back into Paul's office. She left the door open on purpose. He was typing with his glasses down on his nose. He looked over the top of the screen as if he had been expecting her. "Once this next story runs, you should give me a fucking raise, asshole," she shouted.

"The I-Desk should be called 'the Bureau of Great Expectations,'" she screamed, "with this ridiculous pressure. Why don't you try doing some reporting sometime? You probably forgot what it's like."

When she finally stormed out, Paul smiled.

He was as short and chubby as Ollie was tall and thin, with puffy cheeks and a generous belly that he vainly tried to conceal under baggy shirts. He usually wore battered khakis or navy chinos that hung loosely on his legs. So-called relaxed fit, no doubt. He scurried around the newsroom on the balls of his feet, as if ready to pounce at any moment. At the same time, he swung his arms like pistons.

Back at her desk, Ollie channeled her frustration into polishing the newest article. She was struggling with the copy when her phone rang. Recognizing the number, she shook her head in frustration. *This is all I need*, she said to herself. Julie Hoover, the paper's lawyer, the bitchy queen who always played the game of stump the reporter.

"Hi, Ollie, how ya doin'?"

"Fine," Ollie said brusquely.

Julie had a nasal voice and a New York accent that felt like acid dripping onto the eardrums. On the surface, her diction could be confused with Boston's defiled version of English. But the differences between a New England and a New York accent were clear to those who knew. *Maybe you had to grow up in one area and live in the other to really learn the distinction*, Ollie thought.

For instance, Julie would pronounce the word *s-t-a-r* as "sta" in a way that rhymed with "ma" or "pa", but the *Observer*'s readers would say "staaaah" while exhaling and making the "r" disappear altogether, as in "aaaah."

In any case, Julie was the I-Desk's nemesis because she flaunted her veto authority and delighted in humiliating reporters as she pored over their copy in search of potentially libelous statements.

"Did you really look at the rec-uds from *500* hip surgeries?" Julie asked. *Here we go*, Ollie said to herself. *Maybe I can distract her.*

"It was actually 478," she said, trying to stay neutral.

"Then that's a factual error," Julie said, pronouncing the word "err-ah". "You shoulda caught that."

"We can easily change it to 'nearly 500.'" *Good move, concede something*, Ollie thought.

"It's still a factual err-ah," Julie insisted. "It's wrong."

"I know that, Julie. We can easily change it."

"I'm not feeling confident about ya' reporting on this."

"What other changes do you have?"

"How do you know that 67 patients got sick?"

"We've been over and over this," Ollie said. "The advocates group gave us access to the medical records and we saw—"

"Do you have signed consent forms from the patients?" Julie asked.

"We're using the records *anonymously*. But don't worry. The patients signed over their rights to the advocacy group. You know that. Check the release forms I sent," Ollie was increasingly exasperated but knew that showing it would be counterproductive.

"How do you know that the salesman was actually *in* so many operating rooms?"

"Because our sources told us he was like a fixture in the OR." And so it went, for an hour or more. At the end of the conversation, Julie said "Okay," and Ollie knew that was her version of saying "publish it."

When Paul read the copy (and he was always the last one to see their work), he nodded. That was a ringing endorsement. "Make the next one better," he said.

It was the lead story:

Deadline on Arrival

I-DESK REPORT

ARE YOU SAFE IN SURGERY? WHO'S BEHIND THE MASKS?

**BY OLLIE BURNS AND THE I-DESK
WITH RESEARCH BY PAT COLE**

This vicious bacterium has a waxy coating. First discovered in 1882, it causes one of the world's deadliest diseases. It's found in all 50 states and it's still raging. It is spread through coughing, sneezing, shouting, or even singing. Most often it attacks the lungs, but it can also wreak havoc on the kidneys, spine, or brain. We're talking about tuberculosis, commonly known as TB.

A medical device salesman named Alec Moore was infected, unbeknownst to several local hospitals which routinely invited him into operating rooms where he "advised" surgeons on new ball-and-socket hip replacement parts sold by his employer, Analog Joints. With the help of several confidential sources, we analyzed records from nearly 500 hip surgeries that Moore attended over the past five years. We discovered that 67 of the patients who had been healthy beforehand contracted TB after the operations.

Craig Sawyer, whose father perished from the disease following an otherwise routine hip replacement, lays the blame at Moore's feet: "We had no idea he was in the room. We can't understand why the hospital would allow an infected person to come so close to our dad."

When patients are wheeled into the OR, they often see a group of masked personnel. It's hard to tell who's who. Yet device salespeople are often there, especially in orthopedics. Manufacturers claim they often know more than the surgeons about the mechanics of the artificial joints, and they acknowledge that they even help set up equipment in pre-dawn hours. The sales personnel train on cadavers, or on anatomical models called "sawbones" in the industry.

A spokesperson for Moore's company, Analog Joints, said, "Our salespeople are vetted very carefully. They are familiar with proper procedures and are quite skilled."

But are they tested for infectious diseases? The spokesperson declined to say.

Critics say the salespeople spend a lot of time in the OR only to sell products and to convince surgeons to perform more operations. "They bribe, cajole, and charm the doctors," says Alice Roth, from the Surgical Patients' Safety Group. "Even the highest paid doctors are susceptible to freebies, which range from golf bags at the low end to all-expenses-paid trips to luxury resorts at the high end."

Often hired for their looks, the salespeople learn how to ingratiate themselves with the doctors. (There are even consultants who teach salespeople how to get into ORs without an invitation.)

"You can always spot the device reps in the waiting room," said attorney Mitch Yates, who represents several infected patients. "They all look like models, and they're dressed like they stepped out of the pages of *GQ* or *Vogue*."

2

BEGINNINGS

A Few Decades Ago

HER FATHER RUSS always wanted a boy. She thought that was why he called her Ollie instead of Olivia. She barely remembered her mom, who passed away from cancer when Ollie was four. Her dad raised her as well as he could, with the help of his widowed older sister Jessie who had no kids of her own.

Russ learned how to cook, and together he and Ollie would save recipes that scored high on two key criteria: ease of preparation and great taste. Their favorite was pasta with whatever vegetables were on hand. It was quick and satisfying, especially with a bit of black pepper.

Russ Burns was a plainclothes detective in Boston. Ollie loved to ride around in his unmarked car. They'd cruise through their neighborhood in Jamaica Plain, AKA JP, a part of Boston that was then primarily working class. Centre Street (and note the quirky, British spelling) runs through JP like a spine. The architecture is mixed, with ramshackle two-families on some blocks and Victorian mansions on others. Along the so-called Riverway that hugs the Emerald Necklace Park designed by Frederick

Olmstead, of Central Park fame, huge estates seem to strut their style as the traffic snakes through the sinuous road. Around the turn of the 20th century, wealthy families from the fancy Beacon Hill neighborhood in Boston used the mansions as summer houses and weekend retreats, and they'd take the six-mile trip in horse-drawn carriages.

Ollie prided herself on her urban roots. She still lived in her childhood home, two blocks off Centre Street. It was an elegant house, with great curb appeal, as the real estate brokers would say. A turret ran from the first floor to the attic. The siding was painted a tasteful crimson. The windows were fringed with white gingerbread trim in scalloped patterns.

When she was young she loved to climb a ladder and touch up the trim with an artist's brush. Her Aunt Jessie watched with trepidation as Ollie stood thirty feet up on tiptoes on the top step of the ladder to work on the woodwork on the third floor, while her dad just chuckled. He knew she wouldn't fall and so did she.

Her rescue dog Happy, a mutt who was probably a mix of poodle and bichon, looked up at her from the lawn and seemed to be concerned about her. He was *her* pet and he slept with her every night. "It's okay, Haps," she said from up high. "Don't worry, boy. I won't fall on you."

At 13, Ollie took the admissions test and sailed into Boston Latin, a selective high school boasting celebrated alumni like Sam Adams and Ralph Waldo Emerson. "Latin," founded in 1635, is one year older than Harvard. Rumor has it that the university was established so the high school students would have somewhere to go after graduation.

When the time came to write her personal statement for college applications, she wasn't sure what to say. She wanted to describe her dad, but feared that she'd get the reaction "Wow, your father sounds fascinating, but what about you?" She didn't want to be maudlin either. Yet when she sat down to write, she couldn't get more than a car-length from the man she called Pa.

Here's what she wrote:

My Pa Russ was a plainclothes detective in Boston. When he would come home from work, I would run out of the kitchen to greet him and skid to a halt on the worn parquet floor in the living room. I had to pretend there was a force field around Pa, with a radius of about five feet.

If I tried to get too close, he'd pretend to zap me. He wanted to make sure he had time to take off his holster and hang it on a hook high on the hall tree, far beyond my reach. This was his way of keeping me safe.

One day I penetrated the force field and grabbed his leg before he went through the routine. That's the only time he ever hit me. He wacked me hard on my forearm and left a red mark that quickly turned into a bruise. Then he burst into tears that frightened me so much that I ended up comforting him. He was a very gentle man and I think he felt badly about that incident for the rest of his short life.

He carried an old Smith and Wesson on duty because it was traditional, I guess. He also had a Sig Sauer 228, the first compact pistol ever made, but he kept it on a high shelf in the closet. It was too "modern" for him.

Pa had never fired his gun in the line of duty, not once in 20 years on the police force. Apparently, that's fairly common. Contrary to what you see on TV, cops rarely engage in shooting matches with suspects.

That all changed one day toward the end of my freshman year at Boston Latin. I was just 14. I came home from school and let myself in, as always. Aunt Jessie was out shopping. As soon as I walked through the door, I smelled a stranger. A distinctive odor like stale socks. Then I heard a man's deep, scratchy voice coming from around the corner in the dining room: "You don't know me, but your dad does."

The next thing I knew a big guy who blinked more than any other person I've ever met came into the foyer and aimed a gun at my head. He told me that we were going to wait quietly until my dad came home. It was the longest three hours of my life. He was stocky, and unshaven, with unruly sandy blond hair. His baggy sweatshirt billowed over torn jeans. At one point I asked if I could go to the bathroom. He walked me over and made me leave the door open. Just then we heard Pa coming in.

"Ollie?" my dad called. "In here, Russman," I answered. He could tell right away something was wrong because I called him by that nickname, our code for a crisis. By the time he walked over to the bathroom door the stranger had yanked me out. He stood behind me, with his left arm around my neck, and his right hand holding the gun that was pointed at my head. I could barely move because my underwear was down around my ankles.

I knew my father was thinking that the stranger had raped me. I tried to speak to reassure him, but the guy told me to shut up and pressed the gun barrel into my temple with such force that it pushed my neck sideways at a painful angle.

Pa slowly pulled his .38 out of the holster and pointed it toward the intruder. Pa's dark eyes showed no emotion. "Hello, Baby G. What's the game here?" he asked with little inflection.

"Nobody calls me that anymore," he said.

"You'll always be Baby G to me. But you'll be a dead baby if you don't let go of my daughter right now." He said it quietly but with snarling emphasis.

"No chance, man. You gotta pay for sending me up. Time for retribution."

"Big word, Baby G," Dad said. "Did you finally learn how to read?"

The dialogue went back and forth like that for a while. I knew Pa was just buying time and trying to rattle the gunman. He had always told me to stay still and quiet if something like this ever happened. I tried to follow his instructions. But I couldn't.

I took a deep breath, elbowed Baby G in the gut as hard as I could, and ducked away from his gun. He aimed it toward my dad as he staggered and pulled the trigger almost reflexively. The two men shot one another in the head, and both fell onto the hardwood floor. Death came quickly to each of them.

Aunt Jessie promptly took over. She stepped in as a substitute mom and made Ollie stay with her at her nearby home during the funeral. Aunt Jessie did her best to create a sense of normality, as fragile as it may have been, and insisted that Ollie return to school. When the cops were done with the crime scene, Jessie made it the first order of business to remove all physical traces of the murder, starting with the blood stains on the floor. She got down on her hands and wobbly knees and scrubbed the parquet with cleanser, sanded it by hand, and applied two new coats of polyurethane. When that work was done, she brought Ollie back to the home where she grew up and moved in herself. The intense smell of the varnish lingered for weeks but neither of them minded. It seemed to represent renewal, or at least perseverance. After that, the aroma of the cookies and pies Jessie always baked filled the house.

Jessie shepherded Ollie through the rigors of Boston Latin, where the competition was brutal. The school was, and is, a collection of some of the brightest kids in the city.

Whenever she suffered any doubt, she'd think of the compassion in her Aunt Jessie's brilliant blue eyes that almost looked iridescent, especially against her weathered, pale Irish skin. Jessie would joke that a new wrinkle appeared every year after she turned 35. Ollie would swat the comment away with a smile but had to admit that there was truth in her words.

Ollie was a top student and her guidance counselor encouraged her to apply to the Ivies, especially since she had such a "powerful narrative." Ollie liked Brown University best of all because there were no required courses and students were able to design their own majors. Plus, there was something cozy about Providence, Rhode Island, where the school is located. It's a small city, especially compared to Boston, nestled in the smallest state of all. An added benefit was that it was only an hour or so away from home and the comforts of her beloved Aunt Jessie.

Ollie applied early acceptance and was overjoyed when she got in, with a full scholarship no less. That meant the arduous application process was wrapped up in a bow by Christmas of her senior year.

The next September Aunt Jessie drove down with her to Providence during freshmen week and helped her settle in. There was still a touch of summer, and the heat and humidity made them sweat as they lugged Ollie's boxes up to her third-floor double room. The dorm had a brick exterior and sat on the perimeter of a quad dominated by several red maple trees. Ollie was asking herself whether she belonged there, especially after meeting her roommate, who wore a pleated skirt and introduced herself as Harper Cain. "I'm from Shaker Heights," she said.

"Where's that?" Ollie asked.

"A Cleveland burb," she answered.

"I'll bet it's a fancy place," Ollie said.

Harper shrugged and muttered, "To tell you the truth, our house is one of the smaller ones on the street. It's only 3,500 square feet."

"Did you go to private school?"

"Yeah, The Laurel School. What about you?"

"Boston Latin."

"That's hard to get into, isn't it?"

"I guess I test well," Ollie answered.

"What are you planning to concentrate in?" Harper asked.

"You mean what I'm going to major in? That word concentrate seems odd to me."

"I guess you'll have to get used to a new vocabulary. As for me, I'm planning to concentrate in folklore."

"I guess you'll be reading a lot of Grimm's Fairy Tales," Ollie said. Harper chuckled but wasn't sure whether Ollie was kidding or just snarky.

When Harper left the room to register, Aunt Jessie lectured Ollie about minding her manners. "I know, Auntie. I'll be nice, don't worry. I guess I'm a bit nervous. Maybe it's that preppy look that set me off."

"She seemed like a nice kid, so give her a chance," Aunt Jessie said. She immediately took over and put contact paper in the drawers of the dresser, mopped the floors, and left a small vacuum cleaner she had bought for the occasion. When it was time to leave, she had tears in her eyes and told Ollie to pretend she was going to school in California and not to come home until Thanksgiving. Ollie knew she didn't really mean it, so she made sure to take the train up to Boston once a month or so. The visits cheered them both up.

Ollie especially enjoyed cuddling with their rescue dog Happy, because he was in the final stages of a terminal illness. He died in her arms when she came home for freshman summer.

Aunt Jessie passed the next year. Ollie never knew that her aunt had a congenital heart defect that frequently caused arrhythmia. She kept the problem to herself, figuring that her niece had experienced enough trauma already. One day her heart just failed. The neighbors found her on the front porch.

Afterwards, Ollie was terrified because she had no family left in the world. Her dad had no other relatives and she had long lost touch with her mom's extended family.

Mostly she kept her distance from her Brown classmates, many of whom were suburban kids who seemed either overly intellectual or completely immature, or both. *What did they know about life*, she thought. Then she'd chastise herself for judging them. Not their fault that they were sheltered. In a way, she envied them. She got along much better with the students who came from poorer families.

Ollie had a distant, if cordial, relationship with her roommate Harper. When Harper went to class, Ollie would look through her closet and at once admire and mock the wardrobe. Harper had told her, with only a small degree of irony, that she allowed only wool, cotton, or silk to come into contact with her skin.

"Does that mean that you're actually allergic to polyester or rayon?" Ollie asked.

"I suppose so," Harper said, chuckling. "Along with wine with screw-off tops."

"You can't be serious," Ollie said.

"My dad has a strict set of rules for behavior," Harper said.

"My dad had rules too," she said. "I was never allowed to touch his gun or say anything racist." Ollie felt that this exchange summed up the difference in their worldviews.

Somehow, the two roommates found some semblance of common ground so they stayed together for all four years of college. Ollie admired Harper's intellect, and Harper conceded that Ollie was the better writer. She'd often ask her to edit her papers and had to admit that her comments were helpful. Then again, some of the things Harper said were just so "gauche," a term she learned to use. One day, for instance, she told Ollie that it was wonderful that a place like Brown would admit a cop's daughter.

At the same time the open curriculum at Brown, with few course requirements, appealed to Ollie. She invented her own major in criminology and pursued several research projects with the Providence Police Department. When she told the beat cops she was a detective's daughter, they accepted her right away. She wrote her senior thesis about women who deliver babies in prison, with a focus on the plight of the children, who are often put up for adoption shortly after birth. She wrote eloquently and wove poignant interviews with the moms into the demographic data.

To neutralize the intensity of criminology, she minored in art history by looking at beautiful paintings and sculptures.

Ollie naturally gravitated toward the more "diverse" kids—another word whose nuances she came to understand. Her closest friends tended to be either from abroad, or from inner cities. Yet she tended to be a lone wolf for the most part. She didn't have any partners because the college boys seemed immature. *They were midway through the metamorphosis process, just beyond the larval stage*, she thought.

After graduation she thought about joining the police force, but instinctively shied away from any job that required a uniform. That would be too confining and regimented. Journalism was the logical second choice because she liked unearthing secrets. It was part art and part psychology—in the center of her skillset.

3

FALLOUT

Present Day

THE REACTION TO THE ARTICLE about the medical salesman with TB was seismic, with Ollie at the epicenter. Her voicemail and email were full of messages from hospital public relations people complaining that the story was one-sided, from anxious patients who were worried that Alec Moore or other salespeople had infected them, and from those who said they had suspicious symptoms after surgery.

Take that, Mr. Paul Green, she said to herself. At one point he walked by her and smiled. That was the closest he ever came to a compliment. Ollie was planning to head outside for some fresh air when her desk phone rang. She took a chance and answered it.

"Hello, I-Desk," she said.

"Ollie Burns?" a woman asked.

"Yes, this is she."

"I'm Leslie Moore. Alec's wife," the woman said. "I thought you might like to know that he was shot and killed. He wasn't the guy you wrote about, bitch. He just happened to have the same name."

Ollie remained silent.

"You're a bloodsucker and a total sleaze." With that, the woman hung up.

Ollie stared open-mouthed at the phone for a moment, then put it back on the cradle. She was used to people calling and complaining but this was a whole new level of invective. *The Great God of Stories strikes again,* she thought. *We worship it, serve it, feed it, publicize it, but is it a false idol?*

"Need a drink?"

That question came from Jan Watkins, Ollie's boss, the editor in charge of the I-Desk.

Although it was only 2:30, Ollie said, "Yeah, I do."

Ollie was always intrigued by her boss. One of Jan's eyes was slightly lower than the other and her nose was askew, with the asymmetry of a Botticelli portrait. Though she was 48, her hair was still naturally blond, if streaked with some gray, and she wore stylish clothes with no hint of self-consciousness.

In a newsroom of big personalities, Jan was a reserved enigma.

The two women headed to the nearby First Draft bar, which functioned in many ways as an extension of the newsroom. More business took place there than in the cubicles. The place was one of those Boston "taverns" redolent of a men's club. It had dark paneling, a brass foot rail under the bar, tall chairs with red leather seats, pictures of mayors and sports heroes on the walls, a TV always tuned to the latest games, and a strong smell of burgers and fries in the air. On any given day or night, reporters, photographers, political operatives and PR people would meet and gossip.

In many ways Boston is a small town trying to write itself large, with maybe a thousand influential people separated by three degrees instead of the proverbial six. As the older ones die or retire, youngsters enter the group. If you plucked a name out of the now outmoded white pages at random, chances are someone at the bar would know that person and could recount the family's history.

Eddie, the barkeep, owned the place with his wife Betty, who waited on the tables. Eddie had Jan's Chardonnay and Ollie's Manhattan half ready as they came in.

"Beautiful in body, as always, ladies, but heavy in mood today," Eddie said with a wink.

"Politically incorrect, Eddie, but I'll take the compliment," Jan said with a vague smile. "Put it on my tab."

"On me," he said. Eddie always wore a crisp white apron with a blue shirt and a fake black bowtie. His matching black hair was perpetually tousled. His round face seemed to get even more circular when he smiled, which was often.

Jan and Ollie walked over to an empty booth and sat down.

"I heard about the murder. Mrs. Moore called me first. Did I ever tell you about the time," Jan said, "when we spent 13 months building a case against a state rep who—"

"Yeah," Ollie said, "and he killed himself when the story ran. And you told me about the married child molester who set fire to his house with his family in it, then shot himself, after your exposé, and—"

"You're making me feel like an old woman who repeats herself and can't remember whom she told what." Jan said "whom" with precise emphasis. "I have no deep words of comfort. But I—"

"Look, I appreciate your concern, but I'm all right. Just our business, right? I was thinking, I should go and cover the murder."

"Do you think that's a good idea?"

"Sometimes we need to see the effect of our actions," Ollie said flatly. "As long as I don't have to interview the widow."

"Leave that to the police reporters. They have no feelings anyway."

Ollie smiled and they clinked glasses. She took a small sip of her drink and headed out. "What a great business," she said to herself, with all due sarcasm.

Jan sat and savored her Chardonnay. Ollie remembered a remark Jan made a few weeks prior. "I know I drink too much," she told Ollie. "But I'm not an alcoholic."

• • •

At age 28, Ollie had covered a dozen or fifteen murders in her career up to that point. On the surface, she thought they were all the same. The police would cordon off the crime scene, issue bland statements in "cop-eese" about perpetrators, the estimated time of death and so on, saying as little as possible yet trying to create the illusion that they were on top of the matter.

The victim in this case, Alec Moore, had been an assistant headmaster at one of the local schools. As she drove down Fayerweather Street in West Cambridge to his home, Ollie wondered how a guy who probably made no more than $200K or so could afford such a large house now surrounded by yellow tape draped unceremoniously on the neatly sculpted yews that sheltered a porch running the entire length of the front wall. *Must be family money*, Ollie thought. As soon as she got out of her car, she heard a woman yelling and cursing with astounding fluency.

Twin boys who looked to be about seventeen were trying to hold the woman back. Ollie thought she recognized the voice from the phone call she had received earlier.

"You assholes, I want to go back inside. I want to see my husband!" she screamed at the cops.

A policewoman in uniform tried to calm her. "Ma'am, we don't want to disturb any evidence," the policewoman said. Ollie watched this scene unfold from a respectful distance. Just then Terry Keegan, the public relations officer for the Cambridge police, came up behind her.

On the police force we called Keegan "Lieutenant GQ." For starters, he's always overdressed. The running joke was that he was a "ratty" guy with natty clothes. That day he wore a navy chalk stripe suit with a blue spread-collar shirt and a knit maroon tie. His pants fell onto black tassel loafers (yeah, tassel loafers—the most "uncoplike" thing to cover your feet). His hair was always moussed to such a degree that a hurricane wouldn't ruffle it. To tell you the truth, I despised Keegan.

"Ollie Burns, are you back on the street?" Keegan asked.

As Ollie turned to say hello, the woman heard the exchange and ran toward her.

"Liar, slut!" she shouted as she picked up speed. When she got close to Ollie she lunged. Ollie sidestepped and the woman fell face first onto the sidewalk. When she tried to stand up her chin was bleeding. By this time the two boys were at her side.

"C'mon, Mom, it's not worth it," one said.

Ollie knew that the families of murder victims tended to lash out. Sometimes they would treat the press like one of those bop bags with weighted bottoms. She didn't blame her.

"Mrs. Moore, can we give you a ride somewhere?" Keegan asked.

"We'll take her," one of the sons said as they walked toward their car.

Mrs. Moore tried to run toward Ollie again, but the boys restrained her as she collapsed and sobbed. Ollie was trying her best to pretend that nothing untoward had occurred.

"Great way to make a living," a man behind her said in a harsh tone.

That would be me, Ronan Mezini. Ollie turned around and our eyes met. I had investigated probably thirty murders and had butted heads with some of the toughest killers around, but I confess that my stomach turned when I saw Ollie, for reasons you'll come to understand. She was very tall, and I thought she carried herself with a self-assurance bordering on arrogance. My synesthesia immediately kicked in. I sensed a weird smell coming from her even though she was standing ten feet away. The odor was powerful, you might even say muscular, though I could not identify it at the time.

"Detective Mezini," she said quietly. "We meet again. Mind if I ask you a few questions?"

"Yeah, I do mind," I said. "I didn't think the I-Desk ever set foot on an actual street. I thought you did all your work from the office." Later, you'll understand why I was hostile.

Ollie ignored the insults. "When was he killed?"

"We're done here. Talk to Keegan. He speaks fluent reporter, which is a sub-category of English. Good-by, Scoop," I said as I walked away.

Ollie walked toward a trailer that the police had set up on the outer perimeter of the scene, where Keegan was about to address the print, TV, and radio reporters swarming around him. Amy Stout suddenly appeared at Ollie's elbow. She was one of the police reporters at *The Observer*, and no one covered the beat more enthusiastically.

"I guess Mezini's still pissed about your little exposé," Amy whispered.

"'My 'little exposé?'" Ollie replied, with quotes in her voice. "There's more to journalism than fires and murders, you know."

"Touchy, touchy. I didn't think you covered *breaking* news. I thought you only did stories that take *months* to research. Watch and you might learn something."

Amy always reminded Ollie of a spitting cobra, with the ability to shoot its venom into the eyes of its victims with stunning accuracy, but only at close range. She had square shoulders, burly arms, wide hips, and thick legs, in a way that personified her last name of Stout. She wore her hair in a ponytail, probably so it wouldn't get in the way of the spewing venom.

Ollie gave her a long, hard look, then started chuckling dismissively. By then Keegan had started talking so they turned their attention toward him.

"We have a brief statement, then I'll take questions," he said. "The victim was Alec Moore, and he died from a gunshot wound into the back of his head sometime last night, we're not exactly sure when yet. His wife had not heard from him since dinnertime yesterday. She called us to report that he was missing around noon today. Shortly after 2:00 PM one of his sons found him lying face down in the garden in the back yard."

Keegan paused for a moment, then looked at Ollie. "The victim just happens to have the same name as the person recently profiled in an I-Desk story, but I want to emphasize that he's not that man. We have no suspects at this point but we will be pursuing all leads."

A barrage of shouted questions followed.

Ollie raised her hand and Keegan acknowledged her.

"Did anyone hear the gunshots?" she asked.

"Not that we're aware of," Keegan answered. "And, by the way, there was only one shot. Yes, Amy," he said, gesturing toward her.

"Do you think the killer mistook the victim for the medical salesman profiled in the I-Desk story?" she asked.

"Right now, we cannot say."

"Do you think a family member of one of the patients infected with TB did this?" one of the TV reporters asked.

"Once again, we do not know at this time," Keegan said. "We are doing everything in our power to investigate."

"Could it have been a suicide?" a reporter asked.

"Unlikely, given that the bullet came from behind," Keegan answered.

EMTs were wheeling a body bag into a waiting van. The cameramen turned toward them to capture footage of the scene.

Keegan said, "With that, I need to get back to work. We'll keep you updated as frequently as we can."

The reporters clustered around Ollie and fired questions at her. What do you think about this? Will management respond? How did the real Alec Moore react? etc.

Ollie fended them off. "I'm digesting this myself," she said, "and I need some time before I can respond."

For once, Amy came to her rescue. "I'm sure management will have a statement soon." She stared at Ollie with an expression of triumph, as if to say, "now you're a victim too." Ollie caught the glance, turned away, and went back to her car. She never did file a story. She left the spoils to Amy.

4

A DEADLY SPOTLIGHT

FOR KENNY MORAN, writing columns was all too easy at first. Much simpler than covering the news and dealing with the stubborn reality of *facts*. He would finally be free to share his opinions. After all, he had dozens of ideas about current events—probably five dozen of them. Yeah, that first batch of 60 columns came quickly. Then the real work began. He had to start *reporting* again—finding new stories instead of generating what are known in the trade as "thumb-sucker" pieces—sheer opinion only partly buttressed by evidence.

Yet, the truth is more than the square of two facts, he said to himself. *Sometimes, the story lies behind or around the circumstances. Not necessarily in them.* Case in point, this column he had just published, in his inimitable crude style:

Deadline on Arrival

WHIZ KID FINDS HIS MS.

BY KENNY MORAN

Those of you of a "certain age" may remember Wilhelm Stafford, who appeared on a local show called *The Young Wizards*. Of all the weird platehead geniuses who graced the studio, he was the most brilliant, which is saying a lot. Though the social neurons in his brain were dysfunctional, there was nothing wrong with the cognitive cells. This kid could figure out the cube root of a five-digit number in his head in about three seconds. Plus, he was able to translate any passage you gave him into Latin, and from there into Greek, before you could say Albert Einstein. He was only ten years old when he appeared on the show.

He entered MIT at age 13, graduated in three years with a degree in electrical engineering, and then disappeared for four decades. Until now that is. The mother of another one of the "wizards" contacted me recently and told me that her daughter, Uma Din, had fallen in love with Stafford recently.

Now, I know a good story when it slaps me in the face. I did some digging and found Stafford, living on the top floor of his old frat house on the outskirts of the MIT campus in Cambridgeport. He rarely comes out of his room, except at night when he sits on a beat-up office chair on the fire escape. He scrawls untold ideas in a notebook. The kids tolerate him as the resident nutjob.

Since graduating from MIT, he has had a succession of low-paying odd jobs: librarian, landscaper, dishwasher, and most recently, a night watchman at Cambridge City Hall. He was easy to spot, in his wrinkled button-down shirts, with his greasy gray hair pulled tight into a long ponytail.

He and Uma Din stumbled into one another a few months ago at a coffee shop in Central Square. She recognized him immediately and challenged him to figure out the cube root of 19,683. He blinked twice and said, "27," with a grin. The strange thing is that he can't even say how he does it. Uma had an unusual talent herself. If you read a paragraph out loud, she can repeat it backwards instantly, letter by letter.

One cup of coffee led to a romance and …

Though Kenny has been a columnist for 20 years, he had once been one of the paper's best metro reporters, with intricate knowledge of Boston's meandering streets. When he started at the paper as a summer intern, he badgered the news desk so aggressively that they gave him a few assignments. Even then, he a knack for turning out articulate copy quickly. It didn't take the editors long to offer him a job as a junior reporter, at $150 a week.

As his confidence surged, he started sneaking tiny exaggerations into his news stories, here and there. For instance, a 4th of July parade became a "cornucopia of 77 flotillas."

"Were there really 77?" the editor asked. Kenny insisted that he had counted them. Then he'd quote unnamed bystanders who would just happen to utter the pithiest and most colorful soundbites: "The gunshots sounded like the eruption at Krakatoa"; or "The Charles River was so thick with pollution that you could part the water with a shovel." Editors were skeptical, but he'd swear that the quotes were real and that the people simply didn't want to be identified.

Getting away with little lies emboldened Kenny and made him more and more contemptuous of *Observer* management after they rewarded him with a column of his own. The editors tolerated him because he was the most famous personality at the paper and had a sizeable following. A sketch of his rough-hewn face, with a broken nose that skewed to his right, made him instantly recognizable all over town.

His "inventiveness" eventually ran amok. *Hub Magazine*, a glossy that covered the city, started a feature called "Really, Moran?" written by a reporter named Lara Berger, who fact-checked his work every month. Kenny dismissed her with this comment: "If Berger weren't working for *Hub Magazine*, she'd be writing supermarket ads."

Then came the latest story about the Young Wizards, which distressed *Observer* management as never before. For one thing, the paper had "outed" Wilhelm Stafford as a former child genius in a feature 20 years earlier. He sued for violation of his right to privacy because he was self-conscious about his failure to live up to his early promise as a so-called prodigy. The court ruled against him on the grounds that the first amendment took precedence over his desire to preserve his anonymity.

The paper's attorney Julie Hoover told editor Paul Green that Kenny should have never written the story because he surely should have remembered the lawsuit since he had been at the paper at the time. She also chided Paul for lax supervision in the matter.

Even more troubling, there was no credible evidence that Uma Din, Stafford's alleged girlfriend, was even still alive. The tapes of the Whiz Kids TV show had long since disappeared. The *Hub Magazine* team searched every known database and could find no one by the name of Uma Din. When they called Paul Green for comment, he merely said that the matter was under investigation.

When he hung up the phone, Paul strutted over to Kenny's desk. He was muttering to himself the entire time. "Fuck me in a dog's ass," he said loud enough to be heard. That was one of his favorite expressions. No one on the staff knew exactly what that meant, except that his anger was reaching the point of homicide. They knew enough to leave him alone at those times.

"Where the fuck is Moran?" he shouted at the top of his lungs when he saw the columnist's empty chair. "Do I have to run out myself and find him?"

"I think he went to the First Draft," one of the interns said.

"Great. I'm on my way."

He went back into his office, grabbed his jacket, slammed the door, and headed for the exit.

"Chief, before you go—" News Editor Will Cabot called after him. He had a worried expression. He was a weaselly guy known to be panting for Green's job.

"Don't call me Chief, for starters," Paul barked. "What is it?"

"You're going to want to hear this before you talk to Kenny."

"Hear what? They found Uma Din?"

"No. Somebody killed Wilhelm Stafford last night. At the fraternity."

"What?" Green yelled. He sneezed, as he always did, especially when he was angry. "You're telling me this *now*?"

"The news just came in 30 seconds ago."

Paul turned around and went back to his desk.

• • •

My team at the Cambridge Police Department was still investigating the murder of the so-called *other* Alec Moore in the exclusive western part of the city. Now we had to deal with a new homicide on the east side in Cambridgeport. The MIT frat house Zeta Zeta where Stafford had lived was cordoned off as detectives questioned all the students inside. This time twenty-five reporters showed up at PR officer Terry Keegan's briefing.

Speaking to the reporters outside the frat house, he went through the usual details about the approximate time of Stafford's death and the absence of eyewitnesses. He said the "decedent" was found face down in the tiny backyard of the frat house—with a bullet fired into the back of his skull.

"Is this murder connected with the Alec Moore shooting?" one of the reporters asked.

"We cannot say but we are investigating all possibilities," Keegan answered.

"Do you have any idea what the motive may be?" another reporter asked.

"I cannot say."

"Did any of the students hear anything?" was the next question.

"We are speaking with them now. We'll have more to say about that later."

Headlines screamed about the case that night. In *The Observer*: "Whiz Kid's Sad Demise"; in *The Boston Sun*, the city's tabloid: "Gloomy Genius Gunned Down"; from the Associated Press: "The Death of the World's Smartest Night Watchman."

In the aftermath of the murder, Paul Green's white-hot anger at Kenny Moran cooled to red. Rationality returned, if only for a moment. His fear that Stafford might sue again was nullified by his death, but he still wanted to make sure that their coverage mentioned the earlier case. He asked police reporter Amy Stout to mention the litigation in her stories and even asked her to interview the obnoxious station lawyer Julie Hoover about the legal issues. By the time Paul finished working that day, it was after ten o'clock when he headed to the parking lot.

At that moment, Kenny was staggering back to his car—after spending the evening at the First Draft. The mere sight of him sent Paul into apoplexy.

"Hey, Hemingway," he yelled. Kenny stared at him with a glazed look.

"*El Capitan*," Kenny slurred. "We who are about to die salute you."

Paul pulled out his cell phone and dialed 911. "I'd like to report a drunken man who is about to get into his car. I'm in the parking lot behind *The Observer* newspaper offices ... My name? Paul Green. I'm the editor."

He ended the call. "You're suspended until further notice," Paul said. "With no pay."

Kenny walked toward him, stumbling. As he advanced, his balance improved. By the time he was face to face with Green, he seemed almost sober. Without a word, he feinted with his right fist, then swung a roundhouse with his left hand. Paul ducked, but Kenny managed to graze the top of his head.

Amy saw all this as she was emerging from the back door. She shouted at Kenny and ran toward the scene to try to break up the fight. The security guard got there first. He sprinted out of his booth at the entrance to the lot and placed himself between the two men.

Kenny wriggled out of the guard's grip and headed to his car. He started the engine and drove directly into a post on the chain link fence.

The air bag exploded, and he nearly passed out against it.

Paul walked cautiously over to the car. Kenny lowered the window and muttered, "A great career pauses. By the way, do I still get my paid vacation, Chief?"

5

VANITY AND URBANITY

Two Weeks Later, Early June

A MY STOUT WAS ARGUABLY the most relentless hard news reporter in the city. Rumor had it she slept with a flat speaker under her pillow so she could monitor the police radios all night long. She trained herself to separate the routine from the newsworthy. Like a doctor on call, she could emerge fully alert from a deep sleep in an instant. Those who knew her saw a more compassionate side to her personality, which she generally kept hidden as a protective measure.

In a case of opposites attracting, her boyfriend of many years was Troy Carr, who ran a PR agency with the deliberately tacky name "Influence Peddlers." Behind his back, reporters called the company "Influence Pidlers" because he was always pissing about.

He didn't care how deeply he dredged into the swamp for clients. No customers were too sleazy or underhanded, as long they were willing to pay, especially in advance. Troy had represented local politicians who had accepted bribes, restaurants that routinely served drinks to underage kids, executives caught cheating on their wives, and the like. Competitors said he specialized in the sordid, the slimy, and the squalid.

He and Amy were a tight couple even if they were as outwardly compatible as football and croquet. With a reputation for stiff-backed integrity as a journalist, she made a point of rejecting any gift, even a cup of coffee, when she was on the job. Tony never met a freebie he could refuse.

They seemed to enjoy the friction, though their friends were often repelled by the biting banter. Troy would chide Amy for her ample weight and went so far as to call her photos "adiposes" instead of "poses." For her part, she told him that he should arrange a networking event at Concord State Prison for those who might need his "reputation management" services.

There was one particularly cringeworthy incident at *The Observer* Christmas party last year at the Marriott on the harbor in Boston. Amy and Troy shared a table with Paul Green, Ollie Burns, Ollie's boss Jan Watkins, and other media illuminati. After dinner, they were enjoying glasses of port, served with chocolate mousse.

Troy told the story of how he and Amy met. He claimed that he convinced her to bury an article about an indictment that was coming down against an executive he represented. His charm initiative, he said, took the form of a romantic weekend at a lavish resort owned by one of his clients.

"Killing that story was labor intensive for me," he said with a lewd chuckle.

Everyone at the table was embarrassed and tried not to show that they were studying Amy for her reaction.

She quickly recovered and said, "Yeah, you exhausted yourself begging for sex, which I withheld on principle."

Everyone laughed nervously while admiring her deft dodge.

Trying to shift the focus, Amy asked Troy to tell the story of the organic foods client he just landed.

Rising to the challenge, he said the company came to him unsolicited because they heard he had a reputation for getting results. "They call themselves Southern Eco Foods, and they sell kale chips, quinoa, you know, shit like that," he said. "They're from the Florida panhandle, of all fucking places.

"Now I may be a whore," he continued, "but I'm honest about the diseases I carry. I told them straight out that I represent gun companies and foes of transgender rights, just for starters."

"You forgot big tobacco," Amy said.

"Yeah, that too," Troy said, wiping his mouth with the back of his hand.

"Did they refuse to work with you?" Paul asked.

"Negatory," Troy said. Imitating the client's southern accent, he said, "The guy told me, 'Mistah Cah, we don't cayuh who ya other clients ah, as long as you get our legislation pah-est.'"

He paused to revel in the laughter.

"Fifteen K a month, and counting," he said. "Plus all the kale I can eat."

• • •

The Observer's entertainment reporter Anika Mehta was still glamorous at her "mature age." She'd prance around the newsroom as if she were the star of an imaginary movie. She used to dye her hair but one summer got a buzz cut and let the gray grow in. She brushed it back in a dramatic pompadour.

"Age is a state I embrace," she pronounced to the staff.

She believed it was part of her job to be "on" at all times. Now that the paper was encouraging reporters to do Zoom "broadcasts" from their desks, she was beginning to envision herself as a TV star too. Her reviews were breathless and overdone: For instance, "This film displays a super *spirit* but fails to lead convincingly toward a sensible denouement." Or "The ice sculptures at this year's Winter Carnival seem as if they were locked in a frozen stasis."

No one dared to supervise her activities. She had been around long enough to carve out an independent niche in a business that was becoming increasingly controlling. On this day, she told the assignment desk that doled out the day's work that she was going to profile a new filmmaker in town who called herself V 2.0. The filmmaker wrote and directed a short shown at the Tribeca Film Festival. This was Anika's favorite kind of story: a young artist succeeding against all odds.

She drove to a street off Putnam Avenue just outside Harvard Square in Cambridge, a neighborhood full of triple-deckers, many stylishly renovated and turned into condos. Not V 2.0's place, though. It was one of those homes that still looked dilapidated.

From the moment Anika walked down the stairway into a space she hoped would be an artist's "lair," she felt right at home—as a "creative," as she would have phrased it, among creatives. She no doubt imagined that her lead would probably go like this: "Once she emerged from her shabby basement studio, this young filmmaker cast a shadow that might extend all the way to Hollywood Boulevard." Though she could have done the story from her cubicle, to her credit Anika still liked to go out and meet people in person.

"Anika Mehta," she murmured and exhaled with flourish as the young filmmaker opened the door.

"I know," V 2.0 said abruptly. She was wearing a waist-length vinyl jacket, faded jeans, and a T-shirt, all black to match her hair dyed the same shade. A beehive hairdo rose nearly vertically from her ample forehead. Lavender lipstick was unevenly applied, *no doubt deliberately* Anika thought. Scuffed gray sneakers completed the ensemble.

"Thanks for taking the time to see me," Anika said. "Cool place." She was admiring the unframed Basquiat-like paintings on the walls.

V 2.0 was apparently unfazed.

"I get into Tribeca and suddenly you're all over me," she said in an aggressive way. "Do you have any idea how many films I have produced and how many times my crew and I have tried to get *The Observer* to cover our work?"

Anika dismissed the complaint with a wave of her hand. "I was at the festival and heard a lot about your film. There was tremendous buzz after the screening at the Angelika."

"It wasn't shown at the Angelika. You didn't see it, did you?"

"Does it matter?" Anika asked, to distract attention from being caught in a lie. "It's as if you were *anointed*."

"Yeah, and meanwhile, I'm the same person I always was."

"I heard there were over 8,000 short films submitted, and yours was one of just 60 chosen."

"I guess I'm *special*," V 2.0 said sarcastically.

"Look, darling, do you want me to write about you, or not?" Anika asked pointedly.

"Don't call me darling, darling. I'll send you a link so you can actually *see* what I did. Do whatever you want."

"Why do you call yourself V 2.0?"

"Because I'm no longer a newcomer. Some of us actually reinvent ourselves as we go along, and others just keep cranking out the same old copy."

Anika couldn't help acting the part of a celebrity in her moveable fantasy. She convinced herself that she was just as famous, or should have been, as the people she wrote about. *After all*, she thought, *what separates me from the A-listers? Very little, really. When I confer my blessing on a new talent with my articles, I'm like Minerva, goddess of the arts, able to manipulate public interest at will.*

Back in her basement studio, V 2.0 was texting friends about *The Observer*'s interest. She pretended to be blasé but was shrewd about publicity. She played it coy and snarky, but she played it.

Anika's review of V 2.0's movie, "The Cellar Dwellers," noted that the dialogue wasn't synched with the lips, which she found somewhat disconcerting, but made sure to add that the notion of coordination between sound and picture was a 20th-century artifact that just might be going out of style. "After all," she wrote at the end of the review, "our lives are discontinuous, and we often don't hear and see life at the same time. Who knows? V 2.0 may just be in the vanguard of the new cinema."

Though tempted to retch after she read the copy, V 2.0 was pleased with the exposure. Perhaps she really was arriving. She and her friends pushed the review on Instagram—with stills from the film. They celebrated with champagne and Twinkies, her favorite combination.

Three nights after the story ran, she was writing her next script. She made herself a cup of black instant coffee—her rebellion against what she called the Starbucksification of America—because she planned to stay up as late as possible. Sometimes she just chewed on the dry coffee crystals right from the jar.

Apparently unable to focus, she decided to take a walk. She brought her video camera, as always. No sooner did she climb out onto the street, than a bullet pierced the back of her head, ripped through her brain, exited through her forehead, and left a star-shaped wound above her left eye. She was dead before she hit the sidewalk.

6

CHAOS, CHAOS

V 2.0'S MURDER UNLEASHED widespread panic in the city. Two people killed following stories in *The Observer* might be a coincidence, but three could not possibly be random. Readers were flocking to the paper's website as never before, clicking on stories about the deaths of former boy genius Wilhelm Stafford, filmmaker V 2.0, and Alec Moore, the namesake of the sleazy medical device salesman.

The Sun, Boston's tabloid paper, was enjoying every minute of the crisis and running headlines like this: "Profiles in Death: News Coverage Can be Harmful to Your Health." It pushed the notion that the murders might be the grisly work of a sole serial killer. Worse, the paper quickly generated a catchy nickname: "The Headline Hunter."

The next day, local politicians scheduled a news conference at Cambridge Police headquarters in Kendall Square to demonstrate that they were on top of the situation, even if they were completely clueless. An impressive bank of lights illuminated the podium where Governor Jim Decoulos and Cambridge Police Chief Michael Cronin took turns addressing a room full of some fifty reporters, local and national, including *The New York Times* and all the major TV networks. Though the statements were predictable and general, they had been prepared with some care.

From Governor Jim Decoulos: "We are doing everything we can to protect our all-important news organizations and the people they feature in their stories."

Cambridge Police Chief Mike Cronin: "We have never seen senseless attacks of this nature. We are confident that Detective Ronan Mezini and his team will succeed in bringing the perpetrator or perpetrators to justice."

"Any idea what the motive might be?" a network reporter asked.

"We are following every lead, interviewing every conceivable witness, and working tirelessly." Cronin said, dodging the question.

"Are you reaching out to the FBI?" a New York reporter asked.

"We have discussed the cases with their field office in Boston and we'll have more to say about that in the coming days," Cronin said. He certainly did not look happy about the FBI's involvement.

Amy asked, "Do the Cambridge police have the expertise to handle a serial killer on their own?"

Cronin shrugged, as Governor Decoulos took over. "I have every confidence that local law enforcement is up to the task, especially with the assistance of the FBI," Decoulos said.

The public relations industry was sterilized. Their clients would ordinarily be delighted to appear in the news, especially in a dedicated profile. But now they feared reprisal, or worse.

Smart Media Strategies, for instance, a huge PR firm, was touting a biotech startup, boasting a promising new drug that could alleviate Alzheimer's symptoms. *Observer* business editor Nico Lyons was so impressed with their research that he was writing the story himself. He was putting finishing touches on the draft when a young woman from the PR firm called and asked him to bury the story. When he asked why, as if he didn't know, he was told (off the record) that the CEO was terrified that he would become a target.

"I never thought I'd see the day when a public relations person would try to keep a client involved in a *positive* story out *of* the paper," Nico told her.

Meanwhile, *The Observer* itself became a focus of media interest. Ollie had received so many requests for interviews that she routinely rejected them with the excuses that she was busy on her own follow-up stories and that she didn't think a newsperson should comment on an ongoing investigation.

Paul Green had no such scruples. He was only too happy to opine and opine. Newsroom scuttlebutt had it that he even wore makeup for some of the network TV interviews. Anything would be an improvement, the newsroom gossips said. Paul was not noted for his good looks.

• • •

Somewhat reluctantly, Chief Cronin later reached out to the FBI's Boston bureau, which in turn referred them to the BAU, the Behavioral Analysis Unit in Quantico, Virginia, which had broad experience with serial killers. We were told that Dr. Jack Grimes, *the* expert, would help us.

If the field of serial killer profiling didn't exist, he would have invented it. Critics may have called profiling pseudoscience and even compared it to astrology, but few could disagree that Grimes had an impressive record. He had helped 20 major police departments apprehend serial murderers. He held a doctorate in criminal justice from the University of Maryland, and his PhD dissertation "The Killer's Way" was considered a landmark in the field. He was semi-retired in suburban DC, but he agreed to interrupt his vacation in the Caribbean to come to Boston to help. For a hefty fee, of course. He was expected to arrive in two days.

My team and I were working at an absurd pace. I had three other detectives on the case, and I told them to go all out. We had interviewed the medical salesman Alec Moore, from his hospital bed, students at the MIT fraternity where former "whiz kid" Wilhelm Stafford lived, residents on the surrounding streets, and people in the apartments in the vicinity of the filmmaker V 2.0's home. We went back to these people again and again to check for any discrepancies in their accounts.

Despite all this legwork, we could find no apparent motive and no evidence linking the three victims. For one thing, the murders occurred on different days of the week. Why does this matter? It might provide clues as to the killer's domestic situation. If he had a family, for instance, he would probably have done his handiwork between Monday and Friday because he'd be accountable to a spouse or children on the weekends and could not easily break loose. One helpful observation: the murders were committed at night, and that led us believe that the killer may have had a day job.

It would be all too easy, I reminded myself, *to fall back on the notion that the murderer was psychotic. He might be perfectly rational. And, for that matter, how could anyone be sure there was just one criminal? The pattern did have the earmarks of a single perp, though. The ritual was the same in each case. Death for all the victims came from a gunshot in the back of the head.*

If only the reporters would stay off my back. Constantly asking: What have you discovered? Do you have any suspects? Are we all safe? Christ, we just started. Things don't happen instantly, like on the TV shows. One thing we could do was revisit the crime scenes to get to know the victims more intimately, to craft what experts called "psychological autopsies."

Speaking of autopsies, I felt that *The Observer* had done one on me, when I was still alive. I confess that every fifth thought in my head ran back to the story the paper did the year before. I practically had it memorized, unfortunately:

NASTY, BRUTISH, AND BLUE: ARE THE COPS AS VICIOUS AS THE CRIMINALS THEY HUNT?

By Olivia Burns and the I-Desk
With research by Pat Cole

A six-month investigation into police brutality in the Boston metro area has unearthed 27 documented cases where officers mistreated or assaulted people in custody during interrogations, and another 116 allegations not yet substantiated. There is sweeping evidence that these problems are widespread and long-standing ...

In May, for instance, Detectives Johnny Garlowe and Ronan Mezini, both 29, from the Cambridge homicide unit were interviewing Piet Skodor, then a suspect in two brutal murders of young children in West Cambridge that terrorized parents at the time. Gilberto Curtis, Skodor's attorney, claimed that Garlowe pummeled his client with his fists and burned him during what he called a sadistic interrogation that lasted for 10 hours.

Under pressure, Skodor had signed a confession that his lawyer claimed was forced.

A state-appointed doctor examined the suspect and determined that his face and neck were severely bruised in a manner that led to "an inescapable conclusion of battery." The doctor also found severe burns on Skodor's forearms, inner thighs, and genitals.

An internal investigation cleared Detective Mezini, but his partner Johnny Garlowe left the force after his hearing was postponed several times.

Attorney Curtis claims that the investigation was a whitewash because the police went to great lengths to protect their own. He also believes that Mezini may have played more of a role in the brutal interrogation than the department acknowledged.

"Garlowe was known on the street as a cop's cop," Curtis said, "who was always ready to help a friend and smack a suspect. Mezini was his partner and either knew about it or should have known."

The charges against Skodor were eventually dismissed, though he does have a prior conviction for child abuse involving offenses committed twenty years ago. He is now 45 years old.

I'll have a lot more to say about this story later. As is often the case, what you read is only part of the truth. For now, I'll take you back to the newspaper murders.

• • •

I sat alone inside the living room of V 2.0's basement apartment, after the forensics team had finished its work. I breathed in slowly and deeply. I smelled incense, pot, and a faint trace of lavender shampoo, even though she had been dead for three days. *I began to experience these scents as soft music, like a string quartet, with occasional blasts of bass trombones that cut into the melody like unwelcome interruptions.* Over the years, I've learned to pay attention to the eccentricities of my sensory impressions as a source of insight into character.

What did the crossover from smell to sound tell me here? I wasn't sure, but the perceptions were unsettling, as if I were a sensitive receiver absorbing sounds from V 2.0's grave. For some reason I thought of the nouns referring to the five senses and the adjectives describing their sensations: sight (visual), sound (auditory), touch (tactile), smell (olfactory), and taste (gustative). If you think of all of them as elements, then I have compounds made from them, adding up to more than five senses altogether. Sometimes all the organs seem to flash at once, like a TV set with all the channels turned on.

No wonder I couldn't concentrate in school. I can learn only when I have the privacy to let my brain and my perceptions go where they will. *Okay, Mez, let the hourglass pour up instead of down*, I said to myself. Synesthesia sometimes turns gravity upside down if that even makes sense.

Investigation is often a lonely process, but the solitude can make concentration easier. Would you think me vain if I said that my brain keeps me entertained? I suppose I'm at once the performer and the audience. Somehow all the books I've read keep crashing the party, in a way that can be helpful.

I think of ole Montaigne, a nobleman, politician, and warrior who basically retired to his tower to read and think for years on end. I wish I had that luxury.

Let me tell you about V 2.0's apartment: The two long walls of the rectangular living room had surprisingly traditional red and green floral wallpaper. One of the other walls was painted solid black, and the fourth a light blue. Somehow the total effect seemed to work. The bookshelves held an eclectic collection of screenplays (Bergman and Fellini), coffee table art books (Cindy Sherman, Diane Arbus, Robert Frank), and poetry (Sappho, Elizabeth Bishop, Sylvia Plath).

The victim's laptop was still on the black vinyl desk and fully charged. One of the forensics experts had figured out the password so I had ready access. A folder called "Raw Video Footage" had a list of files with the name Jade in various iterations: Jade Beach, Jade Kitchen, Jade Acting, etc.

I started with the last one.

On the screen I saw a young woman in an open field in the morning sun. She was naked, her forearms crossed on her chest, her back arched. A tattoo of a blue butterfly decorated one shoulder. When the camera zoomed in, I saw a look of fear, as if she were uncomfortable in the pose. "How long do I have to stay like this?" she asked, in the footage.

"Until you get it right," an offscreen voice said. The woman I took to be Jade flinched.

"You just ruined the shot," said the voice.

"Having fun?" I heard from a person behind me.

I've been a cop for so long that it's almost impossible to startle me. I turned around to see Jade, or at least that's who I assumed it was, standing before me. I had left the door ajar without thinking. She had walked in so quietly that I hadn't heard anything until she spoke. She was wearing cutoff jean shorts, a shocking pink shirt, and black Doc Martens boots.

"I'm Detective Mezini," I said uneasily.

"I guess you can see I'm Jade," she said. "Good thing I'm not easily embarrassed."

"You're an, uh, actress?"

"Yes, I am an *actor*. And I don't appreciate you peering at the videos. Some things are personal."

"From what I've seen, I like her work. I'm also a big fan of Robert Frank. I saw his book on her shelf," I added, trying to change the subject. "Do you know what Jack Kerouac said about his photos?"

"Yeah, that he sucked—"

"A sad poem out of America," I finished the quote. She seemed surprised that I knew that. I chuckled. "I guess you think all cops are illiterate boors. My mom taught me a lot about literature and art. She used to paint a bit. Mostly watercolors, seascapes, that kind of stuff. She had a good eye, though." I could tell that she was warming up a bit. "My dad's family was incredibly well-read too."

"So, what do you think about Margaux's work?" she asked.

"Margaux?"

"V 2.0 was her professional name. I knew her as Margaux Duran," Jade said.

"Why did she call herself V 2.0?"

"Because she had reinvented herself as an artist."

I didn't say anything. I knew that people tend to talk more when you just wait.

"I know that cop trick. Hang back and let the person fill the silence," Jade said.

I smiled and shrugged.

"Will it work with you?"

"Maybe. Someone was here last night."

"How do you know?"

"Because I've been watching the place."

"How did they get in?" I asked.

"Your team must have left one of the windows unlocked. Are you guys always this careless?"

"Can you describe the person who snuck in?"

"No, they were leaving when I was a block away. Whoever it was had dark clothes. That's all I can say. There was no moon so I couldn't see much."

"Can you guess who it might have been?" I asked.

"She had lots of friends and lovers who came and went."

"If it happens again, please let us now." I handed her my card.

"So serious, so steady," Jade mocked.

I ignored the sarcasm. "Do you mind if I look at the rest of the footage?" I asked as straightforwardly as possible.

"Be my guest. It's all film-schooly. Lots of experimental stuff, different sorts of camera moves. She was always shooting random scenes. I'll stay here, if you don't mind."

Not waiting for a response, she sat down on a sofa on the other side of the room and started reading a book that she pulled out of a large, purple knit bag she carried.

I noticed that she had rolled up her sleeves. She winced when she bumped her arm on the corner of an end table. *Was she hurt*, I wondered. *I suspected something else.*

After about two hours of screening the footage, I took a break. She had been silent the whole time. She even nodded off on the sofa at one point. I had found nothing of interest and no clues. Except that V 2.0 was often barking orders at Jade.

"Was she always this, uh, bossy?" I asked. I did my best to avoid looking at her arms.

"She was a director. Knew what she wanted, as they say." Jade began to tear up.

"How close were you two?" I asked softly.

"We have, I mean had, been dating for the past year or so. Seeing other people too."

"Are your arms bruised?" I asked. I hated to pose such a direct question, but sometimes that was the best approach. "I don't mean to pry."

"Yes, you do. It's none of your fucking business."
"Were you afraid of her?"
"That is *really* none of your fucking business."
"Glad we clarified that."

7

OBSERVING *THE OBSERVER*

AMY WOKE UP ALONE in the loft she shared with Troy Carr on Boston Harbor. She wished that Troy hadn't kept his own house in Concord, a fancy Boston suburb, but he assured her that he used it only as a home office. She suspected otherwise.

That same morning Troy's current companion Amber Burke was relaxing on a lounge chair on the back deck of his home in Concord. Wearing a short robe, Amber had her eyes closed as she thrust her face toward the sun. Her arms were crossed against the early chill and her hands cupped a mug of warm coffee. A shirtless Troy came out of the sliding door a moment later and bent down to kiss her as he undid the strap on her robe and opened it.

Troy did not usually have affairs with clients, but this was an exception. Amber was a young attorney recently named one of the best lawyers in the city by *Hub Magazine*, thanks to his influence. She specialized in maritime law with a narrow expertise in defending those charged with driving boats under the influence. She knew more about the impact of various intoxicants on reflexes than most doctors and could tell clients exactly how much pot they could smoke, how much they could drink, or how many pain pills they could pop and still maintain some semblance of normal reflexes.

She kept one of her recent clients out of jail after he rammed an expensive yacht on Martha's Vineyard with his racing boat. She crafted a plea deal that involved a stay in rehab. No sooner did he emerge from the six-week recovery program than he drove to his favorite bar at noon and got blind drunk. On the way home, he went through a crosswalk near his home in Arlington and narrowly missed a group of grade school kids, but he severely injured a popular crossing guard who was a retired cop.

Somehow Troy managed to keep Amber's name out of the story that ran in the papers and on TV. He bribed a contact in the courts who conveniently buried the records of the boating incident. Then he fed reporters salacious details about the driver to focus their attention on him and away from her. All of this was very risky, but he was an expert in this sort of maneuvering. Amber could have had her pick of Boston's eligible men, yet she was attracted to Carr because she saw him as a lovable rogue.

He wasn't above threatening to expose her if circumstances demanded, and she knew it. In any case, she was enjoying the trysts. She didn't take him very seriously and knew that their relationship would be brief and intense.

That day the two lovers were so absorbed in one another that neither took note of an intruder snapping pictures from the cover of the thick woods surrounding the house.

• • •

Late that afternoon I showed up unannounced at *The Observer*. The receptionist called Paul, nodded briefly, then directed me toward his office. I quickly noticed that he wasn't at all surprised to see me. If anything, he wondered why it took us so long to show up. He hadn't yet invited me to sit down in his office when Pat Cole, a reporter who worked with Ollie on the I-Desk, knocked on his door and entered before he could shoo her away.

"Did you look at the biotech story yet?" she asked.

"No," Paul said.

Her eyebrows rose and her tight lips got even tighter, pressing together hard enough to make them white.

"I know, I'll get to it, Pat."

"When? We want to get it out ASAP. Rumor has it that their new cancer test is a phony."

"Who's the source for this?"

"Someone at the FDA, whom I happen to know personally. In fact—"

"He's your ex, isn't he?" Paul asked.

Before she could answer she looked over at me. She and I clearly recognized one other but had studiously avoided eye contact. She was the researcher for that infamous story about me.

"Excuse me, I hope this isn't a bad time," I said in a mocking tone as I stood outside the office. I couldn't resist.

"No problem," Paul replied. Speaking to Pat, he said, "Find me another source whom you *haven't* dated."

I suppose my body language showed that I was curious about the conversation even though I pretended to be checking email on my phone. I can't say I was dismayed to see Pat's humiliation. Meanwhile, she was motionless, a bit at a loss.

"I'll talk to you later after your big bad editor act is over," she said to him.

Paul ushered me in and shut the door.

"Sorry about that, Detective. It's—"

"Jeez, good thing your people aren't armed," I said. "No wonder you assigned her to work on that story about, uh, alleged police brutality. She doesn't take any prisoners."

"I'm busy, Detective, what's up?"

"Okay, if that's how you want to play it. For starters," I asked as I sat down, "has anyone contacted you to take credit for the murders? Any unusual letters or phone calls?"

"Not that I know of."

"Do you have any idea why anyone would want to kill these three people?"

"None whatsoever. The media aren't exactly popular these days. Maybe killing the people we profile is a twisted way of getting back at us."

"Can't imagine why anyone would have a grudge against the paper," I said with barely restrained venom.

He let the comment pass. "Our investigative team does a feature on a dishonest medical salesman who worms his way into operating rooms, knowing that he has TB. Somebody with the same name is killed. I'd say that points toward a pretty stupid murderer."

"Or maybe somebody who's trying to make a statement."

"And what would that be?"

"No idea. I need not remind you that the other victims are an artsy filmmaker and a whiz kid who turned out to be a loser, both of whom showed up in your pages."

"Not much of a connection, on the surface," Paul said.

"I'd imagine all this is bad for business," I said.

"To tell you the truth, more people are clicking on the stories, but ad revenues are down."

"Where does that leave you?"

"Under pressure, as always. At least our subscribers tend to be well-heeled. I call our people Josef and Salomé Syrah, while *The Sun's* are Joe and Sally Sixpack."

I chuckled. "Do you mind if I speak with Ollie Burns?"

"Ollie?" That brought Paul's eyebrows up.

"That investigation was pure trash. I'd never have anything to do with the putative reporters on the so-called investigative desk if it were up to me, but it's part of the job, unfortunately."

"Putative?" Paul said sarcastically.

"Should I have said supposed, presumed, or alleged instead?" I asked. "I'll talk to Ollie first. She was the writer."

"Given the circumstances, can you be objective?" he asked.

"Are you going to lecture *me* about objectivity? I'll do my best to play it neutral. I'm sure I'll just get BS from her anyway."

"You'll find Ollie at her desk. Do you want me to walk you over?" *I could tell he thought I was smart. He probably thought it was unusual for a cop.*

"No thanks, I can find my way. I'll just follow the rancid scent."

• • •

Ollie was typing furiously at her desk when I knocked on the door of her office. I could see through the small glass window that she was so deep in concentration that she gave a start.

"Detective Mezini," she said as she opened the door. "What a surprise." She was clearly sarcastic.

"Do you know what Napoleon said about the press?" I asked.

She shrugged as if to say, tell me.

"'Four hostile newspapers are more to be feared than one thousand bayonets,'" I said.

"Well, you've only done battle with one paper," Ollie said. "Three to go. Did you come here to complain?" Her tone turned sharp. *That smell came off her again. What was it? As hard as I tried, I couldn't place it. It was sort of metallic, I guessed.*

"I'd like to complain, but I come, hat in hand, seeking information," I said with mock solemnity. "I have three murders to investigate. One of them involves your story. So whaddya say we go to the First Draft and talk about this like two civilized adults?"

Ollie nodded. I could tell she was intrigued. "On the record?"

"Yup," I said. "Plus, there's a fringe benefit."

I could tell she wondered whether I was coming on to her.

"Don't flatter yourself, Burns," I said, reading her mind. "You're not my type. I'll bet Kenny Moran will be there too, from what I hear about his fondness for the watering hole. It'll save me the trouble of tracking him down. I want to talk to him too."

Ollie nodded. "Give me ten minutes."

"What are you working on, by the way?"

"None of your fucking business."

"A lot of people have been saying that to me lately. I'm beginning to get a complex."

"I'm almost done here. Just wait at the First Draft," she said as if dismissing me. "And you're buying."

• • •

It was the end of the workday, and the usual crowd was at the First Draft. Most of the newspaper reporters and editors looked rumpled. The guys wore cotton-poly shirts, many with worn collars and cuffs, over khaki pants that might have looked presentable if their owners had ever visited a tailor. For the most part the women sported bland, "sensible" skirts, in the Ann Taylor or Lands' End mode, utilitarian rather than stylish, with beige or olive shirts. Few wore heels, since flats were much more practical if they ever had to actually grind through shoe leather. On the other hand, the era of spending several days actually *reporting* a story, collecting information in person, was disappearing. Now they rarely left their cubicles. At least their shoes lasted longer if that was any consolation.

It was easy to spot the PR types in the crowd. They looked like they just came from a college classroom, fresh from their lightweight "communications" studies. All enthusiasm and little experience. Reporters I knew told me that they were mostly naive "account coordinators," who pitched stories in a way that displayed negligible understanding of what news was all about. The good ones just schmoozed, with no apparent object in mind.

I was sitting at the bar. When Ollie greeted me, a few heads turned, as if people were surprised to see us together. Curiosity quickly faded, though, because the news business always generated unusual alliances between cops, informants, scammers, reporters, and PR people, all part of the same menagerie at the bar. Everyone was equal in this peculiar demimonde.

Ollie waved to Eddie, and he blew her a kiss. He was a completely harmless charmer, so all the women felt comfortable showing him affection and accepting his.

As Ollie and I headed toward an open booth, we passed the end of the bar where Kenny was holding court. He nodded to Ollie as we walked by and stared after us for a moment, as if to say, what goes on here, then continued with his conversation.

We also saw someone else I recognized because I had seen him speak at the Cambridge Library one night about the art of reading. You might think it's silly to listen to a lecture about reading, but his was clever. He told us that we should read word by word to do justice to a work of literature, just as we should chew mindfully if we're trying to savor a meal. He mentioned that his father would pour him a scotch and expect him to sip it slowly over an hour. "You wouldn't wolf down a fine steak, and you shouldn't just swallow a drink either."

I'm talking about Caleb Baird, and he was sitting a table by himself reading, of course, and nursing what looked like a double shot of whiskey in a small tumbler. He was a former book reviewer at *The Observer* and he got the reward that virtually everyone who practiced his craft received: a pink slip. I heard that the news came six months ago. Most writers who covered the arts could see the axe above their heads, if they had any common sense, but not Caleb. He adored books and could not imagine that a paper could continue to exist without him on board.

I wanted to say hello and find out what he was reading but didn't want to disturb him.

Betty showed up just as we sat down in our booth. "Ollie," she said. "Burger medium and a Manhattan on the way."

Ollie nodded.

"Who's this hunk?" Betty said, winking at Ollie. "Carries himself like a cop."

Ollie smiled faintly and shrugged in a way that meant "if you say so." *I sensed that she was thinking that Betty was right, if I do say so myself.* Then again, you might chalk that up to male vanity.

I introduced myself, ordered a burger, and a Coke.

I sensed that Ollie felt ill at ease, so I tried to start a conversation. "I suppose you feel just as uncomfortable as I do," I said.

"Go ahead, ask me questions," she said, ignoring my comment.

"All right." I was distracted for a moment by the intense gaze in her blue eyes but quickly shook that off. "I understand your dad was a cop."

"Trying to establish rapport, is that the game?"

"Maybe. Do you want me to be more direct?"

"I guess so. I like that in a man," she replied.

Whenever I'm around a beautiful woman, and I confess that I thought from the outset that Ollie was attractive, I see an aura around her. Usually striking women exude tropical colors for me, like pastel orange or lime green. In this case the emanations were blue with an icy crust. I wanted to break through that façade somehow.

"How did you find out about Alec Moore's, uh, unorthodox sales methods?" I asked.

"Through a source."

"Name?"

"No way. Would you tell a reporter the names of your informants?"

"Guess not."

"I will tell you this, though. Lawyers who bring suits for damages, if they have any brains at all, will contact the press. Nothing like some helpful pretrial publicity."

"Note to self, contact the lawyers. When you interviewed patients who caught TB, or their families, did anyone jump out at you as particularly angry?"

"They were *all* pissed," Ollie said. "Wouldn't you be? Hard to tell if any of them were mad enough to kill, if that's what you mean."

I suppose I looked like I was pondering something.

"Go ahead, Mezini. Tell me what you're thinking," Ollie said. *I guess two can play the mind-reading game*, I thought.

"You guys got that story about us all wrong."

"We tried to reach you three or four times and you never responded. So *now* you complain?"

"Off the record?"

"Sure, go for it."

"Our PR guy Terry Keegan clamped down on us. Said *he'd* handle the interviews. I have never liked that asshole. Kind of guy who has a euphemism for everything. He never stuck up for us. Just covered his own—"

"If you want," she said, "we can talk about this on the record sometime, and I can—"

"Yeah, sometime ... but not now. I'm concentrating on the murders."

"Sorry to interrupt this tête-à-tête, Detective Mezini, but I understand that you were trying to reach me," Kenny said. He had waddled up to our booth unannounced. His belly was practically touching the edge of the table, though his shoulders were thrust back.

"Sit down, Kenny. I'm buying," I said.

"I have never been known to refuse an offer for a free adult beverage, me boy," he said as he sidled over next to Ollie in the booth.

"I didn't know you two were so well acquainted," Ollie said.

"I could say the same to you," Kenny replied. "I always make a point of forging deep friendships with those who inhabit the thin blue line between order and anarchy. Plus, you never know when you're going to be pulled over for, uh, overindulging. It pays to have friends on the force."

"I think I'll let you two talk privately," Ollie said.

"And miss the opportunity to acquire new information? You're slipping, mademoiselle," Kenny said.

"All right, I'll stay," Ollie said with a laugh. "Since you insist."

Betty gave Kenny a drive-by lift of her eyebrows, which meant "Do you want another drink?" and he replied with an almost imperceptible nod.

"Kenny, I was sorry to hear about your troubles at the paper," I said.

"Divorce is sometimes a good thing. I should know, I've done it three times," he said.

"There's always PR. We could use a good spokesman."

"Keegan has always been kind of a slimy bastard, to use a literary term. Not my sort of job, though. I'd rather be on the outside pissing in, than on the inside pissing out, as they say."

Betty brought Kenny's drink. He thanked her, raised his glass, and took a large gulp. "Here's to the First Draft. A beached ship of fools destined never to sail again. What do you want to know?"

"Tell me about Wilhelm Stafford."

"I went to the frat house where he was living. Spoke to a lot of the MIT kids coming in and out. They were strangely protective of him. He may have been a weirdo, but he was *their* weirdo. And that's saying a lot for a school with arguably the largest collection of eccentric kids on the planet. Nobody told me much."

"When did you, uh, interview his girlfriend?"

"Are you questioning me or interrogating me?"

Ollie was following the conversation very closely.

"Touchy, touchy. I just want to know if you have any suggestions for me. You may have been the last person to see him." I knew he was dishonest; I suppose everybody did, but he could also be a decent source of information.

"To tell you the truth," Kenny said, "I snuck around the back of the frat house and saw someone who was on the third-floor fire escape. Big, unkempt beard, wrinkled clothes, baggy shirt. I shouted up to him and he looked down at me, gave me the finger, and went back inside."

"What did you say to him?"

"I said, 'Hey, Wilhelm,' if you must know."

"And that was it?"

"Oui, oui."

"Our team has spoken to virtually all of the students and the neighbors, twice," I said. "Not much help."

"The rest of the story will be in my book, Detective."

This made Ollie perk up. "What book?" she asked.

"The one I'm writing about my storied newspaper career," Kenny answered. "Agents are swarming all over me."

Ollie looked at me as if to say, "not happening."

"As long as you're here, Detective," Ollie said with mocking respect, "why don't you tell us what *you've* discovered so far."

"Should we ask Mr. Moran to give us privacy?" I asked. "In any case, we don't know too much yet."

Kenny held out his palm as if to say, "I'll go, if you want me to."

"You let me listen to your conversation with him, I think we should return the favor," Ollie said. "But be careful, you might end up in his column. I think you had some questions for me."

"Yeah, did anyone contact you about these murders?"

"Just the usual crazies. We got some emails saying that it's no wonder violence follows us," Ollie said.

"I get those all the time," Kenny said. "But they're not that articulate. They usually call me a fucking vulture. Sign of a good column, I always say."

"I did get one really strange call just after that artist was shot," Ollie said.

"You mean, uh, V 2.0?" I asked.

"Yeah, whatever name she gave herself." Ollie said. "A woman called me and said that next time someone who happens to be named Ollie Burns might be killed."

I winced. "What did you say to that?"

"I just hung up," Ollie said.

"Scary," I said.

Ollie just blinked and said nothing. *A tough cookie,* I said to myself. *Don't even think that word,* I thought. *A tough woman.* I had to admit, I was intrigued.

Kenny swallowed more of his drink and his eyes moved from me to Ollie and back again, as if he were trying to figure out if anything was brewing between us. Ollie's reaction was harder to read. *An inscrutable character in many ways,* I thought.

8

THE EXPERT PLUS THE PLOUGH AND STARS
Late June

WHEN DR. JACK GRIMES, the FBI's serial killer expert, finally came to Cambridge Police headquarters to meet us, the staff wasn't sure what to expect. He was Black, medium height, elegantly dressed in a blue suit, spread collar shirt, and carefully knotted tie. He carried himself as if he knew he was special. He tended to treat local police with a degree of condescension, like a professor indulging undergraduates who could never hope to achieve his level of insight or intelligence.

"Sorry we interrupted your vacation," I said as I ushered him into a conference room and closed the door.

"That's all right," Grimes said. "It isn't the first time, I'll tell you that," he said in a way that indicated that he was used to being in demand. "Beaches are overrated anyway."

After some small talk, I got down to it. "I read your dissertation a while ago," I said.

"Thanks, but I never look at it because so much has changed since I wrote it," Grimes said. "It's probably out of date. Was it too technical for you?"

I let that arrogant comment pass. *Always better to be underestimated.*

"Can I start with a potentially dumb question?" I asked.

"I'm used to that. The GP asks smarter questions than most cops do."

"The GP?" I asked.

"General Public. Great unwashed," Grimes said. "Go ahead, Detective, try me. I won't bite."

When he said that my synesthesia kicked in. I wasn't sure what to make of Grimes. Whenever he spoke, I experienced a taste I could best describe as "dusty library," as if someone had opened an old book that hadn't been read in years.

"What do you make of the situation, Dr. Grimes?"

"The similarity in MOs indicates an organized killer, not someone who kills at random," he said. "MO means—"

"Modus operandi," I said. "I know. Latin for pattern of behavior. The actions he takes to avoid detection, to coin your phrase."

"Right, but the MO may be different from a ritual," he said.

"Meaning …"

"Meaning that a ritual may meet an emotional need."

"I get that," I said. "The Unabomber carved FC on the explosives he used. It meant Freedom Club, apparently."

"You're a smart guy, uh …"

"You can call me Mez." *The smell of books was getting stronger and stronger.*

"You okay, Mez? You look a bit distracted."

"Fine, proceed, professor." I was starting to lose patience. "What's your best guess, is the killer male or female?"

"It's safe to assume that we're dealing with a male," Grimes said. "Only 15% of serial killers are women. Generally, the killers tend to be glib and impulsive. They're not necessarily loners, though. In fact, most are in relationships. They blend in, which is why neighbors often say, 'He seemed like such a nice, quiet guy,' and all that bullshit."

I was surprised to hear him curse. It seemed out of character.

"They often have jobs and families and own homes. Even go to church," Grimes continued.

"They do crave attention, though." I asked.

"Fuck, yes," Grimes said. "The media doesn't help. They give them stupid nicknames like the Sunday Morning Slasher, the Cleveland Strangler, the Killer Clown, and so on. And now we have the Headline Hunter, thanks to your friends in the papers."

"They're no friends of mine," I said.

"So I understand," Grimes said.

How much does he know, I wondered. *A rude comment in any case.*

"Then again, David Berkowitz gave *himself* the nickname 'The Son of Sam,'" Grimes said.

"Right. He saved reporters the trouble," I said. "Crazy."

"Remember, these guys are sane, in the legal sense," Grimes said. "They may try to plead insanity, but it's very hard to succeed with that in court. Even David Berkowitz, who said he was taking orders from his neighbor's dog Sam, was found competent to stand trial."

"Where does that leave us?" I asked.

"Let me look at the files and I'll get back to you."

"Do you need an office?"

"That'd be great, thanks." Grimes said. "Privacy is necessary." He said this with finality, as if he was already closing an imaginary door.

• • •

It had been almost a week since V 2.0's death, and Anika Mehta was still upset because she had never encountered a murder on the entertainment beat. She reached out to Kenny for comfort. Even though they were an odd pair, they were good friends. She called and asked him to meet her at the crime scene.

Outside V 2.0's apartment, Anika posed like Gloria Swanson in *Sunset Boulevard*. There was a chalk outline on the sidewalk where the body had fallen, with blood stains around the head. Yesterday an up-and-coming filmmaker, today just a corpse on an autopsy table.

Yellow crime scene tape extended from sawhorse to sawhorse on the sidewalk in front of the house. A police officer stood guard outside and others were visible through the open basement door.

Neighbors accosted Anika, mostly in curiosity. Her stylish attire was conspicuous. "You don't look like a cop," said a woman who walked down the steps from the first floor of the house.

"No, I'm from *The Observer*," she said.

"Another bloodsucker," the woman said over her shoulder as she walked away.

Deadline on Arrival

I happened to be in the apartment at that moment. I heard the commotion, walked up the basement stairs, and introduced himself.

"Anika Mehta," she said, as if identifying herself was superfluous.

"I read your story," I said. "When did you interview her, if you don't mind my asking?"

"Am I under oath, Detective?"

"Should you be?" I asked with a trace of annoyance. I was tired and petulant. *These media types are all so self-important*, I thought. "Did you notice anything out of the ordinary?"

"It was a routine interview, Detective. I always try to keep an eye out for new talent."

How would you know about talent, I thought. *Mehta was a pale imitation of Joyce Kulhawik, the woman from WBZ-TV who set the standard years ago for everyone in her profession in Boston.*

"Did, uh, V 2.0 have any reason to fear anyone, that you were aware of?"

"We just discussed her work. I'm afraid I can't be very helpful."

"What brings you back to the house?"

"I feel a connection here that I can't explain." I looked at her quizzically. "Plus, I'm meeting a friend. Someone you know, no doubt."

Kenny pulled up in a red 1984 Oldsmobile 88, a barge-like car that was 18 feet long. He would never win fashion awards (he had the rumpled reporter look down to a science), but the Olds was pristine, as if it had just come off the assembly line.

"Hop in," he said to Anika.

I waved to Kenny, who saluted me in a mocking way. Anika opened the passenger door and settled in.

"Would you like to join us, Detective?" he asked. "C'mon, let's get a drink. We're going to The Plough and Stars. To pretend we're *real* writers."

"Okay, I'll meet you there," I said. *You never know what you can discover when you spend time with reporters who love to talk.*

• • •

The Plough and Stars has been a Cambridge landmark since 1969. Poets like Lawrence Ferlinghetti and Seamus Heaney, and singers like Van Morrison and Bonnie Raitt have hung out there over the years. It's what you might call a "good drinking bar," full of literary and musical ghosts.

I settled into a table with Anika and Kenny. I was tempted to order a water, but I thought that might discourage conversation. We clinked glasses when three Guinness Stouts showed up.

"Luck of the virtuous," Kenny said.

"Here's to the dinosaurs," Anika added.

"You know, the latest stats I saw said that employment in newspaper newsrooms has dropped by almost two-thirds in the country since 2006," Kenny said.

"How many of us are left?" she asked.

"We're down to 30,000 or so, last I saw. We'd all fit inside Fenway Park, with a lot of room to spare. Imagine that," he said.

"How many seats are in Fenway?" Anika asked.

"Thirty-seven thousand, three-hundred fifty-five," I said. *Yeah, my mind is a slag heap of useless statistics.*

"Detective, I'm impressed," Anika said flirtatiously. *Meanwhile I was thinking that she was used to speaking in a flirtatious way to all guys.* "I like a man who can remember things."

"I remember my job," Kenny said. He was surprisingly maudlin. "In a way, I'm glad I got suspended. I always wanted to punch that fucker Paul Green. It was worth it."

"They'll take you back, don't worry. You have too many readers," Anika said. "Just disappear for a while. Speaking of which, I have to visit the bathroom."

When Anika got up to go, Kenny looked even more chagrined. *Maybe that "Really, Moran?" column fact-checking his pieces was beginning to bother him, or maybe he was just drinking too much.*

"You know," he said, "I've been working in the 'biz' for 40 years, is that too long? I remember the days when the paper had 450 editorial employees and we could throw 20 bodies at any story just like that. Christ, every morning a group of interns would dial up the police departments in all 350 towns and cities in the state, from Abington all the way down to Yarmouth. They'd ask if anything significant had happened overnight. If so, a reporter would be on the story before finishing his morning coffee. We had so many people that there were several old writers who were just relics in cubicles, generating copy every few months, if that. They were so revered for their past prowess that it was considered rude to ask, 'What are you working on?' It was almost as if there were putting Quaaludes in the coffee in those days."

I just sat back, sipped my Guinness, and let him talk. I didn't really like Kenny, but I found him amusing. *Musical notation seemed to dance out of his mouth.*

"Now it's all online, slam-bam, with every reporter cranking out three stories a day," he continued. "Get the press release, add a live quote, and call it an article. Just like adding water to a packet of hot chocolate mix. Stenography with a byline. Can't fight a riptide, have to swim sideways or get back on land and find a different beach."

I nodded. "You won't get an argument from me about the craziness in the business," I said.

"Who the fuck am I to talk?" Kenny said. "I'm just a hack columnist with a tired list of contacts. I've been writing the same story with different dates and names for decades. Jesus, Mezini, you're too young to pay attention to these riffs. How's your old partner Johnny Garlowe, by the way? Did he survive the onslaught?"

• • •

The Recovery Through Reflection complex sat on rolling fields in Concord, close to Walden Pond. The buildings were all brick with white cupolas of varying heights that looked like benign sentries. Almost every window had a flower box full of tulips or irises that were blooming now that the weather was warming.

As Ollie walked down the hallway, one dejected person after another passed by. Through a small window in a closed door, she caught a glimpse of what appeared to be a group therapy session. Ollie later told me that she couldn't imagine sharing her story with a bunch of strangers. *Bet their childhood issues are a lot simpler than mine,* she said to herself. She wondered how much cocaine, joints, pills, or bottles of booze patients had snuck into the place.

She stepped into a room so sumptuous that it could have been in a luxury hotel. What appeared to be hand-made rugs adorned the hardwood floor. A couch with red upholstery sat along one wall, with two Eames lounge chairs on either side. Jan Watkins was slouching in one of the chairs.

Framed photos of mountains, in the style of Ansel Adams, decorated the walls. Jan put down her book and looked up at Ollie.

"Hey," Ollie said. "Good to see you."

"Back at you, kid," Jan said in a weak, hoarse voice.

"Are they treating you well?"

"Rehab. Strange word," Jan said. "I call it blab-blab. I talk to my shrink, I listen to people go on and on in group. But I'd rather sit here by myself."

"What are you reading?" Ollie asked. She didn't know how to keep the conversation going.

"William Styron's *Darkness Visible*," she said with a chuckle. "I'm just kidding. I already have that book memorized. This is just a junky mystery." Silence fell for a moment.

"Can I get you anything?" Ollie asked, doing her best to be amiable.

"A big glass of Chardonnay, maybe," Jan said with a faint smile.

"Chilled, or room temperature?" Ollie asked, playing along.

"I'd chug it right out of the bottle, sweetie," Jan said. "What's up, something on your mind?"

"I wanted to see how you were doing," Ollie said.

"And?"

"And I need some advice," Ollie said.

"About what? Tell me. It'll take my mind off my, uh, cravings."

"The brutality story. Mezini says we got it wrong," Ollie said.

"Take that as a sign that we hit him where it hurts," Jan said.

"Maybe," Ollie said. "He's a pretty smart guy. Deeper than you'd expect."

"He is good looking, too, as I recall," Jan said.

"If you like that type," Ollie said. Jan looked at her skeptically.

"Talk to him. See if he'll go on the record. Worth a try, I suppose."

"Maybe," Ollie said. They fell silent for a moment.

"What made you check in here?" Ollie asked.

"You might say I got an ultimatum from, uh, management, to dry out or—"

"Management meaning Paul?"

"Are you two talking shop?" said a familiar voice from the doorway. Ollie turned to see Paul himself. Jan blushed and coughed as he walked over and gave her a kiss. Ollie took in the interaction.

"Do us a favor, and don't tell people about us," Paul said. "We, uh, try to be discrete." He was embarrassed and Ollie was stunned to see him stumble, for once. *Still she wondered why he was openly affectionate. Maybe it was his way of flaunting his imaginary status as a Romeo.*

"Don't worry," she said. "I never breach a confidence."

"I'm glad I ran into you. I was going to ask you to work on the Headline Hunter story. Christ, now they even have me saying it," he said.

"C'mon, Paul, I'm not a crime reporter. Let Amy and company handle it. I—"

"It's not really a request, Burns," he said.

"What about our other investigations?" Ollie asked.

"*This*," he said. "*This* is an investigation. And a big one. Deal with Mezini," he said. "Now can Jan and I have some time alone?" he asked with finality.

"Aye, aye, my liege," Ollie said. She looked over her shoulder and saw Jan's smirk.

9

SARTRE AND FLYING BRICKS

I WAS LYING IN BED and couldn't sleep. I was mulling over the murders and wondering what, if anything, I had missed. If the so-called Headline Hunter was an erratic loner, then it would be difficult to find a pattern. Then again, he might be perfectly sane and organized, as Dr. Grimes had suggested. The only consistent MO was that the victims were shot in the back of the head with .38-caliber bullets, as the ballistics reports indicated. Was the killer reluctant to face them? Perhaps he was fearful or squeamish, or he got a thrill from surprising the victims. I was beginning to think that I wasn't up to this job and that I should consider changing careers and going into corporate security.

It's no wonder, though, that I ended up as a homicide detective because death has always been an inextricable part of my life. Both of my dad's brothers perished from heart attacks, six weeks apart, when I was 14, not to mention several other relatives who left this world during my mid-teen years, followed by my own dad just a month before my high school graduation. Some people don't encounter the utter finality of death until they're much older, but I came face to face with it during adolescence.

I'm certainly not squeamish around corpses—Christ knows I've seen a lot of them—but I always think about all the experiences that disappear with them. Baskets of memories, secret ambitions, failed love affairs, disappointing vacations, birth of children, fulfilling meals, fine wines—their thoughts of all those events fade like morning dew on a hot day. Someday AI may preserve them, but who will go through them? It would take a whole lifetime to relive a lifetime of memories.

In times of trouble, I often turn to Sartre. I've read a fair amount of philosophy, and his ideas never fail to resonate. I think he was right when he said that man is a useless passion. Sartre believed we can make our own destiny even if our circumstances are as immutable as our height and eye color, yet at the same time he poignantly described the quixotic nature of our struggle to find meaning in a world unprotected by any gods. He can be depressing as hell, but he always offers hope, bleak though it may be. I have "Sartred" my way out of many quandaries.

As I was contemplating all this, my cell phone rang, interrupting this morose interior monologue. As it was after one o'clock in the morning, I knew it wouldn't be good news.

The familiar voice that greeted me belonged to the night supervisor at the homicide desk, Charlene Larson.

"What's up, Char?"

I listened for a moment, then said, "On my way."

Ten hectic minutes later my black Ford Interceptor SUV, lights flashing, pulled up in front of a house in Huron Village, an expensive part of West Cambridge. I was the first to arrive and I proceeded cautiously up the steps of the brick house. I knocked gently on the door and kept my hand on my gun. A woman, perhaps forty years old, appeared. Her hair was scraggly, and she looked terrified.

"I'm Detective Mezini, from the Cambridge Police," I said.

"Thanks for coming. I'm Jody Moore, Alec Moore's wife," she said.

"Just to clarify, your Alec is the one that *The Observer* wrote about, the medical salesman?" I asked.

"Yes, unfortunately," she said. *Why did she use that word*, I wondered.

She led me wordlessly into the kitchen, where shards of broken glass had fallen from a window over the counter. She pointed to a brick on the floor. "I had been standing in front of that spot two minutes earlier," she explained, then suddenly sobbed.

I surveyed the scene. The brick apparently landed on the counter, cracked several tiles, then bounced onto the wooden floor where it left a dent. "Is anyone else home?" I asked.

"No, I sent my kids to my parents' house in Lexington after the other Alec Moore was killed. I'm here by myself. I came back for a couple of days to organize some things."

"Where is your husband?" I asked.

"He's still in Barnes Hospital in Boston. He's been there for weeks. Getting treated for his … TB." *Unaccountably, my lungs started to ache when she mentioned the disease. Sometimes my synesthesia causes me to feel other people's pain acutely.*

"I'll make sure we beef up protection for him there. From now on, please stay at your parents' place."

"You're not leaving now, are you?" she asked with increasing anxiety.

"Absolutely not. I'm going to call in backup and someone will drive you to Lexington. I'm sorry this is happening, ma'am."

She started to say something but stopped herself.

"Have you been to see your husband? Is he getting better?" I asked.

"I think so," she said with some hesitation.

"Mrs. Moore, I hate to ask you this. Is everything okay between the two of you?"

She breathed in deeply. I interpreted her hunched shoulders as a no.

• • •

On the following day I drove to Analog Joints, the company where Alec Moore had worked. As I sat in the reception area, I marveled at the ridiculous conversations. All the salespeople who walked through—and it was easy to peg them because they were attractive, athletic, and well dressed—shared gossip or useless information with the receptionist, a no-nonsense older woman who humored them politely.

Don't you guys have anything to do, I wondered. I'm sure I was fidgeting as I waited.

The receptionist, sensing my impatience, said, "He should be right out, Detective." With that the salespeople stiffened. *Were they unhappy I was there, or where they just responding the way drivers do when they see a cop car on the highway? I chuckled to myself and remembered something one of my instructors had said at the police academy: "Most people have a guilty conscience. That's why they freeze up around us."*

A few minutes later a secretary led me down a corridor toward the CEO's office. Along the way I couldn't help noticing that workmen were removing a sign from an office door. I guessed it was Moore's, though I acted as if I didn't notice.

The CEO was Dr. Anton Benson, a former orthopedic surgeon who invented replacement hip joints made from ceramic instead of a combination of titanium and plastic. Benson carried himself like a man who has known a great deal of success. His "bedside manner" was smooth and genial, at least on the surface. *He's good*, I said to himself.

"Detective, what can I do for you?" Dr. Benson asked once we were seated in his office.

I ignored the question. "This is a beautiful office, Dr. Benson. Do you do the manufacturing in the US?" I asked.

"No, most of it is done in Shanghai. I travel back and forth every couple of months. We have a plant in Des Moines, too." Benson said.

"Partially made in America. Better politically," I said.

"Right."

"This must be a lucrative business, with, what, 300,000 hip replacements a year in the US alone," I said.

"Yes," Dr. Benson said, "but not all surgeons use our devices ... yet."

"You sell your hardware for 5-10K per patient, I'm told. Not bad."

"You've done your homework. Do you want to come work for us?" he asked with a smile. *Was he serious?*

"I'll think about it if I ever change careers," I said, playing along. "I'm just curious: why ceramic instead of titanium?" *I was partly stalling, trying to size up the doctor. I smelled disinfectant coming off him. Was that telling me that he needed it?*

"Good question. It wears better than titanium and plastic combos and won't dislocate as easily," Benson said. "Plus it causes less inflammation.

Surely, Detective, you didn't come here to talk about hips. How can I help you?"

"What kind of salesman was Alec Moore? Does he still work here, by the way?"

"No, he does not."

"May I ask why?"

"It's our policy not to comment on personnel matters," he replied, suddenly growing serious.

"I get it. I can imagine why he's gone, though. Did you know he had TB?"

"Of course not, Detective. Do you think we would have allowed him to go into operating rooms if we had known?"

"If Moore knowingly transmitted TB, that would be a felony," I said. *I wasn't sure about that, but I knew it sounded intimidating.* "At the very least, you're liable for his actions since you're the boss. I'll bet you've already been sued. Work with me." I paused to let this message percolate.

"Can I level with you, off the record, so to speak?" Dr. Benson asked.

"Please do. I'm a homicide detective. I'm trying to figure out who the murderer is. I'm not here to investigate medical issues."

"Moore was a great salesman," he said. "He was selling more of our hip joints than anyone else. We gave him carte blanche. He had the biggest expense account of all. But I swear to you, we had no idea he had TB." He raised his voice. "We run a reputable company. I'm a former surgeon, for Christ's sake. I, uh—" His voice quivered.

"I believe you. But just answer one question for me, please."

"What?" Dr. Benson said as he struggled to regain composure.

"What kind of a guy was Alec Moore?" I asked.

"As I said, Detective," he answered, "he was a great salesman."

I nodded. *Benson's meaning was clear. Damning him with a pale compliment.*

"You might want to speak with his wife."

I said, "Thanks very much for your time, sir. Have a great day."

As I walked toward my SUV in the parking lot, I saw Ollie leaning against the passenger door. I was surprised to see her. She was wearing the beginning of a smirk.

I couldn't help but smile back as I stopped a few feet in front of her. "I overheard Amy talking about that escapade with the brick last night and I figured you'd come here," she said.

"I guess dispatch should be more careful on the two-way," I said. "You never know when nosy jerks might be listening in."

"Detective, I want to talk with you about the I-Desk story."

"Wrong preposition, Burns. You want to talk *to* me, not *with* me," I said. I got into my car and drove away.

10

FAREWELL TO A SALESMAN

THE BARNES HOSPITAL for Infectious Diseases, in a part of Boston called Dorchester, is world renowned. The smartest doctors in the field work there. From the outside it looks like a fortress. A central brick building with barred windows, redolent of a mental institution, dominates the structure, with joyless concrete rectangles extending outward like spokes on a wheel. Many prisons are more inviting.

Because of recent events, Alec Moore, the "real one," was in isolation, now under armed guard, while doctors treated his tuberculosis. I later learned a visitor dressed in scrubs, with a matching blue cap covering a short-haired wig, snuck into the hospital through the loading dock when the attendant took a quick break. The visitor must have scurried to the basement, found the corridor leading to Wing C where the TB patients were housed, taken the stairs up to Moore's floor, and donned a hospital mask on the way. Walking by his room, which was easy to spot because of the presence of a uniformed policeman sitting on a plastic chair outside, the visitor somehow found the kitchen where meals were arrayed on shelves on a dolly. This mysterious person grabbed the tray marked for Moore's room, quickly poured some liquid into a glass of juice, and left the room.

We surmised that the visitor no doubt ducked into a restroom, peeled off the scrubs to reveal street clothes underneath, stuffed the hospital garb into a bag, removed the convincing, lifelike mask that had obscured the facial features, put another one on, walked calmly down the corridor, took the elevator to the first floor, and left through the front door. The plan was disturbingly quick and easy to execute.

Ten minutes later, Alec Moore took a large gulp of the juice with his lunch. Within a short time, he began vomiting violently and started hyperextending his arms and legs. He moaned loudly enough to attract the attention of the policeman, who called the nurses and ran into the room. In seconds six medical personnel were involved in a code rescue.

Moore was raving, hallucinating, growling, and sweating profusely. His heart raced at 160 beats a minute. In two hours, he was in a coma, despite the best efforts of the medical team. He was dead by dinnertime.

I had heard about the murder from a source in the Boston Police Department and showed up on the scene within an hour. The toxicology tests eventually identified the poison as Compound 1080, sodium fluoroacetate, commonly used to kill rats, wolves, and coyotes, and easily purchased online. It's colorless, odorless, tasteless, and deadly. In fact, a single teaspoon could kill 100 people.

The area around the hospital is called the "Methadone Mile" because of all the junkies that frequent the area. Because of the drug sales there, there are enough video cameras trained on those streets to fill a TV studio, not to mention the security cameras on the premises of the hospital itself. My team and I spent days looking at all the footage. Given that healthcare facilities are labor intensive, there were hundreds of employees coming and going on the day that Moore was killed. Beyond this, there were 227 patients in the hospital, and each one had many visitors at the time. No one in the footage appeared to be the least suspicious.

I had to admit that I was about a mile from nowhere in the investigation. I decided to take a closer look at the victims once again, in ongoing psychological autopsies. Back at headquarters, I did database searches on both Alec Moores, Wilhelm Stafford, and V 2.0, real name Margaux Duran.

I was astounded to discover that all of them had been arrested, though never officially charged, for domestic violence. The 911 records were quite revealing. They showed that the real Moore's wife Jody had called in hysterics, claiming that her husband repeatedly slapped her face in front of their children; the "fake" Moore's wife said her husband smashed a mirror in the foyer with a baseball bat because he was angry when she came home late; a young woman visiting her brother who was a student at the MIT fraternity claimed that Stafford had cornered her and "invited" her to his room so many times that she was terrified; and Margaux's partner Jade Greenwood said that one evening V 2.0 downed numerous shots of vodka, threatened her with a knife, and slashed a painting that Jade had worked on for months. All four victims refused to press charges for unknown reasons.

Occasionally, when I get stuck, I'll pull a philosophy book off my shelf at home for some insight. This time old Martin Heidegger was elected. He was a 20th-century German thinker who was extremely smart but foolish enough to ruin his career by tying himself up with the Third Reich. I condemn his politics but grudgingly admit that I sometimes find his writing useful. He believed, for instance, that art involved "unconcealment" (his term), leading to a "shining" that shows the truth.

What in the name of Christ does this have to do with detective work, you are probably wondering. A lot, I think. Investigation, in many ways is an art form, a process of "unconcealment," meaning, I suppose, that we struggle to find hidden parts of the puzzle so that the solution eventually reveals itself and shines brightly in a pitiless spotlight.

I sat back and asked myself what I had missed, what lay hidden behind the obvious and what I might be able to predict. Certainly, both Moores, V 2.0, and Stafford weren't the first abusers to show up in the newspaper for reasons that had nothing to do with domestic violence. I felt that my eyes had seen something in the files that my brain failed to register. I reviewed each record one more time, word by word.

Then it jumped out at me: All four arrests had taken place this year. Why didn't I see that right away? Are you still there, Mez, I asked myself. Did the killer start planning the murders recently? All the arrest records were public, but whoever noticed the connection had to be watching the reports for quite some time. Someone on the police force perhaps.

Deadline on Arrival

I was beginning to take the "Headline Hunter" murders personally. At the same time, I was astounded that I was using the tabloid nickname myself. The media got to me, I said to myself. Once again, I went over and over what I knew, and what I didn't.

Let's start with the victims: A sleazy medical device salesman who spread TB in operating rooms, perhaps knowingly; his namesake, with no known connection; a filmmaker who treated her lover shabbily; a nutjob former whiz kid. Three of them profiled in the paper. And...

And, what?

11

OLLIE AND I

Ollie called me from her office phone, no doubt so I'd recognize the number.

"Mezini, it's Burns."

"Yeah, I know." *My first reaction was to wonder why I took the call.*

"I need to speak with you," she said.

"About what?"

"About the story we wrote about you."

She went on to insist that we had to meet to be face to face. As much as she liked the First Draft, it wasn't the right place. If she invited me to the paper, there was sure to be gossip. Ditto the police station, where reporters weren't exactly welcome.

How terrible could one conversation be, I thought. *At the very least, I might convince her that I wasn't a brutal guy.*

We arranged to meet at Magazine Beach on the Charles River in Cambridge the next day.

The mere idea of a beach on the Charles may seem odd, with that famously dirty water, but in its heyday in the early and mid 20th century that stretch of sand was busier than many resorts. Rich and poor alike would gather there to swim, picnic, and fish. Sixty thousand visitors a year, they say. It wasn't exactly the Riviera, but it was close at hand, and it was free. Today swimming is rare, but Magazine beach is a peaceful park sprawling across 15 acres.

Ollie arrived first at the jungle gym, where we had agreed to rendezvous. She must have seen me park my car and waved as I walked over.

We sat down on a park bench, a comfortable distance apart. "So?" I asked. I tend to be monosyllabic if I'm unsure what I want to say.

"Can we speak frankly?" Ollie asked. "We had a friendly discussion last time. Let's try to be civil."

"Why?"

"It's in both our interests."

"Maybe," I said. "Yet in my experience reporters are as stubborn as—"

"Try me," she said, with just the slightest degree of flirtation.

"Okay, you asked for it. This is off the record. Understood?"

She nodded.

"Don't just nod, say 'Yes, it's off the record.'"

"Yes," she replied. "It's off the record."

"You made me look like a thug with that story," I said. "And you had no idea what you were talking about."

"We went with what we were told. As I mentioned, you should have talked to us."

"You get one side of the story, and you call it journalism."

"C'mon, Keegan defended you."

"Yeah, in the most general way possible. What did he say, that we comported ourselves in a professional manner, or something like that? Did us a lot of good."

"Tell me what really happened."

"Why? Are you going to run a correction on page one?" I asked. "That's about as likely as the Headline Hunter confessing on live TV."

"What did we get wrong?" *I think she sensed I wanted to spill. She was right. If I didn't, I probably would have already walked away and cursed her over my shoulder.*

"Do you know anything at all about my partner, Johnny Garlowe?" I asked. "In your story, you said something like, 'he was always ready to help a friend and smack a suspect.' Where'd that come from?"

"That was a direct quote, Detective. Somebody on the force told me that."

"Name?" I asked.

"You know I can't tell you."

"Great. You make shit up and put quotes around it. Too bad you can't patent your inventions. The wall between fiction and non-fiction is porous—"

"Detective, I didn't come here to argue. But I do have a, uh, proposal for you."

"What?" I asked. Now I was really intrigued.

"Let's work together on this Headline Hunter stuff."

"Are you serious?"

"Hear me out, please."

"Okay, I'm going to give you five minutes. Then I gotta get back to work."

"I got a call yesterday," she said.

"And ..."

"From a woman who said she was Alec Moore's mistress."

"Which Alec Moore?"

"The guy who worked for the medical company."

"Okay, so he played around. Big deal. Typical salesman."

"She said he was abusive."

I'm sure my face revealed a glimmer of a reaction. "Go on," I said.

"She said the sex was rough. He got her into S&M as a game, then he turned downright violent." She looked at me. "You're not surprised. Did you uncover something similar?"

"What else did she say?" I asked, deflecting her question. I wondered if she thought I was trying to hide my ignorance or simply avoid giving her the satisfaction of getting ahead of me.

"She freaked out when she learned he had TB, He never told her. It made her think about what else he might be hiding."

"You have this on the record?"

"Nope. She wouldn't give her name."

I smiled. I could tell she thought I was still playing it coy.

"Detective, can I call you Ronan?"

"No," I said pointedly. *I sensed that whatever was going on between us could be dangerous, professionally and personally. I wasn't sure it if was pure intuition, or my synesthesia firing.* "Mez will do." I could tell she was disappointed.

"All right, then," she said, smiling. "Someday I want to hear what really happened with you and Johnny. If that story was false, then—"

"Then what?"

"Maybe we can do a follow up. Where is Johnny now?"

I started to say something, then stopped.

"You'll probably just publish lies again, so why should I bother?"

"Maybe because I care. Did you ever think of that?"

I wasn't feeling much trust and I'm sure I conveyed very little interest in her plan to work together. The whole thing seemed transactional on her part. She was dangling a follow-up story about me so she could find out what I knew about the murders.

"Give me a hint," Ollie said. "Tell me where we went wrong."

At that point I encountered that strange metallic smell again. But I couldn't identify it.

She blurted out, "Mez, have dinner with me and we'll talk about this." I guessed she said it without thinking.

"You figure you'll get me drunk and find out what really happened."

"Maybe," she joked. At last, a hint of a smile.

I was 99% against further discussion. But maybe she could be useful somehow. At least that's what I told myself.

"One dinner, and that's it," I said. "*One dinner,*" I repeated, and I'm sure I sounded as if I were trying to convince myself. "Tomorrow."

I can't believe I'm going along with this, I thought. *Then again, reporters have pretty good sources, and sometimes people will talk to them more readily than to us cops. Maybe I should keep her in the loop.*

• • •

Take my word for it. These events occurred as described. I heard about Ollie's antics later.

At home the next night, Ollie tried on several outfits but was unable to decide. She FaceTimed Jan, who was still in rehab. "Sorry to bother you," Ollie said, "but I'm in a tough spot. And I figured you could use a distraction."

"What's wrong?" Jan asked.

"I need advice about what to wear," Ollie said.

"Must be an, uh, important occasion," Jan said.

"How are you doing, first of all?" Ollie asked.

"Okay. I miss my wine, but I'll live. I'm high on powdered eggs and overcooked bacon. They do have unlimited coffee, though. Small consolation," Jan said. "Before I help you, I need to know *who* it is."

"Mezini," Ollie muttered.

"*That* Mezini?" Jan asked.

"None other."

"Christ, what are you doing, my dear?" Jan asked. She was concerned and borderline horrified.

"It's okay. I found out some stuff about the murders that he may not have known," she said. "We can trade. I figure I can get some useful information out of him."

"That makes perfect sense," Jan said, sarcastically. "We did a scathing piece on him, and now you're working together."

"I know, I know. But he says we got the facts wrong," Ollie said.

"Typical. Never once heard a bad guy say, 'Wow, that investigative piece was completely accurate and I was awful,'" Jan said.

"I have a feeling about this," Ollie said.

"That's exactly what I'm afraid of," Jan said. "Now I *definitely* want to help you pick out an outfit."

• • •

Meanwhile, I was having wardrobe troubles of my own. Khakis and a blue shirt? Nah, too preppy. Black pants instead? Better. Crew neck or V-neck sweater? Leather jacket? *Jeez, Mez, is this a date*, I asked myself. *You can't fall for a reporter, even if she is good looking. She trashed you, and don't forget it.*

Yeah, but she seems open to revisiting the story.

Really? You're a cop, you're not supposed to be gullible. You're acting like a nervous 10th grader.

I finally settled on light gray slacks, a blue shirt, and a blazer. I figured I'd err on the side of conservatism.

• • •

Back to Ollie's FaceTime with Jan: Ollie put on a leather skirt that fell to mid-thigh. Jan shook her head and said, "No good, unless you want to seduce him."

She pointed to her black silk shirt. "What about this?" she asked.

"Okay, just button one more button," Jan said.

"Be right back," Ollie said. She came back with a red skirt.

"Now you look like a teacher in a Catholic school," she said. "Good and bad."

• • •

I found out later that we were both feeling awkward about our rendezvous and promising ourselves that we'd try not to show it. I had suggested Daedalus on Mt. Auburn Street in Harvard Square. The owner Laurence Hopkins is a friend of mine. Besides, I love their food.

When I arrived in the early evening the sun was bathing the red and white umbrellas in a warm glow on the spacious roof deck where Ollie was already sitting at a corner table. The upper floor has the feel of a tree house, with plants and lanterns all around. If you didn't know that you were in Harvard Square, you'd think you were at a resort. Perhaps it was because I felt so comfortable in that setting that it reminded me of a vacation somehow.

Ollie stood up when I walked over to the table. Her long arms peeked out of the rolled-up sleeves of her black shirt, untucked over a short red skirt. We shook hands, somewhat formally, yet she held onto mine for a second longer than is customary.

I made a point of maintaining eye contact but I couldn't help noticing the rest. *There were many colors emanating from her: red hair, blue eyes, red skirt, black shirt, white sandals. They all began to swirl into a pastiche in front of me.*

"Are you all right, Detective? You look a bit dazed."

"Yeah, fine."

Ollie asked for her usual Manhattan, and I did the same. Once the waiter left, there was no choice but to engage in conversation.

"Well …" I said. *Not one of my best opening lines*, I thought. "I'm not sure why I'm here." *Now that definitely sounded awkward.*

"One dinner won't kill you, Mez," Ollie said.

"You never know. The press can be lethal," I said.

"Are you always this talkative?"

"You should hear me when I'm excited. I sometimes speak ten words at a time."

My buddy Laurence came over and wished us good evening in his Irish brogue. I introduced Ollie.

"Pleased to meet you," he said. "Ronan is a good man. I've known him for what, ten years?" I nodded. "Our grandmothers knew each other back in the old country. At least on his Irish side."

"Except my family came from the wrong part of town," I said. "Still struggling, three generations later."

"He always cries poorhouse when he comes here," he joked. "Nice of you to buy dinner, Ollie," he said with a wink. He paused and then added, "On me tonight." Before I could object, Lawrence sped away to the bar.

"I like that guy," Ollie said.

I smiled, despite himself, tapped my fingers on the table and wondered what to say.

I looked up. "Great colors in this sunset. A myriad of shades of orange," I said. *That's such a cliché*, I thought.

The waiter came to the rescue with the drinks. I raised mine and Ollie did likewise. "Cheers," I said stiffly.

"Let's play a little game, Mez. Tell me some of the things cops say about reporters. Don't censor it, just free-associate," Ollie said.

"Is this a psychological test?"

"Don't worry, I'm not going to end up telling you that you're really a woman inside. Just humor me."

"I'm game."

"When you think of the media, everything from *The National Enquirer* all the way up to *The Wall Street Journal*, what adjectives come to mind?"

"Arrogant, biased. Then, slimy, sloppy and subjective," I said, with little hesitation.

"Nice alliteration. Great start. If reporters were animals, what would they be?"

"Snakes, cockroaches, cheetahs …"

"Why cheetahs?" she asked.

"Too fast to catch, but they peter out quickly," I answered. "That's why they never follow a story to the end."

"Fair enough. Now tell me what *you* think *reporters* think about cops. Not what you *want* them to think, but what you think they *actually* think."

"They'd probably say we're stupid, racist, lazy, and overweight."

"Too much time at Dunkin'."

"Yeah, I guess so," I said.

"If I asked a bunch of reporters to compare cops to animals, what would they say?" she asked.

"Sloths, pigs, flounders, maybe."

"Flounders?" she asked.

"Bottom feeders," I explained.

"Do you get what's going on?"

"Yeah, clashing stereotypes and warring preconceptions," I said.

I could tell she was impressed that I got the point of the exchange right away.

"You might say it's dialectical," I added. I was on a roll. "Thesis, antithesis, and all that. Those opposing points of view might somehow come together in a synthesis, maybe a meeting of the minds."

"You know your Hegel," she said.

"German philosopher, lived from 1770 to 1831," I said. "But he never actually said thesis, antithesis, synthesis. Commentators attributed that to him somehow."

"Are you trying to impress me?"

"Maybe. Is it working? Reading the Germans is a good place to start in philosophy."

The waiter came to take our order. Ollie chose the pulled pork, and I asked for the flank steak, medium. I scanned the wine list for a long time, it seemed. *Was I stalling?* I finally chose a bottle of Chianti.

"Lawrence's money, so go big," she said after the waiter left.

"I'm not letting him pay for this," I said quickly.

"Only kidding, relax."

I just shrugged.

"So, you and Johnny Garlowe worked together," Ollie said, picking up the conversation again.

"Do you reporters ever let up?" I asked.

"You go first. Ask me *anything*. No matter how personal it is."

"You sure you want to go there?"

"Go ahead. Don't be shy."

I just shrugged and took a deep breath. *I couldn't believe I was doing this, and I looked around to make sure no one was listening.*

"Don't be too much of a gentleman," she said. She was sensing that she now had my interest.

"Huh," I said softly. "Why did you get into the investigative racket?"

"Because it gives me a chance to do some real reporting, as opposed to just reacting to the news of the day," she said. "I always wanted to write novels, to tell you the truth, but I don't have any talent in that arena. Chasing the bad guys saves me the trouble of inventing their stories."

"Who's your favorite? Beethoven or Mozart?"

"Beethoven. He seemed to wrestle with the music, as if composing was painful. Mozart made it look too easy," she said.

"Jane Marple or Hercule Poirot?"

"Hercule. Arrogant. I like that in a man," she said. "C'mon, go deeper."

"Did you ever…"

"Here we go," she said, sensing hesitation. "Now we're getting somewhere."

"Sleep with a woman?" *I wondered if I went too far. What the hell, keep her off balance.*

"Once, in college," Ollie said.

"And…"

"After I broke up with a short-term boyfriend one of my friends came to comfort me. We drank some wine and cuddled, and that was about it."

"Nothing happened?"

"Just hugging, I swear, I like men too much. I think my friend was disappointed, though. She wanted more."

Now she knew she had my attention.

"One more question, Mez."

"Why do you care about *my* story?"

"Two reasons: You have useful information about these murders. Plus, if I was wrong about you, I want to correct the record. Despite what you think, we reporters do have some integrity. At least I'd like to think I do. You can believe that, or not, as you wish."

"That's an honest answer."

"Well…" she said.

"Johnny Garlowe and I grew up together in North Cambridge," I said. *I wasn't sure why I was opening up, but I suppose I saw an opportunity to correct an inaccurate story. Was I naïve?*

"I'm a stocky guy now, 6'2" on a good day if I stand up straight, but I was scrawny when I was a kid. Johnny was much stronger. One day three guys who had been bullying me pulled me into a narrow alley between two triple-deckers. They started wailing on me."

"How old were you?" she asked.

"Nine," I said. As if sensing my pain, she leaned toward me from across the table. *I was beginning to wonder why I started such a personal story. Maybe I really am naively trusting*, I thought.

"I was standing there with my fists in front of my face, just taking the blows, when I heard Johnny's voice," I said. "He showed up out of nowhere. He blocked the entrance to the alley so none of those assholes could escape. They knew his reputation and figured they were in for it. 'Mez, come over here behind me and watch my back,' he said. I couldn't move. 'Mez, are you deaf? Get the fuck over here,'"

"Go on," Ollie said. *I wondered if she realized how difficult this was for me. I started to see what my mom would have called contrasting colors around her, pink and orange. What did that mean?*

"The three kids tried to run by Johnny, to get the hell out of the alley, but he pushed them back each time," I continued. "I tried to help but he kept shoving me behind him. 'Just watch. You might learn something,' he said.

"He tore them apart and left them lying there bleeding. I asked him if we should call the cops, or an ambulance or something, and he said, 'Nah, they'll live.'"

"On the way home, he grabbed me by the shoulders, hard. 'From now on, stay close to me,' he said. 'I'll always protect you, but you gotta stay close to me.' And I always did. He helped me out of so many jams.

"You know, he was a great student. The teachers wanted him to go to college. But when Johnny went to the police academy, I figured I'd follow him. Mr. Baker, my English teacher was heartbroken. He was the only one in school who believed in me. He was always giving me extra books to read and told me he thought I had a knack for writing, even though I found it difficult. Not meant to be, I guess. Johnny and I joined the force together. And we were partners on the street, just as we had been as kids."

Ollie stayed silent. *I think she sensed that the real story was coming.*

"I can't say any more right now. I'll tell you the rest some other time. I just can't do it now."

"All right, Mez, I can accept that."

"It didn't happen the way you wrote it, though."

"I hope that's true," she said.

"If I tell you the whole story, maybe you'll set the record straight."

"Can't promise that'll happen, but I'll listen,"

We finished our dinner and the wine in comfortable silence. Ollie knew enough not to push for any more disclosures at that moment.

On the sidewalk we walked in different directions. I looked back at her over my shoulder to see if she looked at me. She never turned around.

12

BACK IN THE NEWSROOM

PAUL GREEN HAD his Aeron chair tilted way back. His stocking feet lay comfortably on his desk. He casually drummed on his thighs as he waited for Ollie to arrive for the meeting she had requested.

"Close the door," he said brusquely when she walked in.

She complied and sat down across from him. He left his feet on the desk.

"Great fucking posture, boss."

This was exactly what he liked about her. The profanity, the directness.

"What do you want?" he asked.

"A penthouse apartment overlooking the Charles River, or maybe Boston harbor, an unlimited expense account—"

"Yeah, yeah, don't waste my time."

"I want to follow the cops as they investigate these murders," she said.

"You're kidding me, right? Why would they allow that?"

"Because they'll look like heroes if they succeed."

"And like chumps if they take too long."

"I've already cleared it with Detective Mezini," she lied.

"What? Even after that story? Why would he let you follow him—"
"I think he feels the coverage might rehabilitate his reputation."
"What sort of deal did you make with him?"
"I wanted to talk to you first, boss," she said with feigned deference.
"I don't like it, Burns. I don't like it at all. Did you discuss this with Jan?"
"Obliquely," she answered.
"Meaning …"
"Meaning that she knew I was meeting with Mezini."
"Did you and he talk about how this might work?"
"Uh, not exactly," she said. "I figured that anything I saw would be on the record and that—"
"The cops won't let you tell the world what you see. It would compromise their investigation. They're not that stupid," he said, raising his voice. *That was a good sign,* Ollie thought, *it meant he was interested.*
"Maybe I can promise one thing to make it easier for them to accept the arrangement."
"What?"
"That I hold off on writing any stories until they're done," she said. She improvised this on the spot. She knew she was taking a risk by winging it, but it was working out so far.
"What about all the other reporters here? Will they have to wait too?" She knew him well enough to realize that he was getting so mad that he might lose control. If he did, the conversation would be over.
"Of course not. This doesn't affect them," Ollie said.
"You sure you didn't promise him anything else?" he asked, skeptically.
"No."
"Are you sleeping with him?"
"That's an inappropriate question, and you know it."
"I need to know before I rule on this."
"No, I'm not."
"Would you admit it if you were?" he asked.
"No comment. This is strictly—"
"Business?" he asked. "Is that what you were going to say?"
"No, I was going to say that it's all about the story," Ollie said.
"Burns, I'll think about this and get back to you," Paul said. Now Ollie knew she had him.

She immediately called me.

"We're a go," she said, jumping in without small talk. That wasn't true, of course, but she wanted to get started.

"Wonderful," I said with no appreciable enthusiasm.

Reading my hesitation, Ollie said, "Mez, I don't plan on following you around like some parasite. We can just touch base occasionally."

"I prefer symbiosis," I said. "How often do you think we should talk?" I'm sure I was gruff.

"I don't know, maybe—"

"Remember, I haven't said this was okay. I'm playing along, for now. But I'll have to check with the Chief to make sure and we need to be *very clear* about the ground rules. That comment is off the record, by the way," I said.

"Rule #1, Mez," she said. "You can't say something is off the record *after* you say it. But don't worry, I'm not going to quote you on that. It'd be suicide because you'd never speak with me again."

I grunted in a way that seemed to suggest that I was seriously considering the arrangement.

"I'll bet you were a wrestler in high school," she said. *I guessed she was thinking she'd go oblique for a second to distract me.*

"Only when it didn't interfere with my ballet training. Yeah, I competed in the 175-pound weight class for a few months. Why?"

"Because boxers tend to punch, but wrestlers take you down."

"You mean you see me as the type of guy who's more likely to go for the knees?"

"Yeah, and I'm more the type to sock you in the jaw or poke you in the eyes."

"I'll remember that."

"What have you found out so far?" she asked. "I assume you spoke with the neighbors, family members, lovers, spouses, exes, friends, bartenders of the victims, right?"

"You know something about police procedure. Bravo," I said.

"Any good stuff?"

"Not much. Are we off the record, seriously?"

"Scout's honor."

"Okay, nothing from bartenders. Neither of the two Moores had a favorite bar. V 2.0 just smoked dope, which is legal now. The dispensary nearby said she'd often ask for the strong stuff because it …" I paused as I checked my notes. "… Inspired her work. Doormen? Nope, because this is Boston. Stafford probably never had a drink in his life. Family members: we know that both Moores were terrors at home, that 2.0's lover said she was hell, and that Stafford was weird around women."

"Mmm," Ollie said, "that's news." She was listening without writing anything down.

"I have an idea for you," I continued. "Your technical guys at the paper know what the most popular stories are, judging by the clicks, right?"

"Yeah, and they can even figure out which *parts* of the stories people like best, down to the word."

"But can they identify *who* the clickers are?"

"You mean by name?"

"Is there any other way?"

"Yeah, wise guy, could be by city, or server, or whatever," Ollie said. "I don't know, but I'll find out. Good idea, Mez. You're beginning to think like an investigative reporter."

"That's an insult," I said. She laughed as I hung up.

• • •

That night I had dinner with my Aunt Eleanor, my mom's sister. My aunts and uncles on my dad's side, the Albanian-Italian clan, were all gone. For that matter, so were my mom's siblings, except for the inimitable Eleanor, who was so formidable that she'll probably last forever.

She's a widow with grown-up kids so she's always happy to see me. She lives just down the street from my house. She's not much of a cook but she is always ready to serve up a witty comment and a drink. She also offers a steady dose, sometimes an overdose, of advice.

When I walked into her house I smelled something baking.

"What recipe are you destroying tonight?" I asked.

"Never mind, Ronie," she said. "You don't have to eat my cupcakes if the smell offends you." She's the only one left who calls me by my childhood nickname. I find that both annoying and comforting.

"It's only you that I came to see, Aunt Eleanor."

"Don't try to bullshit me, young man, I ch—"

"I know, I know, you changed my diapers and I can't hide *anything* from you. Time to come up with some new material."

"I can tell that *you* have something new to report," she said. "What's her name?"

"Whose?"

"Don't play the sap with me, boy. Your new, what would you call it, 'love interest?'"

"Who said anything about love?" I asked.

"You don't have to say anything. I can see it in your eyes. You're shrewd in some ways, but you're a chump with women."

• • •

On the way to Chief Cronin's office, I was trying to decide how to explain my plan to let Ollie tag along. He's a decent guy but not noted for his tolerance of creative approaches to police work.

I knocked on his door and heard him say "Come in" without looking up. "What is it, Mez?" he asked. How could he know who I was? "I could tell by your walk, my boy," he said, reading my mind. "Siddown."

I lowered myself into the worn red leather chair across from his carved oak desk, which was as vast as a barge. It served the intended purpose of keeping the underlings at a distance while emphasizing the grandeur of his position.

I figured I'd just explain the situation in simple terms, which I did.

"Let me get this straight, Mez," he said. "You're going to let a *reporter* from *The Observer*, a reporter who slammed you and Johnny Garlowe, watch you investigate these fucking Headline Hunter murders? Is that what you're telling me?"

"Yes, sir," I said.

"What do we get out of this?"

"First of all, she won't write anything until we're done," I said. "If we do a good job, we get free publicity."

"And if we never find this bastard, or if we arrest the wrong guy, or if some overzealous monkey gets rough with interrogations, then where would we be?"

"I think—"

"I'll tell you where we'd be," he said quietly. "We'd be on #1 Shittacular Road and we'd be the only house there. Why would you trust this bitch?"

"Just a feeling, sir."

"A feeling," he said. "She agreed not to write anything until we're done?"

"Yes," I answered.

"Will she put that in writing?"

"I can ask."

"I don't like it, Mez."

I knew him well enough to recognize that meant he was thinking about it.

"Get her to put it in writing. And don't fuck this up. Now lemme get back to work."

13

PRIVATE INEQUITY

AMY STOUT WAS CONVINCED she was pregnant. She was nauseous and her period was late. Though she loved kids and often spoke at high school classes about her job as a police reporter, she wasn't ready to be a mom herself, especially with such a challenging relationship with Troy. It was time to confirm what she feared. She took a home pregnancy test kit into the bathroom.

Two minutes later she watched as the absorptive material turned red. Her first reaction was to call Troy, then she thought better of it. What would she say? That they should get married? Or that she should move to his house in the burbs? Unlikely. Even though they had been together for what, five years now, their relationship had never progressed to a level of traditional commitment. *Maybe I like it that way*, she thought. *Hell, I'm only 36. I still have time to settle down. Probably with someone else. Troy will probably never grow up and take responsibility. Maybe I gave him too much freedom. I should have been tougher sooner and told him what I wanted.*

To distract herself she stepped out onto the balcony and breathed in the salt air blowing off the harbor. She looked at the blue sky over the ocean and felt a connection with things that would no doubt outlast her: nature and the child inside her. *I still have to go to the doctor to confirm this. Don't even think about buying cribs yet, kid,* she said to herself.

She went back inside and poured a cup of coffee. *Is that okay,* she wondered. *How much wine have I drunk in the last few weeks? I should start thinking about my habits, assuming I—. Just focus on the present. Speaking of which, time to get the mail.*

She took the elevator down to the lobby and opened her mailbox. Among a collection of bills and catalogues, there was a manilla envelope with no return address. *That seems strange,* she thought, as she headed back upstairs. She sat down at a table in the kitchen area of the loft and opened the envelope.

The first thing she saw was a typed note saying, "This happened last week." Underneath were several enlarged color pictures of Troy and Amber cavorting on his back deck. Each successive photo was more explicit than the last. Now she *really* wanted to call Troy yet she hated melodrama and didn't want to humiliate herself by acting the part of a jealous girlfriend. Worse, she realized that the person who took the photos, whoever it was, now knew intimate details of her life. Who would do that? And why?

• • •

Elias Olson was *The Observer*'s digital guru. Rarely seen without his cowboy hat, disguising a bald head, he stood out as a "personality" in a business overflowing with characters. He came from North Dakota and had the accent to prove it. "By God" was his favorite expression, which everyone used when greeting him. He pronounced it with a short "u" in place of the "y", as in "Buh-goddd" and played the role of the midwestern cowboy for comic effect. He showed up at the First Draft every single night after work without fail, and Ollie heard the rumor that his life's ambition was to have a drink in each Elk's Club bar in America when he retired. Everyone believed that he would do it. Though he was extremely good natured, the staff approached him with caution because his rapier repartee left scars, though it was cushioned by a smile that seemed to say, "It's fine, we can all stand a little mockery. There's too much pomposity afoot."

Given his status as the software expert, Elias had a large office with a big window that would have overlooked the newsroom had he not filled it with post-it notes with reminders and pithy observations. For example: "People who don't wear safety helmets when riding a bike don't need them." Ollie peeked into one of the few spots of unobscured glass between the notes and knocked gently on the window. Elias waved her in.

"Let me guess, young damsel," he said. "You need my assistance." He loved to speak as if he had just stepped out of an adventure novel from the 1800s. It didn't go so well when he addressed Paul as "Sir Sneezy," but the rest of the newsroom found the quirks charming.

"Elias, I—"

"Hold it right there," he said. "How many drinks do you owe me?"

"Buh-godd, Elias."

"Worst imitation I ever heard. Goes like this: Buh-GODDD, darlin'."

Ollie chuckled. "Seriously, Elias."

"Uh-oh, game face on."

"Can we figure out which readers have clicked most often on the stories about the murders?"

"In a week, or so. Why do you need it?" he asked.

"Because I figure that the killer or killers might have shown unusual interest in those profiles," Ollie said. "Any chance you can do this in a hurry?"

"For you, darlin', of course," he said.

Ollie's cell phone rang.

"Hey, Paul," she said. "Where are you?"

"Never mind. I got 20 seconds. You can work your angle with Mezini. But I want you to keep the arrangement as secret as you can. If people see you together, you just say you're profiling him. And I want frequent updates."

"How frequent?" she asked but he had already hung up.

"You in trouble?" Elias asked.

"Hardly," Ollie said. "At least not right now."

• • •

The next day Paul presided over a meeting of the entire newsroom—about 60 reporters, editors, and support personnel. The tension was palpable.

He stood at a podium and silently looked over the crowd for just a few seconds that seemed much longer to the staff. His pause had the intended effect of attracting even more attention from an audience that was already rapt.

"I'll dispense with pleasantries," he said. "I don't have to remind you that this has been an incredibly difficult time in the news business. Many of you have been here long enough to remember the days when we *owned* this town. We can still claim some of the turf, but not in the same way."

He stopped to clear his throat, sniffle, and sneeze.

"I spoke with our publisher Stuart Allston this morning and he told me that private equity funds are interested in buying the operation. We all know what that means. They'll cut costs by slashing the staff, so they can sell the paper at a profit in three to five years. Right now, we're a bargain for these crass opportunists. The stock in our parent company, Bay State Media, has been hammered. No doubt because of the murders. Meanwhile, our real estate alone is worth tens of millions of dollars.

"I told Stuart that if any fucking private equity firm succeeds in buying this paper, I'll tender my resignation immediately. I did not take this job to preside over *The Observer*'s demise, to coin a phrase."

Sustained applause, which he acknowledged with a sniffle and a nod.

"Are there any questions?"

"Where does the private equity deal stand?" That question came from Nico Lyons, the business editor.

"As far as I know, it's in the discussion phase," Paul said.

"I heard that two different firms were looking at us," Nico said.

"I can neither confirm nor deny that," Paul said with a slight smile. "I'm actually more concerned about the short-sellers—the people betting that stock will drop. It may already be working, since the price of shares of our parent company, Bay State Media, is heading south." He paused. "Let's get back to work, shall we?" he said.

More applause.

He smiled, which was rare for him. He locked eyes with Ollie for a second. Her applause seemed a bit mechanical, as if she didn't want to give him the satisfaction. Yet she looked pensive.

Ollie wrote a brief note to Chief Cronin, on *Observer* stationery, promising not to write about the murders until the killer was apprehended. I'm sure she never told Paul about it, but that wasn't my concern. I had a killer to catch.

14

DEADLY CLICKING?

ELIAS OLSON TEXTED OLLIE soon after their meeting and told her to swing by later that day. She came to his office and found him at his wry best.

"You don't suspect *me*, do you?" he asked.

"Only of bad intent, Elias," Ollie said.

"That's good, because my name came up as one of those who checked the stories many times. Along with just about everyone else in the newsroom."

"Right. Best to ignore insiders. Hard to imagine anyone sabotaging us from within."

"Hmmm," he said and handed her a list of names, emails, and in some cases home addresses. The printout was 20 pages long.

"You'll find this in your inbox, too. Have fun," Elias said, as he pulled a flask out of the pocket of his old jacket that had "Grand Forks Math Team" written across the chest in faded letters. The cork made a loud pop when he yanked it off. "Want a nip?"

"A little late for me, Elias. I generally drink *before* lunch," she said with a smile.

When Ollie forwarded the list to me, I called within seconds.

"Are you kidding me?" I said.

"Too much for you, Detective? How long will this take?"

"I'll check out these people in an hour," I said sarcastically. "Let me see what I can do."

Later that night she called me in a panic. She told me that she was distracted as she walked across *The Observer's* vast parking lot. There were lampposts around the perimeter but the middle, where she had parked, was dark. She pulled her car out into the street and then noticed a warning light indicating that her trunk was open. She got out and walked to the back to close the trunk tightly. She found herself bathed in headlights as a car squealed by, way too close. She said she reacted quickly and jumped out of the way.

By the time she got home, I was at her door in Jamaica Plain.

"How did you know where I live?" she asked.

"Please. I'm a cop. We can find stuff like that instantly." I could tell that on some level she was happy that I showed up.

"You want to come in for a drink?" she asked. "I could sure use one myself."

"Yeah. You all right?"

"Been better," she said.

Once inside, I looked around her house. The foyer had a large hall tree with a built-in mirror, partly obscured by a denim jacket and a leather coat hanging off the hooks.

The living room had a wall of built-in bookshelves, full to capacity. The other walls were painted crimson, and the windows were covered with heavyweight blue drapes, tied with golden ropes. The sofa had blue mohair upholstery, and it was flanked by two overstuffed red chairs. Ollie collapsed into one of them. Even though she was lanky, the scale of the huge chair made her look small. I settled myself on the sofa. I confess that I was feeling—how can I describe it—tentative.

My synesthesia was working overtime. I tasted something sweet as cherry pie in the air and saw pleasant rays of crimson light coming out of her mouth as she spoke. Was this a positive message, or could it be the beginning of something?

"Mez, will you please make me a drink? The stuff's in the kitchen."

"What do you have?" I asked.

"Gin, vodka, vermouth, wine, beer."

"Got lemon?"

"I think so."

"I'll make myself a martini, if that's all right."

"Go for it."

"Should I make it two?"

"Yeah, except I'll take mine with vodka. And go easy on the vermouth," she said. "I'll be back in a minute."

She went to the bathroom. By the time she returned the drinks were on coasters on her oak coffee table.

"So, tell me what happened," I said.

"I've been spit at, cursed, yelled at. But nobody ever tried to run me over before."

"How close did the car come to you?"

"I don't know, two feet maybe, but it felt like two inches. When I jumped out of the way I was pinned up against my own car," she said. "It's a good thing I turned sideways and flattened myself."

"Glad you're safe," I said as I raised my drink.

She swallowed half of hers at once as I sipped mine slowly. "Goes down smooth. Nothing like vodka when you need to *feel* the impact. I shouldn't have bothered you."

"No problem. Better me than 911, I suppose."

"Yeah, the EMTs don't make drinks."

"You didn't get a license plate by any chance, did you?"

"Nope. It all happened too fast."

"Did you see what type of car it was?"

"Medium-sized," she said.

"Color?"

"It was dark," she said with a trace of annoyance. "I should have been more observant. I guess I was just frightened." She sounded almost defensive but quickly added, "I know, you're just being a cop."

"Can't help it, sorry," I said. "Are you going to be okay here by yourself tonight? I can, uh, get someone to come and stay with you."

"Some sort of police matron?"

"Yeah, a 70-year-old former nun who will make you go to bed by 10," I said and she chuckled.

"Just what I need. These murders have me spooked, and I don't scare too easily," she said. "Why would anyone want to kill people that we write about?"

"To get back at all of you, I'll bet."

"Yeah, why not attack us directly."

"Isn't that what happened tonight?" *I was wondering if she was confused because her logic was off.* "I really don't think you should be alone. I'd guess that the person who did this was just trying to intimidate you but we should still take it seriously."

"I appreciate your chivalry, but I'll be fine."

"Well, I should get going then," I said as I finished my drink. "Ping me if you need anything. Are you sure you don't want me to send somebody over?"

"No, thanks."

"All right, see you later, then," I said and got up.

"There is one thing you can do, before you go," she said. "Tell me what happened to your partner."

"I guess you're recovering, since you're back in reporter mode already. He went to a place where it's easy to disappear."

"Where?" she asked.

"Johnny went to Alaska," I said. "His wife told me he always talked about it. Said that was where people go when they want to be forgotten. After a few months up there in the winter, when it's always dark, he walked out into the snow, buck naked. Had enough brandy in him to get an entire frat house drunk. They found him a couple of hundred yards from his run-down apartment, frozen solid."

• • •

When Ollie walked out her front door in the morning, she was astounded to see my car parked right in front of her house. I was dozing in the passenger seat.

She walked up and tapped on the glass. I awoke with a start, turned the key, and lowered the window. *I sensed that she might have felt a twinge of excitement. I could see it in her half smile.*

"You've been here all night?" she asked.

"Yeah. I just fell asleep about an hour ago, I guess, when the sun came up," I replied, yawning.

"Mez, I …"

"Never mind," I said. "I'll check in at the office and see if they have any info about the names."

She was beginning to *react* to me. *And I could tell that she knew that I was responding to her too at some level. Synesthesia gives me sensitive antennas sometimes.*

"Why don't come back over later, so we can chat privately and go over the list? I need to get some rest first, though."

She looked hesitant.

"Don't worry, I have no nefarious intentions." *Did I really say that? Did she sense that I was trying a little too hard to be business-like?*

"I'll be back around noon or so." *She seemed to be OK with that.*

• • •

I woke up about 11:30, showered, dressed, and put the coffee on. I splurged on a high-end machine that made excellent coffee, in any variety you choose.

I prepared two fresh dark roast coffees, each with a shot of espresso and put them in travel mugs. I stopped off at Tatte Bakery on Mass Ave. in Cambridge to buy some chocolate croissants, and I confess I double-parked. One of the perks of the job.

Back at Ollie's house, I offered up my gifts. I had put half and half and sugar in my coffee but she drank hers black. Why was I not surprised at that?

She took a sip and made a sound that could be described as a purr.

"You like?" I asked.

"I like it large. Tastes like velvet."

I bit into one of the croissants and nodded. "These croissants are great too. Where did you get them?" she asked.

"Tatte. Is there any other choice?"

"Excuse me for asking."

We smiled at each other, then she shifted abruptly into business mode. "Did you have a chance to look at the list?"

"I did. My guys went through the the two hundred and forty ultra-clickers, if we can call them that, and they immediately eliminated all those who read the stories less than 20 times. We had to make some sort of a cutoff, and that seemed like a good number. Many of these people clicked 200 times or more. In fact, quite a few of the top clickers have records for violent crimes. Priors are common among serial killers, so this is a good start."

"How many people are we talking about?" she asked.

"We narrowed it down to about 25."

I showed her those names. She studied it carefully, then looked up.

"What do we do now?" she asked.

"For one thing, my guys are fanning out and knocking on doors."

"How many of your people are working on this?" she asked.

"Three."

"That's all?"

"Budget constraints. We're not the FBI, you know. You ready to go? I saved the best suspects for us. We'll take one car. Just let me do the talking."

15

PLAYING HOLMES AND WATSON

WE PULLED UP IN FRONT of a dilapidated house on a back street in Somerville. The railings on the porch were broken. A rusty tricycle sat at the top of the front steps. The paint on the outside walls was peeling off in sheets the size of a laptop. One of the cellar windows was covered with plywood.

As we got out of the car, I said, "Welcome to number one on our hit parade. This guy clicked more than anyone else, it seems. One Scott Goodfellow. An ironic name. He was an accomplice for a serial killer named Zain Leblanc, who had a habit of picking people at random on the street. He'd rob them, then kill them. Leblanc was shot when he resisted arrest.

"Turns out Scott was his childhood friend and helped him hide evidence. Scott should have gone to jail, but the cops couldn't get enough proof to indict him. Happens more than you know."

"Did Leblanc survive?"

"Doing life without parole in Walpole," I said.

I knocked loudly on the door, which opened a crack.

"What is it?" the occupant said.

Scott looked was short and rotund, with big round eyes and a pear-shaped torso. His broken eyeglasses were held together with scotch tape. He seemed to be scared and hostile at the same time.

"Detective Mezini here. May we come in?"

Scott opened the door and motioned us toward the foyer without getting out of the way. It was unclear if he was being obstinate or if he was just awkward. We walked around him to discover a house that was as cluttered as a garbage dump and just as smelly. Even in the dim light we could see stacks of newspapers, crisscrossing cobwebs, and a stained carpet. We remained standing.

"What is this all about?" Scott asked. "And who are you?" he asked, motioning toward her. His lips quivered as he spoke.

"Ollie Burns, from *The Observer*," she said.

"You travel with a personal reporter these days, Detective?"

I ignored the comment. "I'd like to ask you a few questions," I said.

"About the LeBlanc case?" he asked.

"Not exactly," I said. "How have you been since that went down? When was it, five years ago?"

"Something like that," he said.

"I checked with the prison. I guess you haven't been to see him."

"We're not exactly close," he said. He seemed to be covering his fear with sarcasm.

"I guess that's a good thing. He's not what you call a model citizen."

"Detective, I do appreciate your concern," Scott said with as much derision as he could muster, given his timidity.

"Actually, we need your help."

"I'm flattered," he said, again sarcastically.

"I understand you have been following the stories about the so-called Headline Hunter."

"Sure, everyone has."

"Do you have any idea why the killer would be doing this?"

"No," Scott said emphatically. "I am not an expert in these matters." Now he looked really scared. No doubt he was worried that we'd figure out a way to detain him. I wished we could have.

"Our records show that you've clicked on the stories hundreds of times," Ollie said pointedly. I looked at her sternly. She nodded to acknowledge that she understood that she wasn't supposed to speak.

"Is there no privacy, Ms. Burns? Or is that just a disappearing twentieth-century phenomenon?" Goodfellow asked.

"We'll leave that to the sociologists," Ollie said. I looked at her again.

"Because of my, uh, allegedly inordinate interest, you think I might be the guy?" Goodfellow asked.

"Are you?" I asked.

"You have direct experience with murder, don't you, Ms. Burns?" Goodfellow said. "I know all about your dad's death."

Ollie stared at him in disbelief. Apparently, he sensed that he had struck a nerve.

"You wonder how I know your story, don't you?" he taunted.

She took step toward him, and I stepped between them. "Not worth it," I said, trying to blunt the hostility. "Why are you so interested in these stories?" I asked.

"Because I have a fascination with murder, Detective, like you. Is reading a crime?"

"No, but ..."

"Let me guess," he said. "You're going down the names of those who were high on the click list. Nice try. I lead a very quiet life here in the Taj Mahal."

"Can you account for your whereabouts on the days when the murders took place?"

"Yeah, I was right here. Online. I'm sure your computer experts can verify that. I rarely go out."

"We'll be sure to check on that. It's easy to fake your location, if you know your way around the software."

"How was it working with Leblanc?" Ollie asked. She was clearly losing her temper.

"I never worked with him. But if I did, you'd expect me to say it was a big thrill, and that it made me feel special."

"Special how?" Ollie asked.

"I will tell you this, Ms. Burns," Scott said. "If I ever decide to start killing people myself, I'd start with reporters themselves, not with the people they write about."

I stood to my full height, which was easily eight inches above him, and advanced toward him. "Easy, or I'll take you in for threatening her." I looked over at Ollie, who seemed to appreciate the protective move.

"I'll consider myself warned," he said evenly.

Once we got into the car, I let my anger out. "This arrangement is weird enough. But you can't play detective. You do that again and our deal's off, understood?"

"Got it," she said. "He managed to annoy me, I'm sorry. It won't happen again."

"Imagine how it would look if that exchange came out in court," I said. "Some defense attorney would say that the cops and the press were ganging up on the client. We have a hard enough time convicting people as it is."

"I got it, I got it," she said demurely. I looked over at her and saw the tension in her body.

"You're wondering how he knows about your dad, right?" I asked. She nodded.

"Guys like him keep tabs on everybody. He probably has a collection of books on every serial killer and cop killer ever known. Murder's a hobby for him. You can't let him get to you, though."

"Thanks," she said. I wasn't sure if she was being sarcastic or sincere.

"Everybody on the force knows the story about your dad anyway. I hate to say it, but it's common knowledge. No surprise that he has heard it too." Ollie had never discussed that situation with me. I was wondering how to broach it.

"Do you want to tell me about your dad's murder?" I asked, in as neutral a way possible.

Her response was quick and brusque: "Sometime, but not now," and she deflected immediately.

"Do you think he's our guy?" she asked.

"No."

"Why not?"

"Because he's what they call a howler, all talk, instead of a hunter, who'd actually do something. He was terrified of us. Did you notice how his lips were twitching?"

"Of course I noticed," she said.

We wound down the Jamaica Way, past the pond as the conversation flagged.

I spoke to break the silence: "I've always liked JP. Decent restaurants and beautiful architecture." *Really clever,* I thought. *You can do better than that, Mezini.*

Ollie seemed to be pondering something important.

"We'll visit the other key suspects later," I said.

When we pulled up in front of her house she sat still and gave no indication that she was leaving.

"Mezini," she said.

"Yeah?" I replied.

"Come inside."

16

AT LAST

SITTING ON HER SOFA, we kissed for the first time. After a couple of minutes, I started unbuttoning her shirt. She pushed my hands away firmly.

"Take your clothes off first," she said.

I hesitated. No woman had ever asked me to do this. *I remembered a pop quiz Johnny Garlowe had given me when we were 15.*

"When you're with a girl," he asked, "do you take off your clothes first, or hers?"

At the time, I wasn't sure what the correct answer was. "Uh, hers," I guessed.

"Right," Johnny said. "Don't forget that."

Ollie sensed my discomfort and seemed to be enjoying the feeling of control. "Don't worry, Mez," she said. "You won't lose any macho points. I'll still respect you."

"How about if we go item by item?"

"Okay, take off your shoes, socks, and shirt. I'll remove one article of clothing for three of yours."

I shrugged and complied, then she removed her shirt. Before too long I was naked and she was in her underwear and a T-shirt. She stood up abruptly and led me up the stairs by the hand into her bedroom. It had a queen-sized bed with a white quilt, with two end tables on either side with stacks of books. A quick glance showed that she was reading a combination of thrillers, art books, and women novelists. Edith Wharton, Willa Cather, Iris Murdoch, Zadie Smith. I took this all in very quickly since I had my mind on other matters at the time.

She tried to push me onto the bed, but I stood firm, just to play with her, and laughed. She tried to push harder and I let her win and she fell on top of me.

I was hesitant to admit it to myself, but I had been looking forward to this. I have to admit that my synesthesia blazes in various ways during lovemaking. Sometimes, I swear I can feel the partner's nerves tingling in my own body. No question: It was beyond pleasurable to sleep with Ollie, yet some lines from a Pablo Neruda poem intruded into my mind:

> *Leaning into the evenings I throw my sad nets to your ocean eyes.*
> *There my loneliness stretches and burns in the tallest bonfire, arms twisting like a drowning man's.*

Afterwards, we lay still in each other's arms, and she shifted abruptly into reporter mode. "Now tell me the full story, Mez," she said quietly but firmly. "And make sure it's the truth. My bullshit detector is revving."

"Do we have to do this *now*?" I pleaded.

"Yes. I get that you and Johnny Garlowe were friends when you were kids, and that he protected you. But who's protecting whom now?"

"I can't ..."

"You can't what?" she said, as her voice rose in volume. "There are four possibilities: Either you and Johnny are both guilty of abusing that guy, or you're guilty and he's innocent, he's guilty and you're innocent, or you're both innocent. Tell me."

I just sighed.

"I know the, uh, the guy you tormented was not exactly a model citizen. But his prior record didn't give you the right to beat him and burn him. You guys interrogated him all night and forced him to confess to something he didn't do."

Ollie sat up and faced me.

"I was there for maybe eight hours," I said. "Johnny kept at him after that. Do you actually *sympathize* with that lowlife?"

"That guy had a name. Piet Skodor."

"Yeah, his victims had names too."

"And you believe it was up to *you* to punish him."

At that point I had enough. "I have one word for you: aftermath. Do you know the ultimate resolution of the Skodor saga?"

"I know he was acquitted."

"*No*," I corrected her, "he wasn't acquitted. The charges were *dismissed*. Big difference."

"Yeah, but the charges didn't hold up. No doubt because the confession was forced. That's not exactly model police behavior."

"Do you have any idea what that perp did to those boys? He sodomized them with a broomstick."

"And you couldn't prove that?"

"All right, This is off the record. Confirm that right now!"

"Off the record, I get it, Mez," she said. I could tell she was listening really closely.

"You may have heard that Skodor disappeared after the case was dismissed. He took a cruise to the Bahamas and jumped off the boat. His body was never found."

"I never knew that."

"There's a lot you didn't, and don't know about this story. We found out that he used a false identity on the boat."

"Why didn't you make a statement about all this?"

"I wanted to. We talked about it internally but decided not to."

"How do you know for sure it was suicide?"

"He left a note," I said, "which we found in his apartment. Along with a key to safety deposit box. It held some videos, the worst I've ever seen. He had recorded the torture. The boys were screaming and that asshole was laughing the whole time. He probably replayed the videos for his own amusement. A real sick puppy."

"Can we write about this, Mez?"

"No, no, no," I said. "Make that NFW. Am I clear?"

"Why not tell the truth?"

"Because we decided that the families had suffered enough. We didn't want those videos to come to light."

Ollie had been impassive throughout this whole exchange. I was beginning to wonder if the temperature of her blood was sub-zero. Then she surprised me by caressing me and looking at me as if she were the most compassionate person in the world.

"I'm sorry, baby," was all she said.

"I do have to talk about something else," I said. "The truth is that I lied to you. About Johnny. He never committed suicide. I should have told you, but ... He wanted everybody to *believe* that he was gone. He's actually in a hospital."

"So that story that he walked out into the snow in Alaska was made up."

"Yeah. Johnny was always a bit off. Whenever he'd fight anyone as a kid, he went overboard. If someone came at him with his fists, he'd retaliate with a rock. If anyone crossed him, he'd hurt them, bad."

"None of that surprises me," Ollie said.

"Let me finish. We were as close as two guys could be. One drunken night at the academy Johnny told me that had been sexually abused when he was a kid. His dad died when he was seven and his mom invited the local priest over to console him. Some consolation. Johnny never went into detail, but I'm sure the guy had his way and then some. For several years, no less." I paused and rubbed my eyes. Meanwhile, hers were once again as blank as marbles, with the the clinical detachment of a reporter who had covered many horrible stories.

"He had always been the alpha, the toughest kid in the neighborhood. But on the force he found it difficult to answer to superior officers. He had an instinct for the streets, though. A talent for finding the key piece of information that would break a case."

"Even if it meant hurting people," Ollie said.

"Maybe," I said. "Child abusers pushed his buttons. If they even so much as glared at him, he wanted to take them down any way he could. He wouldn't shoot them. But he wasn't above, uh, taking out his anger on the suspects. He couldn't restrain himself. I guess he had too many memories that kicked up," I said.

"Did you try to stop him?"

"Absolutely. I always told him to take it easy. I did the best I could, believe me. He'd just brush it off. 'Fuck it,' he'd say, '99 percent of these perps are guilty anyway.' He'd beat the suspects when I wasn't around. Eventually, he started to get more and more unstable." I paused to collect myself.

"His wife Ashley was his high school sweetheart. We all grew up together. Everything came to a head one Saturday night, maybe six months after the Skodor fiasco. She showed up at my house in tears and said he'd taken a swing at her. She begged me to talk to him."

"Did you?" Ollie asked softly.

"Yeah, I went over to their house. He got incredibly mad and even threatened *me*. I knew he didn't mean it. That next Monday morning Ashley called me and told me she couldn't wake him up. I ran over. He was dead drunk. I practically carried him to the hospital. He came to when we got there and started to get violent. They had to restrain him, which was painful for everybody. Finally, a shrink came and gave him an injection that put him out.

"Turns out Johnny's bipolar. No surprise there. They gave him meds and that helped. But when he went off them, he'd relapse."

"I'm going to ask you again," Ollie said. "Were you there when he abused Skodor?"

"No, while I was there we just kept questioning him over and over. He never asked for a lawyer. I left the room after eight hours. I never laid a hand on Skodor. You have to believe me. I told the night crew to keep an eye on Johnny but they probably had other things to do. Maybe he scared them into staying away. Even the cops were afraid of Johnny. I'm not sure what happened. But when I came back the next morning Skodor had signed a confession." I was choking with emotion.

"Couldn't you see that Johnny had abused him?"

"No. As you wrote there were burns on his forearms and his inner thighs," I said. "I couldn't see any signs of that because he was wearing a long-sleeve shirt and pants, of course."

"I'll bet he didn't have pants on when his dick was burned. You expect me to believe that you didn't know *anything* about the torture?" she asked.

"I didn't, I—"

"You didn't know, or didn't want to know?"

"Ollie, you have to believe that I just didn't know. If I had, I would have done something. I was assigned to another case right away. I saw Skodor in a holding cell, then I went out to another crime scene."

She looked into my eyes without blinking.

"Looking back, I probably should have reported Johnny to the department's psychologist."

"Why didn't you speak up after the story ran if you didn't do anything?" Ollie asked. "After all, we did say that you were cleared. You could have given us your version of the events."

"That fool Terry Keegan wouldn't let me. He knew the truth. He told me the force would edge Johnny out and let me stay. The department wouldn't let us talk directly to the press."

"Where exactly is Johnny now?" she asked.

"At mental institution out in the sticks in New Hampshire," I said. "Drugged to his ears. I go and see him as often as I can. He begged me to tell everyone he was dead because he couldn't stand the shame of being put away. On the way to the hospital internal affairs took his badge and his gun away, which made him feel totally helpless. I guess I felt I had to protect *him* for a change."

"Mez, I'm sorry you went through this. But if you ever lie to me again it's all over. Clear?" Ollie said.

"Clear," I answered.

After a few silent minutes, she asked, "Now where were we?"

I was surprised that she was ready to get intimate again so soon. It seemed that she could turn her desires on or off, almost at will. That made me a bit uneasy.

She did stop caressing me for a moment. "Mez?"

"Yeah, I'm right here."

"You realize it may be impossible for me to write about the murders now," she said. "I do try to have some ethics—"

"Ethics in journalism? Isn't that an imaginary concept, like the square root of negative one?"

"Glad to see you hold our profession in such high regard."

"Look, there are a lot of sleazy reporters, just as there are bad cops. The majority of the people in both fields are reasonable professionals."

"Great Chamber of Commerce analysis, Detective. In any case, sleeping with a source is taboo. I could get fired, but your pals at the station would probably high-five you."

"Maybe so," I said sheepishly.

"I guess I can still collect info and follow you around. Does that make me corrupt?"

"As long as you don't blackmail me."

"No, be serious."

"Ask your editor."

"Right. I'll just say, 'Paul, I slept with Detective Mezini. Can I still work on the series?' Not happening."

"I hope I'm worth it," I said with a smirk.

"I'm not sure yet. I'll let you know in the morning."

One thing is sure. I had never slept with a more, how should I say this, enthusiastic woman. At the time I doubted I ever would again.

17

A DELICATE DANCE

"SO HOW ARE YOU and Mezini getting along?" Paul asked Ollie. He was smirking. *Did he really know what was going on?* Ollie wondered. *The guy had fingers and spies everywhere, it seemed.*

"Uh, fine," Ollie said as she sat across from him in his office.

"What have you discovered so far?"

"Well, we really just got started," she said, and the irony of that statement was not lost on her. "We've been going down the list that Elias gave us. It shows the most, shall we say, enthusiastic readers of the murder stories. We're trying to figure out who hates us the most."

"That would be difficult to determine," Paul said.

"We're also looking at the clickers' social media profiles."

"So why are you sitting there? Get on it."

That was Paul's way of saying that he liked what she was doing, Ollie thought. She stayed at her desk into the night and checked the Facebook profiles of twenty-five of the people I had flagged with police records—

even the ones I had ruled out. She was distracted, though. It seemed as if every other thought turned to me, she later told me.

She really couldn't determine exactly how she felt. For one thing, she barely knew me. And when she thought about her "ideal man" in the abstract, yours truly wouldn't come to mind. Yes, she thought, ahem, Mezini may be handsome, tall, smart and all that. Very smart. Then there was that Ivy League thing that seemed to get in the way all the time. The notion that a woman who went to a school like Brown could be satisfied only with another guy from an elite school. At least a lot of her classmates seemed to think that way. But that sort of snobbery went against everything she believed.

She didn't seem to care about educational credentials, which was unusual. Ordinarily it was a deal breaker because most guys seemed to fear smart women, for whatever stupid reasons ingrained into our culture. Mezini seemed secure with himself, she thought. Unlike the others.

Even so, her dad's words kept coming back to her: "Never date a cop. They care only about each other, and their jobs. I've seen so many of them cheat on their wives and girlfriends."

"What does that say about you, Dad?" she asked him.

"I'm different," he said.

"Yeah, you're weird."

A typical father-daughter conversation. That memory was no help. Mezini seems cool and we're working together and ... Yeah, it's the "and" that gets you every time.

Back to work, she said to herself. Keep looking at the Facebook profiles. The stupid things that people do on social media are amazing. Like posting photos from their vacations while they're away. To me, that just invites break-ins. Then there are those who post a picture without any context. We see a shot of a kid in school with no ID. Ever heard of a caption?

When Ollie's phone rang it was a welcome interruption.

"Were you thinking about me?" I did my best to sound at once confident and playful.

"No, I completely forgot you, Z," she said, using a nickname she had given me.

"Figured as much, O," I said, playing along.

"I think I narrowed down the list to two potential suspects."

"On what basis?"

"Based on social media posts. Can we go visit them tomorrow?"

Was this a professional partnership, or personal, I wondered. *Was she interested in me, or just the story? Or both?*

"Pick me up at 9 in the AM, okay?" Ollie said.

"Yeah. See you then."

"Z," she said coyly.

"Yes."

"See you in the morning." With that deflection, she knew she got my attention.

She could tell that I was disappointed, I said to myself after I hung up. I wondered if she really did want to see me again. Not cool for a reporter to sleep with a source, she had mentioned, but there was no restriction like that for cops. Hell, a lot of the guys in homicide have had relationships with reporters. It's almost a badge of honor.

Do I push it harder, and just show up at her house tonight? Ignore her signals? Will she be disappointed if I don't, and will she think I don't care that much?

But what happens if she loses her job because of a conflict of interest? Wouldn't she resent me forever? After all, *The Observer* isn't exactly chopped liver. Hard to get hired there. Especially as an investigative reporter at a time when the business is shrinking.

If we wait until the last story is published, then get together again, I guess it would be permissible. Christ, I'm not a journalism professor. I don't know how to analyze all the nuances.

I decided to stay away. That seemed to be the smart move.

18

BY HER OWN RULES

OUR FIRST STOP in the morning was the office of Kat Orsino, a tall, no-nonsense probation officer responsible for the next suspect. She was wearing a gray pantsuit with a gun in a shoulder holster visible under her jacket. Her manner was flippant but very deliberate.

"Mezini," Kat said. "Great to see you. Who's the sidekick?"

"Ollie Burns, from *The Observer*," I said.

"You're trusting a *reporter*?" she asked, looking at me. Then she turned to Ollie. "Is he good?" she asked, with an impish glint in her eyes.

"Excuse me?" Ollie said.

"Come on, honey, don't tell me you haven't unwrapped that candy bar." *I'm sure Ollie was wondering if it was that obvious.*

"We're here …" I muttered.

"On business, I know. Whassup?"

"What can you tell us about Reed Mason?" I asked.

"Reed Mason. What do you want with him? You're homicide."

"Trying to find the serial guy."

Kat threw her head back and laughed out loud. "And you think *he* might fit that bill?"

"He did smash the front window at the *Sun*'s offices," I said. "Other than that, he's harmless."

"Yeah, and I once punched my boyfriend when he came home drunk and disorderly," Kat said, pushing herself away from her desk. "Follow me."

Fifteen minutes later we were on a back street in Dorchester, an area of Boston that was gentrifying along with almost everything else in the city. But this particular block hadn't improved and probably never would. We pulled up in front of a rundown triple-decker. The front door was unlocked. Kat led us up the rickety stairs to the third floor. She pulled a key out of her pocket and unlocked the door.

"You just let yourself in?" I asked.

"That's how I roll with my, uh, clients."

"How do you get away with that?"

"They do as I say. You sure you're ready for this?"

As Kat opened the door, the smell of Lysol was overwhelming. We entered a railroad apartment with all the rooms on one side of a long, narrow hallway—a small kitchen, a tiny bedroom, a bathroom, and a living room with no furniture other than cushions in the middle of a bare floor.

The place was sparkling and spare, except that every wall was covered with newspaper articles about the four victims: Alec Moore, the medical salesman, and his namesake, V 2.0 the filmmaker, and Wilhelm Stafford, the whiz kid. Editorials about the abuses of the media covered the rest of the wall space: a mélange of headlines like "Fake News: Myth or Reality?; Independent Study Shows Liberal Bias in Media; Have all Publications Gone Tabloid?" and so on.

"You think he's your guy?" Kat asked as she studied the expressions on our faces. "Let me show you one more thing."

She took us into the kitchen, empty except for a small table with a manual typewriter on it. The paper in the carriage had the word vision, in all caps, over and over. "Would you believe this guy has a master's in creative writing?" she said.

"Where is he?" I asked.

"Does she ever speak?" Kat countered, looking at Ollie. "Or does she just walk in your wake?"

"Back off. I don't have to take this cr—" Ollie said.

"Save it, sweetheart," Kat said. "I'm just a ball-buster. Let's go talk to our boy."

She turned around summarily and took us to a nearby park, really a vacant lot, with a rusty metal bench missing two of the four slats on the back. There sat a clean-cut man of about 30, wearing a black T-shirt with the word "Staff" in white letters across the chest. He was writing in a reporter's notebook on his lap.

"Officer Orsino," he said, without looking up.

"This is Detective Mezini and Ollie Burns, from *The Observer*. They want to ask you a few questions, Reed," Kat said.

"Let me guess, they think I am the Headline Hunter," Reed said.

"Are you?" I asked.

He just laughed. "I wanted to be a killer, really I did," Reed said. "Then I became a writer instead. My career was just about to pop when they started tapping my typewriter."

"How do you they tap a typewriter?" I asked.

"They can do anything now, you know. They read my mail, they read what I type, they read my mind. It's a conspiracy of blues, ooze, and views."

We quickly realized that he was either deranged, or a very good actor.

"I sent several manifestos to journals, but they won't publish them," Reed said. "I try talking to editors, even at your paper, Ms. Burns, but they hang up on me. One of them asked me if I was seeing a psychiatrist. I told him that several psychiatrists are seeing *me*, isn't that right, Officer Orsino? I'm like a transparent piece of film that records everything that has ever been said or written."

He looked at his rapt audience with a smile. He turned his head to the side and yelled "Shut up!" to no one in particular. "That's enough."

We watched this performance without commenting. He suddenly quieted down and sat statue still.

"Do you want me to take you home now?" Kat asked.

He didn't reply so she grabbed his elbow gently and walked him back to his apartment. Five minutes later she reappeared with an expression that could possibly be smug.

"Got a good story, Ollie?" she asked. "This guy won't harm anything except the germs in his apartment. When we got back, he washed his hands three times and asked me if he had been rude to you two."

"Yeah, but some killers are really kind on the outside. You know the drill, the neighbors say, 'But he was such a nice guy,'" Ollie said.

"You learn that in psychology courses in college, honey?" Kat asked.

"At least I *took* some courses," Ollie said. Her left eyebrow headed skyward and the right one moved down.

"Relax, I'm just playing with you," Kat said. "Mez, good to see you." She turned and headed back to her car.

When she was out of earshot, Ollie vented. "What's with her? She must terrorize the guys on probation. I was about to smack her myself."

"Never mind Kat," I said. "She's just a hard ass. Keep taking notes. Start your story with, 'Handsome, debonair homicide Detective Ronan Mezini seemed to generate one startling discovery after another and—"

"Get over yourself. I may have to take credit for everything before this is over." I wasn't sure what she meant but I let it go.

19

MORE ROUTINE, THEN THE MASTER

OUR NEXT STOP on the suspect parade was a car wash in nearby Waltham where Jacob Paros was working. He had been convicted for selling drugs and threatened a local reporter who was covering his trial. Paros was on parole after serving four years. When Ollie and I drove up to the entrance to the car wash, Jacob came to the driver's side window.

"Regular, Supershine, or Ultimate, sir?" he asked.

"The one that comes with information," I said.

"You look like a cop, but she don't," Jacob said. "You want a wash or not?"

"Give me the basic." I handed over a twenty. "Keep the change, Jacob. Five minutes of your time is all I want."

"I'll take a break after your car comes through," he said. "But it has to be quick. Not everyone's on the public's dime, know what I mean?"

While my car was drying in the sun, Jacob, Ollie, and I sat at an aluminum picnic table in the shade. He was eating a peanut butter and jelly sandwich and drinking coffee from a thermos that looked like it was 20 years old.

"Because I allegedly said some, uh, things to some scumbag reporter years ago, you think I had something to do with the murders?" Jacob asked.

"Maybe," I said.

"Why would I hold a grudge against the whole fucking business?"

"Don't know. But we do know you've been reading the Headline Hunter stories again and again."

"Wow, that's enough to make a guy paranoid," Jacob said. "So you put two and two together and got seven? I *read* about the crimes, and that means I *do* them?"

"With your record, that's a reasonable assumption," I said.

"Lemme tell ya', when I first got out, I went to my local bar where a couple of guys I knew asked me if I wanted to make a quick ten grand," Jacob said. "All I had to do was drive a car down to the Cape. Just drop it off at a house on the beach."

I had heard stories like this before. Temptations for easy money were always present for ex-cons. No doubt a drug deal, or maybe a gun sale.

"And?" I asked.

"I just laughed and finished my beer. I like sleeping in my own bed, instead of some mangy bunk with a worn-out mattress full of bedbugs in jail. Why the hell would I risk everything to kill some fucking people who just happen to show up in the paper?"

Back in the car, Ollie and I compared notes.

"I'm beginning to think that tracking the clickers is getting us precisely nowhere," Ollie said.

"Copy that," I said. "As you can see, investigation isn't exactly glamorous."

"Yeah, just like being a reporter."

"Speaking of that, do you know anyone else who would have a grudge against the paper right now?"

She didn't answer right away. "Not sure …"

• • •

Next came a meeting with Dr. Jack Grimes, the FBI's serial killer expert, who had decided to spend more time in Boston. Grimes was staying at his brother's home on Belmont's Lincoln Street in the presidential district, so named because the area features stately homes on streets named Madison, Adams, and so on. The house was a typical central entrance colonial with a brick front and a slate roof with three gables. Belmont always struck me as a town with manicured lawns and equally manicured attitudes.

Grimes ushered us into a study dominated by a lime green sofa with a scalloped back and two beige wing chairs. Old fashioned all the way. He got right down to business once introductions were made.

"I understand that you two are working *together* on this," he said with ill-disguised distaste.

"Not exactly, Dr. Grimes. I'm following Detective Mezini and hoping to write a story about the investigation when it's all over."

"Wonnnnderful," he said. "Are we on the record now?"

"Do you want to be?" she asked.

"Ms. Burns, at this stage in my career I am indifferent to publicity. Let's get one thing straight, though: this is all on background."

"Meaning that you don't want to be quoted by name?"

"Meaning that I don't want to be quoted *period*. I don't want anyone to confuse me with the story. Detective, why don't you tell me what you *think you know* so far?"

I gave him a summary of our investigation, with the details about the murders of the two Alec Moores, Wilhelm Stafford, and V 2.0.

"Any similarities in the victims?" Grimes asked.

"We discovered they were all abusive toward their partners, or would-be partners," I said. "One more detail. The bullets all came from a .38."

He stared directly into Ollie's eyes. He had a piercing gaze under bushy salt and pepper eyebrows. His forehead was wrinkled though the lower half of his face was smooth as polished stone. He used gestures economically, as if trying to preserve energy.

"You may have heard the concept of a frame," Grimes said. "That's a way of looking at the world, often an emotional approach. It can even alter the chemistry of our brains ... and make us ignore facts that contradict what we think we believe."

"I get it, you're telling us that we're thinking in stereotypes," Ollie said.

Grimes seemed surprised that she would catch on that fast. He was probably thinking reporters weren't usually that sharp.

"You might say that," Grimes said. He seemed surprised that she understood what he meant. "For instance, most people think that all serial killers are white men and crazy geniuses. The truth is that only about half of them are white. And by and large, they're not geniuses, that's for sure. They tend to be average in intelligence, except for the bombers for some reason. Take the Unabomber. He was only 16 when he went to Harvard. Later he taught math for a while at Berkeley. Bright guy."

With that he walked over to a side table and poured a brandy into a snifter. "Care to join me?"

"Thanks, brandy doesn't mix with guns," I said.

"I'm unarmed, so I'll have a light one, please," Ollie said.

"I like a woman who won't refuse a drink," Grimes said. "It shows that she knows how to handle it. Now, where were we?"

"I understand that many of the killers are social creatures," I said.

"That's right, on the *outside* they often seem to be upstanding citizens," Grimes explained. "For every Unabomber who lives alone in a cabin in the woods, you have many others who have wives, kids, houses in the suburbs. That means our boy could be next door, so to speak."

"Why would he pick on the press?" Ollie asked.

"I don't know, easy target, I guess."

"I assume you're kidding," she said.

"Only partly. A lot of people blame the media for everything these days. But that's beside the point. Research shows that about a third of serial killers murder people because they enjoy it ... They do it to satisfy some crazy lust or to exercise a twisted form of power. It's a thrill for them, I suppose. Another 30% or so do it to make money, through extortion or what not. You know, pay me and I'll stop. Only about 18% are motivated by anger."

"What's your guess here?" I asked.

"Hard to say."

Grimes took a sip of his brandy and thought for a minute.

"Chances are he'll contact you, Ms. Burns," he said. "These guys love notoriety. As I told Detective Mezini, David Berkowitz came up with the nickname 'The Son of Sam' himself. Ditto Dennis Rader with 'BTK.'"

"Bind, torture, kill," Ollie said.

"That's what he did to his victims," Grimes said. "Don't be surprised if there's a long lull in the action, though. The BTK case went cold for 13 years, then he started sending letters to the media and contacting the police. They finally traced him from a floppy disk of his writings that he was stupid enough to send to the cops. It had some hidden metadata from a deleted Word document that mentioned his first name and a Lutheran church in Wichita where he was active. Careless, careless."

"Didn't his daughter write a book about him?" Ollie asked. She looked like an eager grad student trying to impress a professor, yet at the same time she was eerily detached.

"Very good, Ms. Burns. I carry it around with me to remind myself that convention hides a lot of sins," Grimes said. He reached into his satchel, took out a well-worn paperback, and leafed through the pages.

"Let's see, this is what he said about his daughter: 'I broke her heart. I taught her how to garden, love of plants, animals, fishing, camping. We hiked the Grand Canyon. I shed a tear the day she was married. My girl had finally grown up.'"

"Gets you right here," I said, tapping my chest. I meant it sarcastically, of course.

"Yeah, model dad," Grimes said. "I need tell you something. I've been called away to another case in Chicago. I'm leaving in the morning."

We were shocked. Grimes could see the anxiety in my face and the curiosity in hers. "I plan to work with the team here remotely, don't worry," he said. "I'm happy to look at profiles of any potential suspects. Feel free to contact me if I can help. In the meantime, I have faith in your ability to figure this out. Even if the rest of the city doesn't share my confidence." The last comment stung and Grimes knew it.

"I appreciate your support," I said with no small degree of scorn. "Do you have any parting advice?"

"Don't rule *anybody* out," Grimes said as he stared at both of us.

"Does that include you, Dr. Grimes?" Ollie asked. Her expression indicated that she was joking but in a pointed way.

"You never know," he answered. "That would make a *really* good story, wouldn't it?"

20

QUESTIONS WITHOUT ANSWERS
One Month Later, July

FAMOUS FOR ITS GREAT UNIVERSITIES and frigid winters, Boston is also known for vicious humidity, which had the city in its savage grip in mid-summer. As fears of the murders subsided, businesses returned to some semblance of normality. On Route 95, which rings the city, the traffic was heavy all day long, as it always had been. Commuters going north on Route 93, AKA The Southeast Distressway, cursed their fate in the morning. At the same time, those going east on Route 2 from the western burbs toward Boston ate exhaust and were no doubt wondering how many years of their lives were wasted behind the wheel.

The bartenders served drinks, the lawyers rang up billable hours, and the news still came out every day. Reporters were ever vigilant as they worked on their stories just in case their copy might somehow give rise to violence. Many of the people they tried to profile still politely deferred and asked for rainchecks. Others refused to be quoted at all, period.

As a result, news stories took on a detached quality without any named sources. Phrases like "one eyewitness said" or "a high-level employee told us" became routine. Politicians reacted in one of two ways: Either they courted the limelight to show how courageous they were, or they were "unavailable." One state senator even went so far as to tell *The Observer*: "I have no comment, and that's off the record."

Paul Green did his best to rule an empire that was under threat every day from the private equity vultures and the Headline Hunter. One day he ordered everyone in the newsroom to work every possible angle on the murders. He knew Ollie was working the case from the inside, albeit in secret, but he wanted to stage a blitzkrieg. He made a particular point of singling out Amy Stout and asking her to badger all her contacts.

Amy had secretly coveted a post on the I-Desk, though we have seen how she mocked the slow pace of their investigations. Ollie conceded that Amy was the better reporter, in terms of her ability to stay one step ahead of the news, but Ollie was a much more eloquent writer and was able to reduce complicated stories to their most essential elements.

Their styles were quite different. Amy often went commando, attacking the jugular straightaway. As Paul explained, "She would have done well in a cage fight where the object is to KO the other guy as quickly as possible, even if meant leaving a lot of your own blood on the mat."

Ollie, on the other hand, was usually more subtle in her approach, though equally competitive. Her dad had warned her many times about the danger of thinking of yourself as the smartest person in the room, but she frequently believed it even if she did her best to conceal her vanity. She had studied Aikido in college, where she learned to transform a foe's linear thrust into a circular motion by spinning in a smaller, concentric circle, thereby flipping the enemy over so quickly that she never knew what hit her. It was all about using the opponent's strength against her.

Yet the two rivals were both smart enough to vary their approaches, as circumstances might warrant. Amy could display finesse and Ollie blunt aggression. As soon as Paul's all-hands-on-the-Headline-Hunter order went out, the game was on. He often wished he could combine Amy and Ollie into one person, yet he was conniving enough to see the benefits of pitting them against each other. All for the glory of the Great God of Stories, a deity he worshipped above all else.

After his call to war was issued, Ollie was on her way to the coffee shop downstairs. (Free Java had long since disappeared in the era of cost-cutting.). Amy got up and followed her.

"I'll buy you a coffee," Amy said.

"Okay," Ollie said as her guard automatically went up.

"I figure you'll need it now," Amy said.

"And why is that?"

"Because we have some real deadline pressure here. Paul wants results ASAP, and that's not in your DNA," Amy said. "You probably have the highest income *per story* in the newsroom. Let's see, you make about $75K, and you crank out, what, three stories a year? That's $25K per. Not bad."

"And if you do 150 stories, that'd be $500 per," Ollie countered. "That's about what they're worth. By the way, I'll buy my own fucking coffee." Ollie headed downstairs without turning around.

On the way back to the newsroom, she saw Amy doubled over in pain in the hallway. She was sobbing.

"Hey," Ollie said. "What's wrong?"

"What the fuck would you care?"

"C'mon, kid, let me help you," Ollie said. She grabbed her elbow, took her into an empty office nearby, and closed the door. Amy collapsed on a chair.

"I think I'm hemorrhaging."

"No kidding," Ollie said as she looked down and saw that she was bleeding through her dress. "Are you pregnant, kid?"

"Yeah. I've been having really bad cramps. Now it hurts everywhere."

"Stay right there," Ollie said in a commanding tone. She went out into the hallway and called 911, then ran into the newsroom and told Paul what was happening. She told him she'd stay with Amy. He nodded, which, for him, was a sign of his concern.

Ollie wrapped a sweater that someone had left behind in the I-Desk office around Amy's waist to soak up the blood and rode with her in the ambulance all the way to Mass General. Amy moaned during the entire trip. When they arrived at the Emergency Department, Amy was whisked quickly into treatment. Ollie told the nurses that she would stay in the waiting room.

After several hours, the doctors said Amy's condition stabilized, and Ollie went in to check on her. She looked pale and exhausted.

"Now *that* was pretty dramatic," Ollie said.

"You mean your transformation into a nice person?" Amy said, in a weak voice. They both chuckled.

"What did the doctors say?"

"I almost went into sepsis, you know, blood poisoning. They put me on an IV antibiotic right away, They want me to stay here overnight, at least."

"Are you feeling any better?"

"Yeah, that horrible pain stopped. But I lost the baby."

"So sorry."

"Just as well," Amy said, sobbing.

"Why?"

"I never told Troy."

"Jeez. Does he even know you're here?"

"No, and I don't want him to know either."

"I thought you guys were tight," Ollie said.

"So did I," Amy said with a sigh. "So did I."

"What happened?"

"I threw him out. He always said he liked his own place in Concord. I just never wanted to think about what he was doing there."

"I get it. Why are they never satisfied with just *one* of us?" Ollie asked.

"Good question."

"Is there anybody you want me to call?"

"Yeah, a hit man."

"Hey, you're the police reporter. You probably know more killers than I do. Seriously—"

"No, I'm all right. My folks are down in New York, and I wouldn't want to worry them. They had no idea I was pregnant. My brother's in California. And I'm sure as hell not calling Troy. He's probably not alone anyway."

"Men. You can't live with 'em—"

"And you can't shoot 'em," Amy said.

"That's debatable," Ollie said.

Amy laughed. "Whoever thought we would be this kind to each other?"

"Don't worry, I still think you're a ruthless bitch."
"And I still think you're an overpaid hack."

• • •

Two days later, Paul received a letter in a plain white envelope, with no return address. The typed message was in all caps: AACDDNLWYE GSLTLTAAOR IIUHIEINUA FMEENRNDRD TPFHEIVBPI OLIEHNIIAE FENAUPEDPU. He immediately showed it to us.

My team determined that the document was untraceable. The sender must have used gloves so there were no fingerprints, DNA, or otherwise identifiable elements. The postmark said it was mailed from Dorchester, but that wasn't much help because that neighborhood covers six square miles.

We certainly didn't have a cryptographer on staff, and there was no money to hire a freelancer, especially because we were devoting so many resources to the case already. Cambridge Mayor Daria Cardenas was calling me every day for a progress report and reminding me that the murders were, in her words, "besmirching the reputation of a city that was a major tourist attraction."

Deans at Harvard and MIT were pressuring me too. I learned that the parents of prospective students were concerned. Reporters from all over the country wanted to interview me. Worse, the families of the victims left emotional voicemail messages exhorting me to find the killer. I could not remember ever being so tired and edgy. I decided to channel some of that anxiety into decoding the letter.

Cryptography was one of my hobbies. I had read a couple of books about it, simply for amusement. As I said, I'm a voracious, but omnivorous, reader.

The first thing I noticed was that each word in the message had ten letters. I thought this might be a substitution code, with each letter representing another, but I couldn't find a pattern. I know that E is the most common letter in English, followed by T, O, A, and N, that the two most common one-letter words were "a" and "I," and that the most common two-letter words were of, to, and in. Beyond that I was stumped.

• • •

At a meeting in his office, Paul showed a copy of the letter to Ollie, who read through it carefully.

"If he wanted to make an impression, he should have put it in plain English," she said, in a vain attempt at humor. "Then again, using a code in its own way attracts attention."

"Right," Paul said. "Serial killers like notoriety. Even Jack the Ripper sent letters to the police. Sheer ego, I suppose."

"Maybe so." She looked quizzical.

"What are you thinking?" he asked.

"I'm wondering what his next move will be."

"Aren't we all. What's your guess?"

"What would you do if you were the guy?"

"Get back on my meds."

"And after that …" Ollie said, playing along.

"I'd be wondering what I had accomplished. It can't be easy killing all these people. I'd think about retreating for a while. By the way, I have been meaning to ask you: Can you write a story summarizing what Mezini has done so far?"

"Not much to report," Ollie said.

"Let's put *something* out there. Maybe it'll flush this asshole out. Can I convince you to add a piece of, uh, information that might help?" Green said.

"What exactly are you saying?"

They had a long debate. Would she be willing to lie, just a bit, to help find the killer? For instance, would she write that the cops had a possible suspect just to rattle him? Was *The Observer* duty-bound to be truthful, no matter what, or was it permissible to ignore the facts to further the greater good? After all, people were dying. Was their first loyalty to the readers, or to the truth?

Ollie pointed out that she'd have to run all this by me because I'd be the one most affected, not the paper. She asked Paul why he wanted her to write it.

"Because you're our best-known reporter, and the story will have more impact with your byline," he said.

"Don't try to con me with flattery," Ollie said. "I'm not some rookie right out of J-school. If I do it, it'll be—"

"Think of your dad."

"Cheap shot."

"What would he tell you to do?" Paul asked. "Wouldn't he want to do something to provoke the killer into showing his face, or making a stupid mistake?"

Ollie thought back to all the discussions she and her father had over dinner about his work. He hoped that she might end up involved with criminal justice somehow, so he figured he'd start her training early. He was a fair cop who never strong-armed anyone, as far as she knew, yet he admitted he'd push it hard during interrogations to make a perp think the police had more info than they really did. He'd tell a suspect that eyewitnesses put him on the scene, even if there were none. Or, he'd lie and say that the accomplice in the next room had already turned. "Do you want to go down alone?" he'd ask. "Why protect a guy who already fingered you?" Ollie wondered if "Baby G," the ex-con who pulled a gun on her, had succumbed to this kind of manipulation. Maybe that's why he was so angry.

Later she explained all this to me. I just smiled and that made her wonder if her father's maneuvers were tame compared to what I had seen, or whether I was just amused at the naivete of her attempt to wrestle with ethics. In the end, I gave my consent, but told her to downplay the lie. Anything to further the investigation and help us nail the perp.

In my experience everyone wanted to play detective. A prompt in a news story might, in effect, put the readers on the police payroll. A carefully worded story can convince people to come forward with information, especially those who might otherwise be reluctant, or those who knew something but aren't sure if it's relevant or useful. Occasionally what they think is trivial might be helpful to us.

The result of all these maneuvers was a story that ran under Ollie Burns' byline explaining that detectives had done exhaustive interviews with neighbors, family members, and co-workers connected with the victims, that they had spoken with men who had committed acts of violence against the media (without mentioning our investigation into their reading habits), and that editor Paul Green had received a disturbing, anonymous letter. The kicker was that the authorities were zeroing in on a suspect and that they were convinced that he was a bright, creative person with highly developed organizational skills. I confess that I helped her write that detail, and I was proud of it. *Perhaps this last bit of flattery might cause the killer to be careless,* I thought. *Sometimes you just have to be a bit, uh, flexible with the truth.*

21

LIVE FREE *AND* DIE

*N*EW HAMPSHIRE *is one quirky state*, Ollie said to herself as she headed north.

It was one of the original thirteen colonies, with the operative word being original. New Hampshire's presidential primary is the first in the nation and the legislature is determined to keep it that way. They wait for the other states to schedule their voting days, then preempt them if necessary. It's hard to imagine why the New Hampshire primary is thought to be a key indicator of the strength of the candidates, because the population there is arguably the least representative of the rest of America.

Here's a partial list of unorthodox features of the state: for starters, it has nine state songs. Though this is not well known, some of the highest winds on earth have been recorded there, up to 230 MPH, at the top of Mount Washington, which is only 6,300 feet high. New Hampshire has no income tax, but it owns and operates the liquor stores. The state motto is "Live Free or Die," but Ollie thought it should be "Live Free *and* Die," since there are no laws mandating seatbelts or motorcycle helmets.

1.4 million people live there, and they certainly pride themselves on their independence. But on this day, Ollie was interested in only one resident: My ex-partner, Johnny Garlowe. It was time to meet him.

Standing outside the Mountain Refuge mental hospital in Manchester, she felt despondent as she contemplated the plight of the patients. *I guess I'm in better shape than they are,* she thought, *then felt guilty about her smug attitude. But why is it that all mental institutions seem to look the same? Brick with beige trim around the windows. Green lawns whose serenity mocks the suffering inside.*

After signing in at the front desk, Ollie walked down a long corridor with shiny linoleum that smelled as if it had been swabbed with copious amounts of Pinesol. She stopped outside Johnny's room and saw a woman she assumed to be his wife Ashley, reading a paperback. She was sitting on a vinyl-covered easy chair right next to the bed where he was napping. Ollie's first thought was that this place looked like a cheap motel compared to the luxury of Jan Watkins' digs in rehab in Concord, Massachusetts.

Ashley was obviously startled to see Ollie, who motioned for her to come out into the hallway. Ashley tiptoed out and shut the door of the room behind her.

"I'm Ollie Burns." She extended her hand but Ashley didn't grab it. She kept her arms folded on her chest.

"I know who you are. You have some gall coming here," Ashley said. "That hatchet job you did on Johnny was pretty awful. My husband's in a stupor thanks to the bullshit you published."

Ashley was wearing jeans and a billowy gray sweatshirt that looked like it had been her husband's. Her unkempt brown hair hung down to her shoulders. Ollie sized her up as the "I'll-stay-by-my-man-no-matter-what type."

"I, uh—"

"You, uh, what? Did you want to interview Johnny? You won't get much out of him now. He was off-the-charts hyper yesterday, so they gave him something to calm him down. I think they overstated the case, though. It knocked him out."

"Does he stay here all the time?"

"Theoretically, he's free to go. As long as he signs out. But he's so full of drugs that he wouldn't know what to do on the outside. Still, I worry sometimes that he might try to leave. He always says he wants to go back home."

"He can really sign out anytime he wants?"

"Yeah, he committed himself, so they can't keep him here. They have a log at the front desk—just a piece of paper on a clipboard. The guards are pretty lax. Half the time they watch TV with their backs turned to the door." *Ollie sensed that Ashley wanted to unburden herself,* yet she abruptly shifted into a aggressive mode again. "Why did you come here, just to torture us again?"

"I wanted to ask you a couple of questions about the story we ran. Mez said it was inaccurate."

"In what way?"

"He felt we overstated his role in the...uh...interrogations."

"And I suppose you feel that Johnny got what he deserved, and that Mez was blameless, right?"

"I'm not sure at all. What do you think?"

"I'll tell you what happened," Ashley said. "Johnny was a good cop who believed he was dispensing justice. And if it hadn't been for you bloodsuckers at *The Observer*, he'd still be on the force." There was venom behind her words.

"So, it was all our fault?" Ollie couldn't help getting defensive.

"Johnny's troubled, for sure. But he's *not* a monster."

"What about Mez? Did he really try to stop him?"

"Look, sweetheart. No one could control Johnnie. I know Mez tried. We're done now. Get the fuck away from me."

"I'm sorry if I upset you," Ollie said.

Ashley just scoffed, through her tears.

With that, Ollie decided it was politic to leave.

On the way past the front desk, she found that Ashley's description of the shoddy security was accurate. One sheet on the clipboard listed patient arrivals and departures, and the second page showed the visitors' activities. The guard barely looked up when she signed out.

Christ, we have tighter controls at The Observer, she said to herself.

22

LIQUID INSPIRATION

AT THIS POINT in the investigation, I was more determined than ever. It seemed that the ordinary rules didn't apply to this creep, whoever he was. And I was convinced it was a he. Was I right? After all, women can kill too. But probably not this wantonly, I thought, then wondered if I was being sexist or gendered, as they say. In any case, we're dealing with a beast, that's for sure.

I sat by myself in the detectives' unit at headquarters where ten of us worked in an open area. I always try to keep my work area neat, to avoid distractions. My metal desk had nothing but a plastic rack holding manilla folders, a lamp, a phone, a cup of pens and pencils, a laptop, and an ample array of rusty scratches from previous occupants. I pulled out a long pencil and tapped the eraser end on the desk, in the hope that the rhythm would help me think. When all the detectives were there, the bass hum of conversations could be unbearable. Now that I was alone, I took advantage of the solitude by talking to myself.

Deadline on Arrival

I went over the standard stuff in my mind, though this situation was anything but standard. When we arrive at a normal murder scene, what's the first thing we ordinarily do? Look for signs of forced entry. Broken windows, doors pried open with crowbars, that sort of thing. Check to see if anything is missing. Cash, jewelry, etc. "If so, we can be pretty sure the culprit was a burglar who was a stranger to the victim," I said out loud.

If there's no forced entry, then the killer might be someone the victim knew. Maybe a domestic situation. A quarrel between spouses, or two lovers, that turned violent.

But these ordinary scenarios were largely irrelevant. For one thing, the murders took place either outside or away from the victims' homes. Alec Moore the headmaster was found in his own back yard and Stafford in the back yard of the frat house. V 2.0 was shot on the street, and Alec Moore the medical salesman was poisoned in the hospital.

What about a motive? There has to be a motive.

But that would be in a conventional murder case, whatever that was. We may be dealing with a psycho way outside the range of normality. Maybe killing made him feel better. I recalled what Jack Grimes said: one-third of the serial killers do it for enjoyment, out of lust, or a deranged desire for power. Another 30% want money, but there haven't been any ransom demands yet. Maybe that will come later. Maybe it had already occurred, in the coded note that we haven't yet deciphered.

Then again, maybe our guy just kept waking up with a headache that aspirin couldn't lay a glove on, so he got rid of it by knocking off a few people.

But why this string of victims? They had two things in common: three of the four had appeared in *Observer* stories and all of them had been involved in domestic incidents. They were abusive toward their partners, or, in Stafford's case, women he targeted.

Fingerprints or DNA? I always call to mind what they taught us at the police academy, the Exchange Principle put forth 100 years ago by Edmond Locard, AKA the "Sherlock Holmes of France": Every contact leaves a trace. Whether it's sweat, skin cells, dandruff, whatever. We lifted a couple of stray hairs and some miscellaneous organic matter from the crime scenes, but none of the samples matched any known criminal in our databases.

Okay, Mez, I said to myself: Look at this prismatically, breaking down the light into constituent parts, to try to see the real colors, so to speak. Try to use your synesthesia. Any visions coming to mind? I wish I could turn it on and off at will, but it comes and goes randomly.

Investigation isn't like a crossword puzzle where they give you clues. Speaking of clues, take another look at that letter Green received, I thought. I pulled a copy out of my desk drawer and read it for the 100th time: AACDDNLWYE GSLTLTAAOR IIUHIEINUA FMEENRNDRD TPFHEIVBPI OLIEHNIIAE FENAUPEDPU. The more I studied it, the less it made sense. Each word has 10 letters and there are seven words. 70 letters altogether. Brilliant. You can do simple multiplication, genius. What's next?

For want of a better approach, I cut a couple pieces of paper into 70 small squares, copied the letters onto each one, and kept rearranging them on my desk. Chief Mike Cronin pushed open the office door at that point and the rush of wind blew half of the scraps of paper onto the floor.

"Mez, what the fuck are you doing? A jigsaw puzzle?"

"I was trying to decipher a message that the killer sent to *The Observer*, Chief," I said.

"Yeah, well let's try deciphering the identity of the bastard while you're at it. Everybody's on my ass about this and you're sitting there playing cryptographer. Let me see that note," he said firmly.

The Chief looked at it quickly. "Nine Es. That figures. That's the most common letter, right?"

"Yeah, I noticed that too."

"If this guy isn't a genius, then you should be able to figure this out, Mez. Maybe you need some stimulation. Why don't we have a drink?"

"Are you kidding me?" I asked.

"I'm serious. A little bit of booze can loosen up the mind. Just one drink, though. You have my permission," he said with a smile. I liked Chief Cronin. He was a hard ass, but he was fair.

"Open up Detective Samson's bottom left drawer. He always keeps a flask of whiskey there." Noticing my shocked look, he said, "You guys think I don't know what goes on around here? That son of a bitch is old school. Good detective, though."

I nodded and pulled out the flask. "Give that to me."

Deadline on Arrival

He took a swig and handed me the flask.

"Whaddarya sittin' there for? I told you to have a nip."

I followed his order, swallowed some whiskey, coughed, then picked up the pieces of paper that had fallen on the floor. He nodded and left.

I took another look at the seemingly random words on the note: AACDDNLWYE GSLTLTAAOR IIUHIEINUA FMEENRNDRD TPFHEIVBPI OLIEHNIIAE FENAUPEDPU.

Sometimes synesthesia helps me see patterns. As my friend Robyn Platt once told me, look at it as a bug, not a feature. It suddenly occurred to me to arrange the strips in a square. At first, I put the words in separate rows like this:

A	A	C	D	D	N	L	W	Y	E
G	S	L	T	L	T	A	A	O	R
I	I	U	H	I	E	I	N	U	A
F	M	E	E	N	R	N	D	R	D
T	P	F	H	E	I	V	B	P	I
O	L	I	E	H	N	I	I	A	E
F	E	N	A	U	P	E	D	P	U

That made no sense whatsoever. Then I tried rearranging the words in columns:

A	G	I	F	T	O	F
A	S	I	M	P	L	E
C	L	U	E	F	I	N
D	T	H	E	H	E	A
D	L	I	E	E	H	U
N	T	E	N	I	N	P
L	A	I	R	V	I	E
W	A	N	D	B	I	D
Y	O	U	R	P	A	P
E	R	A	D	I	E	U

Now I was able to decipher it. Reading from left to right, starting in the upper left corner, the message was: A GIFT OF A SIMPLE CLUE FIND THE HEADLINE HUNTER IN PLAIN VIEW AND BID YOUR PAPER ADIEU.

Progress. Now what? The killer's trying to destroy the paper. That's no revelation. But he's hiding in plain view? That could be a taunt. Maybe it didn't even come from the killer. But who else would send it?

I arranged a Zoom meeting with Ollie and Paul and told them what the letter said. Paul's reaction was harsh.

"This fucking guy is playing us, and you know how much I hate being played."

"At least we have some insight into his personality," Ollie said.

"Yeah, and where does that leave us?"

"A few feet above ignorance, Chief," Ollie said, knowing that he didn't like it when she called him that.

With no warning, Paul left the meeting.

"Is he always this charming?" I asked.

"This is a good day for him. He admires your work, that's why he was hostile. If he didn't respect you, he'd probably be polite."

"Superb management style," I said. "By the way, why did you go visit Johnny? Ashley called me up and screamed at me. I won't tell you what she said, but she was like a bulldog."

"Would it help if I apologized?" Ollie asked.

"It would help if you don't do something outrageous without telling me first."

"OK, I promise. I was just doing my job."

"To quote a great line from a movie I once saw, doing your job doesn't make it right. Ashley has suffered enough. Whatever Johnny did, or didn't do, she is blameless. Her problem is that she loves him."

"Z, I'm sorry. I'll make this up you somehow."

"Let's get back to work. What's next?" I was anxious to get on with things.

Ollie suggested that we talk to Caleb Baird. She said he was one of the brainiest guys who ever worked at the paper. As the former book reviewer, he just might have some ideas. Maybe this was what they call a Hail Mary pass in football, where the quarterback just hurls the ball downfield to no one in particular, in the hope that someone on his team will catch it. We didn't know what else to try at this point.

Ollie described Caleb as the cultural soul of The Observer, even after his departure from the ranks.

She did say that he made her uneasy because he seemed to be incapable of feeling any emotion except anger. He railed against management for the demise of culture in daily news, against the book publishers who had rejected his novels, and most of all against anyone who did not think exactly as he did. The odd thing was that he had maintained a friendship with Paul.

The closest he came to publishing anything other than book reviews was a novel aptly titled Oddity, about a culture writer (whom else could he depict?) who stumbled across a conspiracy by bean counters to reduce the head count in the English department at a prestigious university. Ollie had read the manuscript. She found it to be eloquent but bloodless. A literary agent whom Caleb had contacted wanted him to add more intrigue, perhaps even a murder or two, or some romance. In a huff, he pulled the manuscript out of circulation and seethed for years afterwards.

Ollie had always thought Caleb was harmless though she remembered some disturbing things he had said about wanting to destroy the Luddites who ran media organizations. He became a right-winger, in a way that embraced disruption for its own sake.

As for myself, I had seen this phenomenon many times: Liberals, disaffected with their lives, turning to doctrinaire conservatism out of anger or frustration. If he had lived in the 1930s or 1940s, he would have embraced fascism just as the philosopher Martin Heidegger and the poet Ezra Pound did, possibly for the sake of flexing imaginary muscles that most people thought intellectuals lacked. Or maybe they were just looking for a simple doctrine to cling to, without regard to the morality.

Like many lonely, smart, disaffected men, Caleb admired Nietzsche and his brand of poetic, misogynistic anger, what today might be called the angst of the involuntary celibates, AKA incels. Ollie said that Caleb believed you should "Burn alone, if you aren't lucky enough to find a soulmate." He even visited Nietzsche's favorite haunts in Switzerland and Italy and climbed the same mountains to try to experience the philosopher's insights.

Ollie and I wondered if Caleb was truly capable of the kind of violence that had befallen the paper lately. If pushed, would he ever be desperate enough to kill?

The fixation with Nietzsche wasn't surprising. "Remember," I told Ollie, "People see whatever they want in his works. The Nazis saw a kindred spirit, which was pure fiction because he despised anti-Semitism. The misogynists see a fellow traveler, the poets see an eloquent partner, and the philosophers don't get him at all because he's so hard to understand or categorize."

"Are you mansplaining Nietzsche to me?" Ollie asked.

Like most guys who are accused of this sin, I didn't get it. I thought we were just chatting.

"I have to tell you, professor," she said, "I've read all of Nietzsche, and I love his ideas."

"Even the part where he said, 'When you deal with women, bring your whip?'"

"If we women judged you guys on the basis of every stray comment, we'd have to eliminate practically all of you," she said. I let that go.

Changing the subject, I suggested that we go and see Caleb right away.

Ollie said she had never been to his home in Watertown, right next to Cambridge, so she was game. I picked her up and we drove to his ramshackle house, where we saw paint peeling off the worn siding, a roof missing so many shingles that it looked pockmarked, and a chain link fence rusted so badly that a child could punch through it. Ollie knocked on the door and we waited a long time before she saw something flash behind the peephole. When the door opened, the scruffy occupant blinked at the light.

"The I-Desk is here. How exciting," he said with a sneer. "And who is this gentleman?"

"A fan of your reviews," I answered.

"I thought I recognized you."

At 55 or so, Caleb was the very essence of shabbiness. His circular, rimless glasses were so dirty that it was hard to see his eyes, much less determine what color they were. His bushy, sandy blond hair stuck out in formless tufts toward every direction of the compass. His faded cotton shirt, once salmon in color, appeared to be vintage L.L. Bean, and the elastic in the waist of his sweatpants had long since worn out. The pantlegs dragged on the floor and obscured most of his dirty bare feet.

His idea of décor was bookshelves made of planks bowing between cinder blocks. Even the kitchen was full of books, in teetering piles in the middle of the floor. We walked through narrow pathways between tomes. The organization, if you could call it that, was haphazard though he told us he knew where everything was.

As we stood in the kitchen, Ollie was afraid to touch anything because the room was so filthy. We sat down on mismatched folding chairs around a stained wooden table.

"I assume this isn't a social visit," he said. "Are you on the case, Lois Lane?"

"Are you writing any fiction?" Ollie asked, just to get a conversation started.

"Not really. I think my work is not of this time," he said. He barely acknowledged me.

For no apparent reason, Caleb started prattling about Hemingway, whom he was rereading. Figures, Ollie thought, all the wimps revere the macho guys. When he finally mentioned Hemingway's bullfighting book, Death in the Afternoon, she had an opening.

"Speaking of death, Caleb, what's your take on the Headline Hunter?" she asked.

"In what sense?" he asked.

"Do you have any thoughts about the situation?"

"Thoughts about the situation," he muttered, as if talking to himself. "I think you have to watch the quiet ones."

"Meaning?"

"Meaning killers don't often broadcast their intentions."

"Do you speak from personal experience?"

Caleb's laughter was awkward. "Did you know that many serial killers are fetishists? That could be some sort of a metaphor."

"Do you mean that a fetishist uses the object of his obsession, a body part like feet, for instance, to represent the person he loves?" I asked.

"Or lusts for," he added. "Do you know what Aristotle said about metaphor?"

"That it's a sign of genius. An equation between things that are dissimilar, as in saying that a book is a window to a new world."

"Excellent, excellent," he said. I think he was impressed. "And the less obvious the metaphor, the greater the impact: 'Jocund day stands tiptoe on the misty mountain tops.'"

"Romeo and Juliet," I said. "Only Shakespeare could write like that. 'Day standing tiptoe.' Amazing."

I asked him if he had read any decent books lately. His response was, "The novel is dead, long live the novel" and proceeded to lecture us about the insubstantiality of modern literature, the microcosmic emphasis on minute aspects of experience, the mindless embrace (his phrase, not mine) of social themes, and the ubiquitous bad grammar.

I did manage to perform one truth check. I read the decoded quote from the letter that Green had received, just to see his response: "A gift of a simple clue, find the Headline Hunter in plain view, and bid your paper adieu." He reacted like someone who had never heard the words.

Ollie and I later came to the seemingly inescapable conclusion that he was a howler, not a hunter. All talk. I hoped we were right.

23

MONEY MATTERS

AT THAT POINT, Ollie did what any good investigative reporter does, or at least tries to do: She followed the money. The trail led directly to the Allston family, owners of *The Observer*. She decided to call the eldest son and heir apparent, Stuart.

The voice that greeted her was formal, Boston Brahmin, crisp. "Ms. Burns." He pronounced it "Buhhns."

"I hate to bother you, sir, but I have some questions about the murders," she said.

He invited her to come to his home in Brookline the next day. On a map of the metro area, it looks like someone cut a cigar-shaped swath out of Boston to create the town of Brookline. And it's not a cheap cigar. Fourteen percent of the population of 60,000 hold doctoral degrees, more than any other town in America. It boasts the birthplace of JFK and a golf course simply known as "The Country Club," the oldest and one of the most exclusive in the country. The initiation fee there is said to be a cool $250,000 or so. As expected, Brookline is home to many wealthy families, including the Allstons.

Like most of the so-called landed gentry, they had a "family office" of professional managers who supervised their investments and kept a tight control on younger relatives to prevent them from doing anything stupid or impulsive. That was certainly not a problem for Stuart.

He had worked at *The Observer* ever since he graduated from Harvard 40 years ago. At first the staff resented him as a rich kid born to the manor, literally, but he quickly proved himself. He asked for the most dangerous assignments: gang murders, riots, organized crime stories. He used to get mad at the news desk if they *didn't* wake him up in the middle of the night when the criminals came alive. Even grizzled photographers, who had seen everything and forgotten nothing, respected him. No one worked harder and asked for less recognition.

The Allstons had run *The Observer* since his great-great grandfather started it back in 1872. Rumor had it that Stuart was dismayed that none of his four children had any interest in the business. Yet he recognized that journalism isn't the *career* it once was. Besides, they'd be better off putting their money into an S&P 500 fund than watching it dwindle year after year in *Observer* stock. Besides, they had so little sense of duty anyway. "The people need to know" and all those slogans were just words to them.

Ollie turned her car into the long, sinuous driveway at the Allston manse, and in 30 seconds she could no longer see the street. A vast expanse of lawn and forest lay behind her, obscuring the rest of the world. *That's the whole point*, she said to herself.

No sooner had she alighted from her car than Stuart walked down the wide marble staircase and greeted her with an awkward smile. The mansion loomed behind him, all brick and slate. It looked like a college dorm. Ollie counted eight gables on her way to the front steps.

"Hi, Ollie," Stuart said.

"Hello, Mr. Allston."

"Quint, please. That's my nickname because I'm J. Stuart Allston the Fifth. Not much imagination when it came to names in my family," he said. He was tall, probably about 6'4", and ungainly. He tried to be genial but didn't know how. *No doubt all those financial advisors told him to be on guard around people with less money, which would be 99.9% of the world,*

Ollie thought. The rich learned caution of that sort from mother's milk. Always at the ready to refuse requests for investments or contributions.

Quint was dressed in starched summer khakis, with a blue oxford button down shirt, and Sperry boat shoes. He looked like he was on his way to his yacht club for lunch, yet he was probably prepared for a serious meeting, as he was carrying a white manilla folder under his left arm.

He led her into a huge foyer with a shiny marble floor. A spiral staircase with a thick red runner swept gracefully toward a balcony. A crystal chandelier hung overhead. They passed through a dining room into the kitchen, which had glasses hung in racks over copper countertops, then proceeded down a long hallway leading to the semicircular back porch that looked out over a back lawn that must have been two acres.

Quint offered Ollie a seat in one of the wicker chairs surrounding a wooden table and he placed the manilla folder in front of him. A young woman wearing a white apron over a blue silk shirt served tea and cakes. Ollie felt very middle class in this setting. She wondered how many of her classmates from Brown lived like this.

"My dad thought highly of you, Ollie." Quint had a habit of clearing his throat quite often. *Probably a nervous tic*, she thought.

"The feeling was mutual," she said.

"Do you like your work?" Quint asked, obviously struggling to make conversation.

"Yes, I do. I wish I could have limo service to and from the paper, but I'll muddle through." Quint chuckled.

Now it was Ollie's turn to sound uncomfortable. "Has this house been in your family for a long time?" she asked.

"Yup," he said. When Quint used that word it sounded strange, like an uncle trying to be cool. Even though he was probably in his 60s, he seemed even older.

"Can we stay off the record here?" he asked.

"Sure."

"My dad said you could be trusted, and that's good enough for me. I want to share a few things with you. Sensitive matters. Do you know what short selling is?"

"I think so. You sell shares of a stock that you don't own, and buy them later to complete the transaction."

"Right," Quint said. "It's complicated and risky. Unlike most investors who 'go long,' that is hope the price of a stock will rise, short sellers make a bet that the price of the shares will *drop*. Let's say a particular stock is priced at ten dollars a share right now, and the shorts, as they are called, agree to sell one hundred shares at that price, for a total of a thousand dollars. Shares, as you said, that they don't own. The sellers borrow them from a broker, who gets the full price up front from the buyer, and they agree to pay for them at some point in the future. Needless to say, this is all done digitally these days."

Ollie nodded. She was with him so far.

"If the price drops," he continued, "say to six dollars a share, the short sellers are ecstatic. When the deal closes, maybe in ten days, they buy the one hundred shares they agreed to deliver for just six hundred dollars, and they get the thousand dollars the broker got at the beginning. A decent profit of forty percent."

"What if the stock goes up?"

"Great question. They still get only a thousand bucks, because that's the deal they made, one hundred shares at ten dollars a piece. But they are obligated to buy the shares that they made a commitment to deliver at the *higher* price. That can be *frighteningly expensive*. The math becomes the enemy. Let's say the stock doubles, up to twenty a share. Then they have to pay two thousand dollars, and they get back only one thousand, and that hurts."

"Takes a strong stomach."

"Sure does. Potentially, their losses could be infinite if the stock rises and rises. They can minimize the risk, though, by spreading false information about the company—"

"To make *sure* the stocks plummet," she said. "I assume you're talking about the paper. Things are bad enough with the murders. They're just piling on more bad news."

"No wonder you were my dad's favorite reporter."

"The mind of a cop's daughter. 'Look for the financial angle,' my dad always said."

"Indeed. Our parent company's stock, Bay State Media, has *already* fallen forty percent. And the murders are making it worse by the day. That's why the private equity firms are sniffing all around us. They can buy our company at a bargain price now."

"Which firms are involved? Paul said something about this at a staff meeting but he wouldn't tell us who they were."

"That's confidential, but I suppose I should give you enough ammunition to research this. They're called Persephone. I know you're not taking notes, but remember that name."

"Are they working with the shorts?"

"We're not sure, but it wouldn't surprise me. The shorts have thrown gas on the fire, and the buyers are trying to take advantage of the situation. If the stock goes lower and lower, they can buy our company at a fire sale price.

"Take a look at the shorts' report," he said, handing her a thick document that he pulled out of the folder. "They have been passing this out quietly. By the way, our conversation may be off the record, but these shenanigans would make a great story, don't you think?"

He said the word "shenanigans" in a schoolmarmish way, as if it burned his lips.

"Why share this with me? Why not with Paul Green, or Jan Watkins? Or take it to the police."

"I just figure that you'll know what to do with it. I'm sure you'll handle it appropriately. I can't say that about the rest of the staff."

• • •

When Ollie opened the report at home, she began to understand the craftiness and sophistication of the short sellers. Their document was like a professionally produced brochure, with a tasteful color scheme, sumptuous graphics, and articulate analysis—spread out over 35 pages. If you didn't know any better, you'd think the writers were savvy analysts.

They called themselves Fast Accurate Complete Truth (FACT) Investors. The chapter headings were beyond sensational: "*Observer* Management as Starchy as the Family's Brook Brothers Shirts"; "Stiff Upper Lips Quiver," and so on. Their headlines were as crass as *The Sun*'s. *Tabloids 'R Us*, Ollie thought.

The copy fluently outlined all the business issues *The Observer* was facing: the demise of print, falling ad revenues (despite the recent upward tick from the publicity surrounding the murders), competition from dot-coms, and so on. And, of course, they noted the adverse effects of the murders on newsroom morale. There was just enough truth to make the report believable, but a lot more innuendo and exaggeration.

FACT made it sound as if *The Observer* was about to go bankrupt any day. The revenue figures they cited were ridiculously low, the costs overstated. Worse, they cited "intelligence" that the staff was about to go on strike, which was decidedly not true. Ollie had read that these manipulators "distort and short," and they certainly were living up to that slogan.

For more insight she reached out to her personal lawyer Joel Baldwin, who understood more about the media business than anyone else she knew. He had successfully defended the paper in a couple of libel suits. He also had a finance background—very unusual for lawyers, who often render opinions on business issues only because they're asked, not because they know.

On the phone she summarized the report for him. "Is this legal?" she asked.

"Tough question," he said. "The short sellers may spread lies, but they would argue that they're protected by the First Amendment."

"So are we, but we can't lie with impunity. If we do, we get sued for libel."

"Different situation. Basically, the paper would have three options: Number one, report the shorts to the SEC, but the government tends to be flatfooted and understaffed. Two, take them to court, but lawsuits of that sort are expensive and hard to win. The last option is to speak to stock analysts and tell their own side of the story. The problem is that the shorts publish slick reports that *seem* to be true, or at least have a kernel of accuracy. That's why these bastards get away with it most of the time."

"How much do they typically invest?" Ollie asked.

"Maybe ten million," he said. "Then they can make two or three million in a matter of days. Not bad considering they haven't really done much except write a report and lose some sleep worrying about whether the stock will drop."

That night Ollie was doing her best to explain all this to me.

"Hell, if I were greedy, I'd short the stock myself," I said.

"Right now, that might be a good idea," Ollie said, with a sigh.

"Let's go back to the murders," I said, "to figure out a potential link. We can guess *what* the killer might be doing. That is, trying to destroy the paper. We know *when* and *where*, as in now and here. We know *how*, with one murder after another. And possibly now we may know *why*, to short the stock and make a quick buck. But we don't know …"

"*Who*. FACT wrote the report. You think they may have something to do with the murders?"

"Maybe. I can try to find out how much money they've moved."

"We should also check out the private equity fund that's sniffing around too," Ollie said. "It's called Persephone. Hades's wife, and queen of the underworld."

"Yes, but she was also the goddess of springtime growth and flowers," I said. "An odd combination. Hell and spring."

"Fitting, huh? Springtime for them. Hell for everybody else."

24

MAKING MARKETS MOVE

WHEN WE VISITED Persephone's office, the people I saw struck me as a collection of pin stripe suits who probably approached finance as a big game. And not a common sport like football. More like squash or water polo. Some of the ruthless wonders there had actually been water polo stars in college, and the more pretentious members of the staff had been fencers. The place reeked of testosterone, of an elite strain.

The fund's investment manager was Aldous Denby. He had been a classics major at Princeton before attending business school. He peppered his speech with Latin and Greek quotes just to let you know how erudite he was. When Ollie and I showed up unannounced and introduced ourselves, he was not just polite but unctuous.

"Well, well, well, it's not every day that I am visited by a real live detective *and* a reporter," he said.

I am visited. Who says that, I thought. *I hate that manner of speaking. Pompous asshole.*

"Well, it is not every day that I am addressed by a captain of finance," I countered.

"How can I help you?" Aldous asked, as he ushered us into an office that was only slightly smaller than many homes. It was full of nautical paraphernalia. Photos of sailboats covered the walls. A four-foot-long silver anchor sat atop an end table. A salt-water aquarium with a full rainbow of tropical fish gurgled in a corner of the room. The back of his chair was a huge captain's wheel with a cushion in the middle. The spokes extended sideways beyond his shoulders and upwards over his head as he settled into the seat.

Visions of white caps emanating from his head filled my brain. I have to admit, that was a bit distracting. I did my best to pull myself back from the chaos of synesthesia.

"It seems you have been quite successful, Mr. Denby," Ollie noted.

"The finance gods have been kind to us," he said. "But that could change in an instant. A few bad trades and Dame Fortune's daughter Miss Fortune might just appear."

"I guess it's easier when you have your finger on the scale," I said. I sensed that he was enjoying himself. He had stared down some of the greediest people in finance. His attitude seemed to convey that a mere Cambridge cop was no challenge.

"Surely you didn't come here to debate the morality of the markets," he said.

"Mr. Denby, are you working with FACT?" I asked.

"Detective, we don't discuss our investment strategies. That's why we succeed. And, if I may ask, why are you here, Ms. Burns? Isn't it unorthodox for a reporter to accompany a detective on his rounds?"

"I'm doing a story about the investigation. I'm here mainly as an observer," Ollie said, "but I do take this personally. We want to preserve our paper."

"Very noble, Ms. Burns," he said. "Very noble. You're a warrior in the quest for the elusive *real story*. Let me assure you that I do business the old-fashioned way. I'm a value investor. That means I look for the hidden, the hated, and the misunderstood. The properties no one wants. I buy them at rock bottom and wait."

"It helps if you drive the price down first with misinformation," I said.

"Your words, not mine," Denby replied. "Let me say this: whoever pushed *The Observer* into oblivion did a good job. The buyer will trim the excess. They'll leave just enough people in place to cover a fraction of the news to fool readers into thinking that the paper still has some semblance of the old magic."

"Smart, maybe," I said, "but cold."

"I appreciate that compliment, Detective. Now, I trust I have answered all your questions."

It was time for us to leave.

I always wished I had infinite subpoena power, just as Ollie wished she had any at all. Wouldn't it be great, we both thought, to be able to stroll into the offices of a suspect and search everything in sight, without regard to civil rights or privacy?

At least I knew what my next target was: FACT. This time I went alone. As I stood outside their office in a non-descript building in Lexington, I reminded myself that it meant Fast Accurate Complete Truth. *Great irony*, I thought, *and dreamed about a search warrant. No chance.* First of all, stock manipulation was a federal crime, about twenty light years beyond the jurisdiction of a Cambridge cop. Plus, offenses were hard to prove. Not to mention that I really didn't know much about the markets.

"Eff it, just go in," I said out loud. A mom pushing a stroller stared at me, but I didn't care.

A tiny FACT logo was etched into the glass door, which was incredibly easy to open, as if it were responding to my will. The carpet was soft underfoot, so much so that I left footprints behind. The artwork spanned several styles. An abstract mélange in red and blue, a portrait of a young woman with a piercing stare, and a minimalist black oval on a white background.

The receptionist peered at me through oversized glasses with a neon red frame.

"May I help you, sir?" she asked.

"I'm Detective Mezini from the Cambridge police and I'm wondering if I might see Mr., uh …" I paused and looked down at my notebook. "Terrell, Liam Terrell." I found that name on their website.

"May I say what this about?" she asked.

"Investments," I said with as much authority as I could muster.

"Please wait a moment," she said as she stood up and walked into the inner offices. I sat down on the slick leather sofa, which was not very comfortable because I immediately slid into a slouch.

A man emerged. "Detective, come on in. Liam Terrell," he said, extending his hand. His lips were smiling but his eyes weren't. He led me into a conference room.

"Would you like still or sparkling water, coffee, or tea, Detective?" asked the receptionist, suddenly appearing in the doorway.

"Nothing, thank you, I'm fine," I said as she smiled and closed the door.

Liam interlocked his fingers, turned his palms toward me, and cracked his knuckles. His black hair was pomaded and combed straight back. He wore a navy suit with white chalk stripes that were very wide, a blue shirt with a white collar and French cuffs, and a pale yellow tie. He was handsome, with sparkling blue eyes, though there was something predatory about him. Perhaps it was just the way he carried himself.

"Let me guess," Liam said. "This isn't a social call."

"Fair assumption."

"Well, have at it."

"I'm curious, Mr. Terrell, how long have you been in business?"

"Well, if you include my job as a courier on Wall Street in high school before the days of email, I'd say 25 years."

"Things have changed a lot over that time."

"Yes, indeed." His manner abruptly shifted from polite to brusque. "Detective, I'm a busy man. Please tell me what you need."

"Let's get down to it, then. Why did you write a report berating the stock of Bay State Media? Needless to say, that's the parent company of the *Boston Observer*."

"Are the local police clipping at the edges of SEC territory now?"

"Hardly."

"FYI, you don't use the term berate with regard to stock, only people. You should say belittle, since stocks are inanimate."

"Just like dead bodies."

Liam chuckled. "Do you suspect us of murder?"

"Mr. Terrell, I just want to ask a few questions, then I'll go. Is that fair?"

"Sure. Do I need a lawyer?"

"Up to you."

"I deal with enough of them in my business, I think I can handle myself. Shoot. Sorry, bad word choice. Go ahead."

"I won't ask you to account for your whereabouts on the nights of the murders. Even if you were involved, you wouldn't be on the scene."

"This is outrageous, Detective."

"Relax," I said, changing the subject. "I'm legitimately curious. How did you get started in this business?"

"Are you asking or investigating?"

"Both, I suppose."

"Do you know what it feels like to place a ten million dollar bet that a stock will go down?" he asked. "You do seventy percent of the analysis and you're seventy percent sure you're right, so you press a key that initiates the trade. But there's always that thirty percent of doubt, even on a good day. Remember, it's *not your money*. A lot of very rich people have given you their funds to invest. Can you imagine the fear and trembling?"

I chuckled. "Not even close. For me, a fifty-dollar blackjack table is a stretch. Why not just take a long position, and wait for the stock to rise?"

"Strictly plebeian, Detective. Besides, there are so many badly run companies out there that deserve to be, uh, 'berated' in our reports."

"Or sometimes they're just the innocent victims of a psycho killer who helps destroy a reputable business that is already in a—"

"Dying industry, like newspapers?" Liam said. "Did it ever occur to you that the whole news business is a dinosaur?"

"And it's up to you to see that it goes extinct."

"I don't take moral positions, Detective."

"What does that mean? That you ignore the consequences?"

"I'm strictly clinical, Detective. We make a bet that stocks will move in a certain direction. The companies we target are failing because they have made foolish decisions, or they're run by incompetent people. We don't create the problems; we just profit from them."

"Matter of opinion," I said. "The reports you write may contain a scintilla of truth, but they're mostly invective."

"Did you come here to engage in a debate, or do you have some real questions?"

"Can I see the list of your investors?"

"Not a chance," Liam, replied. "I will tell you that you would recognize many of the names. People who would never admit that they're giving money to short sellers. Our track record is pretty good. It's a quick way to make money, or, of course, lose it in a nanosecond."

"I could subpoena the list."

"Go ahead and try. I don't think you'd get too far. Isn't that what lawyers would call a…"

• • •

"Fishing expedition, it'll never work." That's what Greg Bauer, one of my contacts at the Secretary of State's securities division, told me on the phone. All the cops liked him. He tended to think like we did. But he couldn't do the impossible.

"You can't just start rooting around in the hope of finding evidence," he said. "No court would allow that."

"Nothing we can do?"

"Nada. You know I'd give you the go-ahead if you were even close. Can you figure out a specific reason to search?"

"Not really. Between us, we believe that someone was engineering the murders to hurt the company and drive down the stock. I'd bet my badge that FACT knew about it and took advantage of the situation. Chances are the Headline Hunter has made a, uh, killing, on the stock too."

"Bad choice of words."

I thanked him, hung up, and immediately called Ollie.

"Don't you know any cat burglars?" she asked, after I explained the situation.

"Where's Kat when we need her?" I asked.

"Kat?"

"You know, Kat Orsino, your favorite wiseass probation officer," I said.

"Yeah, she probably knows someone who could help us. A professional who could go in there with a flashlight and start digging through files."

"That's a great fantasy. Speaking of which, can I come over?" I asked offhandedly, to avoid showing any enthusiasm, or desperation. She didn't say no.

The first part of the evening was fantastic, then the mood turned.

"I have to ask you something," I said.

"Kiss me first."

I complied. "Tell me what happened the day your dad was shot."

I could feel her body tensing next to me. "What do you want to know? That it was a nightmare? That I have had PTSD ever since?"

I let that pass and waited a minute. "Can we talk about it?"

"NO." She was practically shouting.

"Is the subject entirely taboo?"

"I'll tell you what, Z. I'll let you read my college essay, which I have never shown to anybody. After that, no more questions, no more discussion. Deal?"

I assented, reluctantly. I read the essay you saw at the beginning of this narrative. Then a curtain fell between us.

25

THE SEARING *SUN*

JAN WAS BACK AT WORK. Yet even before she smelled the wine on her breath, Ollie could tell that she had relapsed. She knew right away when she stepped into Jan's office to give her an update about FACT's machinations behind the scenes, the short selling, and her conversation with Quint. Jan's voice had a sparkling quality, a slight shimmer, a telltale sign. Ollie worried whether she was sober enough to absorb the complexities of the information she was sharing.

"Jan, I hate to ask you this, but …"

"Yes, I'm drinking again. Just a little bit," Jan said. "I'm following you, don't worry. Shorting stock is dirty business. I feel badly for Quint. He's always been a decent guy."

She reached under her desk, picked up a wine bottle, filled the red plastic cup on her desk, and took a long sip.

"What do we do with all this?" Ollie asked.

"Spend more time with your detective, Ollie."

Deadline on Arrival

Ollie stared at Jan and realized there was no point in denying that the relationship had progressed.

"Don't worry, I won't say anything. I have no right to judge. Nobody knows about Paul and me, so I guess we're even."

I called Ollie on my cell just then and told her that I had to see her right away. "What's up?" she asked.

"I have to show you," I said.

"Where are you?"

"In the car. I'll pick you up in front of the First Draft in five minutes."

"Do we have to do this now?"

"Absolutely," I said. "It's something you *have* to see."

"Meet me at the side of the building. I'm on my way."

Jan asked Ollie "What's happening?"

"I don't know, but I have to go," she answered.

"Be careful. I don't like the sound of this."

Ollie shrugged, rushed out the back door, then down the street to the bar. She was hidden against the side of the building when I pulled up.

"Hop in. I'll explain in a minute," I said.

I drove quickly to a nearby industrial area and pulled into a parking lot behind one of the buildings. "I don't think we'll attract any attention here," I said. "Look at this."

I opened my laptop to reveal a still frame from a video of Johnny Garlowe in an interrogation room at the police station. He was wearing sweatpants and a dirty T-shirt, and his eyes kept darting about. "This was recorded this morning," I said.

I hit the space bar to start the video as Ollie watched closely. Johnny was speaking very quickly, though coherently. She heard my voice in the background asking questions. Here are some excerpts from the conversation:

Me: "Why did you do this, Johnny?"
Johnny: "Because I wanted to even the scales."
Me: "What does that mean?"
Johnny: "They have too much power."
Unidentified voice: "Who are you talking about?"
Johnny: "Them."
Me: "Who's 'them' Johnny?"

Johnny: "The press."

I looked over at Ollie who seemed dumbfounded. "Do you believe him?" she asked.

"Keep watching," I said.

More excerpts from the video:

Me: "What can you tell us about the victims, Johnny?"
Johnny: "The people they wrote about."
Unidentified voice: "Who?"
Johnny: "That salesman, the filmmaker, the crazy genius guy, you know."
Me: "What was the salesman's name, Johnny?"
Johnny: "It's a secret. But there were two of them."
Me: "Two salesmen?"
Johnny: "No, two with the same name."
Me: "And what was that name?"
Johnny: "Can't say. Don't want to speak ill of the dead."

Ollie was watching quietly. "He seems pretty evasive to me. I suppose that means one of two things."

"Go on, Detective."

"Are you mocking me?" she asked in a serious tone.

"Maybe."

"As I was saying," she said irritably, "he's either being coy as he's confessing or he's just playing a game."

"Meaning that you don't believe him?"

"I'm not sure, We know he's crazy, so maybe he's confessing to crimes he didn't commit because he's looking for a place to attach his guilt. Or maybe he wants attention too, in a twisted way. What do you think? *You're* the detective."

"I don't think he has any idea what he's saying. When we questioned him about the details of the murders, he was vague. He's just scrambled. Just to be safe, we gave him a polygraph test."

"And?"

"Clear results that the confessions were a lie."

"What are you going to do?"

"Ashley is driving him back to the hospital, along with a couple of patrolmen. They went along as a courtesy. She said she'll make sure the docs adjust his meds."

"Just like that, you exonerate him?"

"Do you have any idea how many crazy people come in and confess to crimes for their own wacko reasons?"

"Yeah, I know, but how can you be sure he's not really guilty? Polygraphs are totally unreliable."

"Not when the results are so clear cut. Besides, I know Johnny."

"Maybe *that's* the problem. Your friendship is blunting your objectivity."

"Ashley told me that he's been spewing all sorts of nonsense lately," I said. "When he gets manic, he's liable to say anything."

"So, you send him back to New Hampshire and leave him at the hospital?" Ollie asked.

"They're going to put him in a locked ward."

"You can do that?"

"Yeah, now that he has indicated he might be dangerous."

"I guess everybody in the department knows what happened to him now. He must be humiliated."

"Whatever's left of him."

• • •

Amy had taken a few days off after her miscarriage, but she was now back on the job. She summarily threw Troy out of their loft and told him in no uncertain terms that she was done with him

In the meantime, work was keeping her sane. She thought she might get somewhere with the Headline Hunter story. She had pretty good sources in the Cambridge Police Department. She heard a rumor that a suspect had confessed. When she contacted several of the people she knew, no one would confirm it. She left a message for me. To tell you the truth, I never returned her call.

Amy walked into the I-Desk office one night when they were the only two people left in the newsroom. She asked Ollie point blank if she had heard about the confession.

"What confession?" Ollie asked, with a deliberately innocent look.

"I heard that someone admitted he was the killer, but the cops didn't believe him."

"Sounds pretty ridiculous. Even if it did happen, it was probably some nutjob looking for publicity," Ollie said evenly. She looked directly into Amy's eyes.

Amy shrugged. "Yeah, that's probably what it was. How are you doing with your work on this? You getting anywhere?"

"Not really. My sources in law enforcement aren't as good as yours." Amy smiled and Ollie wondered why.

"Maybe we should compare notes. We might be able to help each other."

"Good idea. Once I have something to share," Ollie said with a smile.

"Ditto," Amy said. They were speaking cordially, but carefully, to one another.

• • •

As soon as she walked into the newsroom the next morning, Ollie sensed that something was amiss. Her colleagues looked at her and quickly looked away.

Am I being paranoid, she wondered. *The one guy who would tell her the truth was Oscar Sosa, the sports editor and wise guy supreme. He had a pot belly, thinning hair, and a perpetual sardonic grin.* Ollie walked over to his desk and found him on the phone. "PR guy," he whispered, as he rolled his eyes. "Listen, pal," he said into the phone, "I'm about to go into a meeting. Can I call you back? ... Excellent."

"Burnsski, what's up? Working on your Christmas piece ... for next year?" He was always making fun of the scant output of the investigative unit. "This is a *daily* paper, remember?"

She chuckled awkwardly.

"You don't know, do you?" he asked softly.

"Don't know what?"

"Check out Melissa Pugh's column in *The Sun*," he whispered. "Sorry to break it to you, kid. They're a trashy tabloid all the way."

She made a point of walking slowly toward her office in a way that wouldn't attract attention. She sensed that everyone was surreptitiously watching her, and she didn't want to give them the satisfaction of seeing her upset. She'd catch people looking over their monitors, then averting their eyes.

She sat down, stretched, turned on her computer and went right to *The Sun*'s website. There, on the first screen, she saw a photo of her and me standing very close together. *Christ, that was before we even slept together,* she thought. I was escorting her into my car, in gentlemanly fashion. Then she read this:

THE BABE AND THE BADGE
By Melissa Pugh

Once again, *The Observer* has proven it's allergic to two things: objective journalism and ethics. So-called investigative reporter Olivia Burns has been, uh, carrying on with Detective Ronan Mezini, who's honchoing the Headline Hunter case at the Cambridge Police Department. The partnership between the sexy scribe and the hunky cop extends from the streets to the sheets.

Did Burns make an agreement to keep anything the I-Desk discovers secret? Did Paul Green give the cops editorial control? Has our rival rag become the public relations arm for the Cambridge police?

Only *The Sun* will shine its merciless light on the *real story*.

Ollie felt as though a corkscrew was twisting into her gut. She and I had been very careful not to show public displays of affection, but apparently that didn't matter. The story was out, and her reputation was compromised. Ollie always liked to be in control, to maintain the impression that she was holding sway instead of sway holding her, as her dad used to say. She yelled "Fuckers" as loud as she could, then regained her composure and strolled slowly and deliberately toward Paul's office.

He looked as though he had been expecting her. She closed the door and sat down.

"We seem to have a situation," he said superfluously.

"That picture is misleading," Ollie said.

"Doesn't matter. I have to ask you point blank: are you sleeping with him?"

"That's my eff-ing business."

"No, Ollie, it's *The Observer*'s business. You two are working together on a potential story. And it was supposed to be a low-key arrangement."

"That's right," she said. "And you *approved* this deal, remember? Are you going to change your mind about that now?"

"The plan didn't include a romance," Paul said.

"I told you, that picture is bullshit. We were walking to his car."

"Why were you so close to him?"

"He was about to open the door for me. That's what polite, old-fashioned guys do."

"Then tell me you're not involved with him, and I'll issue a statement denying it."

"I'm not commenting on my personal life."

"Is that your position?"

"Affirmative."

"Reporters will be swarming all over this. We don't need this kind of publicity. We're done here." With that, he turned his attention to his computer.

"Bear in mind, chief," she said with full sarcasm, "*you* asked me to lie in a story. Do you want that to come out?"

"No one would believe you," he said, with no sign of wavering. "I'll simply deny it." He was still staring into his computer screen.

"Mezini would back me up," she countered.

"No one would believe him either. You said it yourself, he's a gentleman. It would look like he was lying to protect you."

"If it comes to that, I won't get aggressive, Paul," Ollie said quietly. "But my lawyer will." She got up, turned around, and walked away.

Fifteen minutes later Paul sent this statement to the staff and the media: "Investigative Reporter Olivia Burns has taken a paid leave of absence of indefinite duration. Although Ms. Burns is a brilliant journalist and we continue to respect her considerable talents, we cannot allow even the appearance of bias to taint the objectivity of our coverage."

Ollie stayed in her office for about half an hour to contemplate recent events. Resolving nothing, she took a quick look around her office, packed up her laptop and some essential folders and headed directly out the back door to the parking lot.

Deadline on Arrival

A TV reporter she didn't recognize accosted her. He and his cameraman pursued her all the way to her car. As she was opening the door, she saw that Melissa Pugh, the gossip columnist who had written the story in *The Sun,* was there too. Pugh was known to stop at nothing. Her lurid style was a sharp as the stiletto heels she always wore.

"Ollie, do you have *anything* to say?" she asked.

Ollie's first thought was to ask her if she had ever used her heels as weapons but thought better of it. Instead, she said, "That photo is misleading. Instead of assassinating my character, all of us should be working to determine the identity of the assassin who is terrorizing our city."

"What exactly is your relationship with Detective Mezini?" the TV reporter asked.

"I refuse to submit to this sort of interrogation," Ollie said. "I plan to continue the investigation on my own, regardless of my status at *The Observer.*" Ollie stood up straight and tried to look as defiant as possible, as though the whole escapade was inconsequential.

"Will you continue to see Mezini?" Melissa asked.

"I will tell you this," Ollie said. "If I find out anything about the killer, I'll share it with any reporter who does *not* work for *The Sun.* Now I ask for privacy." She noticed that Amy had just emerged from the back door, though she kept silent and looked at her sympathetically.

Ignoring more shouted questions, Ollie got into her car and pulled away.

I called her a moment later.

"I got reporters all over me—" I said.

"Yeah, tell me about it," Ollie said.

"Where are you?"

"In my car."

"I'll meet you at my house. They won't bother you there."

She knew I was right. Cops always had unlisted numbers and kept their home addresses private. Oddly enough, Ollie herself hadn't been to my house yet.

On the way there she checked her rearview mirror frequently to make sure no one was following her. In ten minutes, she was pulling into my driveway. My house is on a quiet street in North Cambridge, a working-class part of the city, where the homes are crowded together. Mine was indistinguishable from the others except for the teal front door. *She waited near the vegetable garden in the back yard and couldn't help noticing that my tomato plants were flourishing. Odd what you observe in tough times*, she thought. *Here my career is imploding and I'm admiring the fucking tomatoes.*

I drove in a moment later. She shushed me when I started to speak.

"Wait until we get inside," she said. She had rarely been so emphatic.

Once we closed the back door, she exploded in anger.

"Z, we're done. If I posed naked for *The Sun* I'd be less exposed."

"What are you saying?" I didn't know how else to respond so I hugged her. She felt stiff in my arms and pushed me away.

"I'm not sure, Z. I think we need to stay apart, at least for a while."

I wasn't at all sure what that meant. I hoped she was just angry and upset.

"Are you sure about that?"

"I don't care what people think. But I do care about my professional reputation. They're two different things."

"This isn't exactly a picnic for me either," I said.

"Don't pressure me now. I just need time alone."

"Fine, I get it," I said. *Was that how I really felt, or was I just pretending? No doubt this was a painful day.* But that was nothing compared to what was coming.

26

REQUIEM FOR A NEWSPAPER
Late August

SUMMER WAS STARTING to fade in Boston. The leaves were drying up and turning brown at the edges. Many of the 160,000 college students, who make up one-fifth of the population in the city during the school year, were coming back to campus. U-Haul trucks, double-parked for unloading, were common sights. The parents of the freshmen looked more nervous than the kids. Restaurants and bars were enjoying vigorous business after the summer doldrums.

Sweater weather descended on some nights. On those chilly evenings it was time to pull the covers up to your chin, snuggle with your lover, or both. *But not me*, Ollie thought. *I'm keeping Mezini at bay.*

Things may have been quiet in our bedrooms, she thought, *but not at The Observer.* One crisp Tuesday morning this editorial ran on the paper's front page and first screen:

Deadline on Arrival

LOVE THAT DIRTY WATER

**An Open Letter from
Editor Paul Green**

Where are the Standells when we need them? Most Bostonians are familiar with the band's 1965 hit with the infamous refrain "Love that dirty water. Oh, Boston, you're my home."

I'm chagrined to report that the newspaper business is much filthier than the Charles River ever was. I hereby resign. On my way out the door, I'll have my say.

We learned that Aldous Denby and his wingtip minions at the private equity firm Persephone staged a hostile takeover of Bay State Media, the parent company of this paper, the venerable *Boston Observer*.

The new regime asked me to remain at the helm, a position I have been proud to occupy these 12 years. In exchange for keeping my job, I was told that I had to implement a ridiculous "staff adjustment," a crass euphemism for their plan to lay off most of the union reporters and editors and replace them with freelancers right out of college. That's a slick maneuver to allow management to KO the unions.

Copy editing, one of the core jobs in news, will be outsourced, God knows where. That means there will be no face-to-face dialogue about the content, tone, and intent of the stories. Get ready for a barrage of overlooked typos, bad grammar, and mediocre journalism.

Persephone plans to discontinue the print edition immediately. From this point forward, there will be no *Observer* as we know it. Just a website called *NowBoston!.com*. I particularly despise the exclamation point, which highlights the vulgarity of the new owners.

I hope the wonderful people of Boston will survive without a real newspaper. They deserve much more than these greedy capitalists will offer.

Newsrooms are generally noisy places, a cacophony of fingers clacking on keyboards, conversations spilling over the low walls of the cubicles, telephones pinging, and what not. But not this day, Ollie later told me. After the editorial appeared on *The Observer* website, there was a total hush, broken only when ruthlessly efficient security guards appeared to escort Paul Green out of his office. He was no doubt prepared since he had a small box of personal effects under one arm as he strode proudly out the door. Just before exiting, he turned toward the newsroom, yelled, "Excelsior!" and left for the last time.

Persephone's Aldous Denby came in minutes later to address the anxious staff. Ollie had been invited to the spectacle, even though she was still on leave. She sat with arms folded on a windowsill at the side of the room. Columnist Kenny Moran was there as well, acting as though he had never been suspended.

Denby's blond hair spilled over his collar. He wore a crisp button-down shirt with a red and yellow striped tie and no jacket. Suspenders held up his gray cuffed pants. Black slip-on loafers completed the outfit.

He cleared his throat and spoke quickly. His expression carried no hint of friendliness.

"Good morning," he said. "I know you think I'm evil incarnate. A private equity guy who is going to decimate your paper and turn what you regard as an important calling into a commercial enterprise. Believe it or not, I care deeply about the news."

The staff was stunned. People exchanged glances that seemed to say, he must think we're idiots. There were even a few groans. Sports editor Oscar Sosa laughed out loud.

"I know you are concerned about your fate, and we understand that," Aldous continued. "If you open your email, you will see personalized messages explaining where matters stand. Now, if you'll excuse me, I am going to meet with your new editor, Will Cabot, who has been second in command for too many years. As of today, by the way, the Allston family becomes part of *The Observer*'s past. We are the new owners."

He left and headed upstairs.

Everyone dived into email. It was quickly apparent that the casualties included the I-Desk: Ollie (who was permanently relieved of her duties), her boss Jan, researcher Pat Cole, Anika Mehta, the entertainment reporter, Kenny Moran, and Oscar Sosa, the sports editor.

Elias Olson, the technical editor, Nico Lyons, the business editor, and Amy Stout were all survivors. Out of respect for those who were laid off, they tried not to show any emotion, but they couldn't help leaning back in their chairs with relief. Those who were dismissed sat with hunched shoulders. Some of the younger staffers learned that they still had jobs, though they were reassigned to remote beats.

Deadline on Arrival

Jan's sobs released a cloud of wine vapor, but she didn't care. Kenny hugged Anika. True to form, Oscar spoke out: "Elias, take the cash out of your hat band and treat us all at the bar."

Elias nodded somberly as the crowd headed for the First Draft.

• • •

When Ollie walked into the bar, Eddie was already starting to make her a Manhattan.

"Sorry, Eddie," she said. "Make me a Dark and Stormy today. That sums up the mood."

He obliged. "All drinks on me!" He poured himself a shot of rum (rare for him) and raised his glass: "Here's to unions, may they last forever." Everyone cheered. "I'll close this fucking place down before I serve any scabs," he added.

He quickly threw down his shot and everyone applauded.

"And one more thing," Eddie said, as he poured himself a second shot. "Remember what we always say: 'What happens at the First Draft' …"

All joined in for the second line: "Is corrected on the second!"

Eddie downed shot number two with a quick motion.

Once the "party" was in progress, Eddie's wife Betty walked around with trays full of burgers and big salad bowls overflowing with French fries and onion rings. After an hour or so, people started to leave and asked for their checks. She waved them off. They all hugged her and promised they'd stay in touch.

"Come and see us and spend lots of money," she said with a wink. "Drive carefully, kids." The staff left ample tips, which she said she'd donate to the union.

As morning dragged into afternoon, the only ones left were Jan, Ollie, Kenny, and Anika at a back table. Amy, who lingered by herself at the bar, gave Ollie a guilty look as she finally left, as if to say, "no hard feelings."

"Wonder what kind of deal she made," Ollie said to Jan. "I always suspected that she was bucking for an I-Desk slot. Anything's better than playing cops and robbers."

"Yeah, but there *is* no I-Desk anymore," Jan said. "Denby will never give anyone time to do in-depth reporting. The reporters who are left will be doing three or four stories a day, and they'll all be superficial." Ollie had never seen her so angry.

Anika sat serenely, nursing her Campari on the rocks. "Here's to an extinct species," she said as she lifted her glass. "There is some good news to report, though. Our own Kenny Moran is joining the ranks of authors. He just signed a book contract." The three of them cheered.

"What's it about, Kenny?" Ollie asked.

"You, darling," he said.

"Now I know you're drunk," she said.

"It's called *Misfitting In*."

"Marvelous title," Anika said. "I should know. I came up with it."

"Fiction or non-fiction?" Jan asked.

"Is there a difference?" Kenny asked, and everyone laughed. "I think I'll shy away from reporting, though. It seems to be a dangerous business these days."

All four fell silent.

Ollie said, "I should be taking off. Not feeling so hot right now."

"Where to, kid?" Anika asked.

"My front porch. The most inspiring place I know."

She wasn't kidding.

When she pulled up to her home the sight of the porch made her feel better, even though her beloved Aunt Jessie had died at that spot years before. On this sad afternoon Ollie sat in the sun on a chaise lounge and nursed a cup of steaming coffee. *She always thought that sitting and staring into space were underrated.* She looked to her right to watch the traffic go by on Centre Street, Jamaica Plain's main drag, half a block away. The neighbors were used to seeing her like this, so they paid little mind. She watched their activities throughout the lazy afternoon. Moms and dads pushing toddlers in ever more high-tech baby carriages. Old women swaying on gnarled legs. Young boys and girls skateboarding by.

At that moment she felt as if she had ceased to exist as a separate consciousness. She merged with the surroundings and felt no separation from the world. She was the porch, the sidewalk, the neighbors, and the traffic.

27

UNINSPIRED

AS I SAT IN MY OFFICE, I was convinced I was a failure. At any minute the brass might step in and start badgering me. I could imagine the questions: "How long have you been on this case, Mezini? Are you distracted because you're involved with the reporter? Why didn't you tell us you were sleeping with her?" etc., etc. They could fire me at any moment.

Was it worth it, after all, for $75K a year? I could make twice that, or more, in corporate security. Maybe I should just try to write instead. I always wanted to be a writer, so why not do it now?

What would Johnny say? Maybe something like this: "Think about this from the outside in, not from the inside out. If you were the killer, what would you do now? You say you want to be a novelist. Create the character of the killer."

I imagined my sad reply: "I don't know anything about him."

"Try to figure out what motivates him, what scares him," Johnny would say. "How can you get to him?"

The only good thing was that the killer seemed to have taken a break.

It's hard to wage war with someone you can't see. The killer was probably right in our midst. Yet the truth was a shy bird that hid itself and rarely extended its wings.

My day got worse when Chief Cronin called me into his office. "Sit down," he said. It wasn't a request.

I was cringing as soon as I sat down on the other side of his massive desk.

"Now, my boy, on one hand I might be tempted to congratulate you on sleeping with the enemy. Tell me you did this for professional reasons, and I might be more sympathetic." I wondered what took him so long to confront me about this.

"Chief, I know it's strange but—"

"Strange? That's what you call it. It's downright ridiculous. You've been bringing her along on investigations?"

"Yeah, and—"

"And nothing. Are you trying to sweet talk her into retracting that story about you and Johnny?"

"No. I figured we could help each other."

"Help is a four-letter word, Mezini. She gets access, which is great for her, and what exactly do you get?"

I told him about the false information we had planted in the paper, about zeroing in on a suspect. I explained that we made sure to flatter whoever he was by referring to him as a bright, creative person with highly developed organizational skills. All in the hope that we might flush out some clues.

"And did this genius plan work?" the Chief asked.

"Not so far."

"Mezini, you're one of our best but I have to say that I don't like this whole arrangement. It's like inviting a whore to church, for Christ's sake."

"Are you calling her a whore?" I was ready to walk out.

"Jesus, Mez, you are smitten, aren't you?"

I just shrugged.

"I'll take that as a yes," he said. "Let me leave you with this. I don't want her to accompany you on any more rounds, *capish*? What if she gets shot? We don't need that. As for you, you're expendable. See ya' later, Mez."

With that, I walked away. At least I still had my job. For now.

• • •

Meanwhile, Ollie felt like an investigator without a portfolio. No job, no purpose. *Gotta stop feeling sorry for myself, she thought. Now that I'm out of the paper, I can do whatever I want.* "The babe and the badge" are finally free to maneuver. Just keep reporting, even if you're just going through the motions.

She started "googling around" yet again in search of organizations that were avowed enemies of the media. She sifted through numerous sites until she stumbled across one called SMITE, standing for "Silence Media Intolerance Terrorism and Exploitation."

Perfect, she thought. The address was on Fawcett Street in an industrial area of Cambridge. She drove by and parked around the corner. When she opened the car door it almost hit me.

"Are you a street cop now?" I asked.

"Thinking about it. You scared the hell out of me."

Together, we both asked, "How did you find out—"

"From the smartest person in the world: Google," Ollie said.

"We've known about SMITE for a long time," I said. "They're on the domestic terrorism watch list. You shouldn't be doing all this by yourself. These guys might be ..."

"Dangerous? And I'm just a girl?"

"I don't think of you that way," I said in a level tone that brought her up short. I'll bet she wondered why I seemed so dispassionate.

"Shall we go in?" I asked. "For the record, we're not working together on this visit."

"Yes, sir."

In lockstep we headed toward the office, climbed the steps to an unmarked door, and knocked. We heard a click as someone slid the cover off a peephole, then the door opened suddenly to reveal a lanky young man.

"Well, well, well, if we wait long enough the elite come to us," the man said. "Welcome, Ms. Burns and Officer, or should I say, Detective Mezini? Please come in."

Everybody reads the fucking Sun, Ollie said to herself.

We entered a surprisingly sleek office. A French library lamp sat in the center of a horseshoe-shaped table with five ergonomic chairs all around. The décor was redolent of a high-tech company.

"My manners must have fled in the night. I'm Josh Salinas. May I offer you some coffee?"

"Sure," I said. He disappeared and returned in a few minutes with a carafe, three cups and saucers, a small pitcher of cream, and a bowl of sugar, all on a silver tray.

"Help yourselves," he said as he sat down and started to roll a cigarette. "How can I help you?" he asked politely. "I hope you don't mind if I smoke."

"What if we did?" Ollie asked, with a smile, as if she were joking.

Josh smiled back, finished rolling the cigarette, and put it down.

I figured I'd start the conversation obliquely. "How long have you had this office?" I asked. "It's beautiful."

"Thanks," Josh said. "We try to maintain a businesslike image. It makes fundraising easier."

"Who funds this organization?" Ollie asked. I was trying to figure out a way to signal that she should tone it down, but she didn't look in my direction.

"Wow, Ms. Burns, you certainly don't waste time in small talk," Salinas said.

"No, I guess not," she said. "Somebody has been attacking us and the name of your group doesn't exactly make me feel warm and fuzzy. Silence Media Intolerance Terrorism and Exploitation? Come on."

"Do you have any idea how long we worked on that acronym, Ms. Burns?"

"Stop calling me Ms. Burns, Josh. Ollie will do."

"Okay, Ollie. Just because we use the word 'silence' you assume that we want to take the media down by force. Is there anything to suggest that we have harmed anyone? There are those who engage in violence, and those who take advantage of an atmosphere already poisoned by fear."

"And you're in the second category?" I asked.

"Precisely. Detective, if you're looking for clues that will point the way toward the serial killer, you're in the wrong place. We trade in information, not terror. I consider myself a Christian," Josh said.

"Do Christians preach hate?" Ollie asked.

"No, they spread the truth."

"Only as you see it. Do you really think reporters are terrorists?"

"Compared to whom?"

"Compared to Bin Laden, or the Boston Marathon bombers, for starters," I said.

"Different ballpark," Josh said. "But you must admit that one man's anarchist is another's revolutionary. The British thought the American rebels were terrorists back in 1776," he said. "We prefer to think of ourselves as warriors in the battle for accuracy. We are fighting the mainstream media monopolies."

"Fighting with what?" I asked.

"We combat propaganda with the truth, Detective."

"Your diatribes are hardly the truth," Ollie said. "They're full of innuendo, invention, and inaccuracy."

"Three words beginning with 'i'," Josh said. "Very clever."

"Let's see," I said, pulling a piece of paper out of my pocket. "Among other things your website asks followers to resist the media by any means necessary. That sounds like a call to arms."

"Does that include killing people we write about?" Ollie asked.

"We think our followers are intelligent enough to choose their own form of resistance," Josh said.

And so it went.

• • •

Outside, Ollie and I compared notes.

"Not our guy," I said.

"Why not?" she asked.

"If you're going to kill people, you don't set up a website with all that anti-media bullshit first. It's like putting up a sign that says I'm guilty."

"Maybe he doesn't care what the police think."

"Disagree. I think he'd be overjoyed if his organization became a suspect. That would be great publicity. I had a strong impression that he'd rather fight with words instead of bullets though."

"Why are you so sure?"

"He seemed too, uh, *polite*."

"So was Ted Bundy. He was all charm. He was once a counselor on a suicide hotline."

"Yeah, I know. But my cop's instinct says Josh Salinas is no Ted Bundy. Trust me on this," I said.

By this time, Ollie had arrived back at her car.

"What else does your 'instinct' say?" she asked, with ironic quotes in her voice.

"It tells me that I miss you and that you miss me too," I said.

"Maybe so, but maybe we still need to give the separation some time," she said.

"Sounds like lawyer talk."

"You know what I mean."

"Yeah, I do, and I don't like it," I said. She could tell I was angry. "You pull me in with one hand and push me away with the other."

"I didn't expect to meet you here. And I certainly don't need your protection."

"I'm not trying to *protect* you. I'm just—"

"Just what, Z? You want to be my *boyfriend*?" She said the word as if it were a curse.

"Yeah, does that threaten your precious independence? You're on your own," I yelled as I walked to my car, slammed the door, and sped away.

I was hoping that she was fighting me only because she cared.

I drove around the corner, stopped the car, made a U-turn, and came back. She hadn't moved. I asked her to get it in and we headed to a secluded area a few blocks away. Without speaking, we squeezed through the gap between the front seats and made our way to the back of the SUV.

"How many times have you done this in this car, Mez?" she asked as we got started.

"Not enough. Don't worry, the windows are tinted, to protect the privacy of those we arrest, and those we—"

"Say no more," she said.

28

AUTUMN LOVERS
Early October

WELLFLEET, CAPE COD. Paul had decided to retire and was spending his time in a cottage on a bluff overlooking the ocean. He had bought the house long ago, before prices soared. He wasn't well off, but he was comfortable. At 67, he felt that he had no more to contribute to the business, especially after his scorched-earth exit from *The Observer*.

Jan was sharing his bed—scraping by on unemployment—and trying to line up part-time gigs teaching journalism at local colleges. She had considered a couple of dot-com jobs, but the salaries were too low. She thought she was way past that. Those positions are designed for kids making their age (23-year-olds pulling down a salary of $23K) or veterans who couldn't let go of the business and who were willing to settle for crumbs. She couldn't bring herself to lower her expectations that far.

Meanwhile, I was still toiling on the case, with no new developments, and Ollie was on her own. On a whim, she called Paul. Even though he was obnoxious, he might have some insights. After all, he had been a police reporter back in the day.

Deadline on Arrival

He answered on the second ring. "Aren't you surprised to hear my voice?" she asked.

"Surprised and happy," he said. "I thought we'd never speak again."

"I guess I thought the same thing. Listen, I know you used to be a great crime reporter."

"Why do you use the past tense?" he said, with a touch of defensiveness.

"Maybe you've lost a yard or two off your fastball, but I'm sure your insights are valuable," she said. She knew he was the type of guy who would respond to a bold opening gambit, mixed with a bit of flattery.

"You're still want to talk to me, after what happened?"

"I suppose I was out of line," she said coyly.

"Maybe. Can I tell you something?" he asked.

"Not stopping you."

"I would have reinstated you soon enough. I just had to make an example. Standards, and all that. Come see me and let's make amends," he said.

A two-hour drive the next day brought her to his door in Wellfleet. The tourists were long since gone. There was more than a hint of winter in the air and that was refreshing. Definitely jacket weather.

Paul gave her a hug when she arrived and held it for a couple of seconds too long. He was clearly excited, and eager to show off his place. "Let's sit outside, if you won't be too cold. There's a great view of the ocean from the back porch.

"You look wonderful, Ollie." He broke eye contact to check out her body as they walked through the house toward the porch. She let that go. If she made an issue every time a guy leered at her she'd never have any conversations.

"Do you want a glass of wine, or is it too early?"

"I'll just take a cup of tea, please," she said.

She sat down and heard him clinking around in the kitchen. He brought out a tray with her teacup on a saucer, his wine glass on a napkin, and a plate of cheese and crackers. "The local general store has great brie. I hope you like it," he said as he sat down. He sneezed, as usual.

"I can see why you moved here, Paul," Ollie said. The water was dappled with sunlight and the waves whispered with a calming rhythm.

"How's Jan?" Ollie asked.

"Fine," he said. "She said to say hello. She's upstairs—resting." *Ollie sensed his embarrassment. She was no doubt drunk.* "What's on your mind?"

"I want to talk this out," she said. "The murders have very little in common except for the connection to *The Observer*."

"That's significant, don't you think?" he asked.

"Yeah," she said, "but police have talked to the neighbors, checked for prints and DNA, looked up the license plates of cars on the crime scene, and tried to identify photos of people in the crowd in case the killer was stupid enough to return to the scenes. And what have they got? Nothing."

"What about the financial angle?"

"We're still looking at that. Persephone and FACT were probably working together. It's very, very hard to prove, though. And it's unlikely that they'd be killers. Maybe they just took advantage of the murders."

"Did you ever read the Sherlock Holmes story called The Gang of Four?" he asked. "He said something like, once you've eliminated the impossible, then whatever remains, including the improbable, must be the truth."

"But how do we distinguish the impossible from the improbable?"

"Yes," he said, and smiled, as much as to say that he had no answer. "I'm afraid I'm not very helpful." He said this deliberately, as if he really wanted to change the subject. Then he excused himself to "use the facilities," as he said.

Ollie walked into the living room and noticed a collection of art books on the coffee table. One in particular caught her eye: *Conceptual Artists: Working Outside the Canvas*.

She opened it to a page tagged with a Post-it Note. It was a bio of Chris Burden with a picture of his performance in 1974 when he had himself crucified onto a Volkswagen.

Paul suddenly appeared in the hallway outside the room and noticed what she was reading.

"That isn't for the squeamish," he said.

"I know all about it. You forget that I minored in art history in college."

"That's right, I think you mentioned that once."

"My favorite conceptual artist is Marina Abramowicz. She once cut a star into her stomach with a razor blade at the Guggenheim."

"Is that creativity or endurance?"

"Maybe art *is* endurance," she said.

"Or maybe endurance is a form of art. Sometimes I think the whole news business is one big conceptual art spectacle. A bunch of kids pretending to be grown-ups, writing about stuff they can't control, influence, or even understand."

"Yeah, and sometimes blood flows in the process," Ollie said.

They mostly gossiped after that. Comparing notes on the characters they had known.

After she left, Ollie thought about Paul for a long time. *Never figured him for an art guy.* She wondered why she had bothered to visit because she didn't get any useful information. She was so wrong about that.

• • •

Without the pressures of the news business, Ollie was more relaxed, especially with me. One morning she was lying on her side, with her head on my chest, and her left leg straddling me. She said she felt safe and comfortable as she listened to my breathing. Unaccountably she said she had been thinking about religion and the crazy stuff the nuns had taught her when she was a kid.

One of them, Sister Mary Catherine, who never smiled, had a bizarre explanation of the soul, Ollie said. "It's not part of your body, children," the nun explained. "You won't find it if you cut open your chest. But it's there. It's definitely there."

Ollie said that the nun then drew three circles on the blackboard. The first one represented a pure soul, she said. She put dots and short dashes in the second one and explained that those marks were venial sins, such as disobeying your parents. Then she turned the chalk sideways and made big blotches inside the third circle.

"Those are mortal sins," Sister said, pointing to the last circle. "Much more serious. Like not going to church on Sunday or killing someone."

"Isn't it amazing that the church equated those two things?" Ollie asked me.

"Here's the clincher, Mez," Ollie said. She went on to say, "When you go to confession, children, your soul is wiped clean." Then she picked up an eraser and wiped away all the blemishes—leaving three empty circles on the board.

Ollie said she could feel the marks of sin somewhere inside her chest and she knew the other kids could too.

"Olivia, you look so serious,'" Sister said with a trace of contempt.

"Serious?" Ollie said. "I was scared shitless."

The nun went on to explain the concept of original sin, and once again added big blotches of chalk to the third circle. "You remember that God told Adam and Eve not to eat the apple," she said. "Well, the devil tempted Eve and she took a bite. That's what we call original sin. All babies are born with it, besmirched, as they say, even though they didn't do anything wrong themselves. Eve's misdeed was handed down to them."

She turned the chalk sideways and put more big blotches into the other two circles too.

"Of course," the nun said, grabbing the eraser again, "Baptism washes that all away. Unfortunately, people who aren't baptized can never get to heaven. Even if they're good, they end up in limbo when they die."

Even as a child, Ollie said, she wondered why an innocent baby should carry the burden of something Eve allegedly did in the Garden of Eden who knows how many millennia ago. "Catholic catechism left an indelible mark," Ollie said.

"Is something on your conscience?" I asked.

"Is there ever a time when a Catholic girl's conscience is clear?" she asked.

29

REGIME CHANGE

WILL CABOT EASED into his role as editor of *The Observer*. He had long sought the position and now it was his. He was too selfish to feel any sense of survivor's guilt. Besides, running the paper was easier than he thought it would be with the new management. The staff was smaller, there was less copy to massage, and less responsibility because the new owners had such low expectations. Not to mention that they had no taste, no news sense, and no interest in current events.

Though he was in many ways Paul's stooge, Will did have a scintilla of pride left. It occurred to him that there was an easy way to restore a vestige of the old *Observer*: Bring Ollie Burns back. She had been on leave for about three months, since the debacle with the *Sun* article about her relationship.

Ollie doesn't produce that many stories, he thought, but they tend to have huge impact. In case critics accused the paper of relaxing our ethics, he could counter she had been sufficiently punished during her leave, even if she had been paid. Besides, in these lean times no one worried too much about principles, least of all the new owners.

When Will contacted Ollie, she hesitated at first. Like many people in the newsroom, she had little respect for him. *Why would I want to work for that guy,* she thought. *He's Paul Green, Jr., without the brains. Besides, I'm enjoying this break, though I suppose they won't let me continue to collect a paycheck for doing nothing. I'm sure they'll take away my salary soon.*

When she called me for advice, I told her to take the offer. "That'll make it clear that you're still viable," I said.

"You know, Mez, sometimes you make sense by accident," she said.

Even so, she wanted to negotiate, in person.

Ollie felt strange sitting down in Paul's old office, with Will behind the desk. Paul may have been reptilian, but he didn't pretend to be anything else, and that was somehow comforting. Will was just plain smarmy. He blinked constantly, as if trying to shut out unpleasant sights. His suits hung loosely on his skinny frame and his complexion was always sallow. His face was flat as a plate, with small features that added little topography. All in all, a bland bureaucrat.

After small talk, she took charge.

"What job title did you have in mind?" she asked.

"How about Editor at Large," Will said.

"That sounds like I'm retired. Why not just resurrect the I-Desk name? That's the franchise," she said.

"Let's go for Investigative Editor. I want to make a fresh start. The new owners don't believe in investigative journalism, but I do."

Whenever any boss talked about his beliefs, Ollie immediately became suspicious. Her experience showed that those with power in news organizations rarely spoke forthrightly. They always seemed to have a hidden agenda. He was probably just trying to impress her by pretending to care about real reporting. With the finance guys in charge, that was a foreign concept.

Sensing her misgiving, he said, "It doesn't matter what we call you, Ollie. You'll be free to report as you please."

"Meaning—"

"Meaning that I want you to keep working on the murders."

"Why are you doing this, Will?"

"Because you're one of our best, and it's something Quint would have wanted."

Time to be aggressive, she thought. "In that case, I want you to send out a public announcement," she said.

"Straight away," he said. "But there will be some ground rules."

Uh-oh, here it comes, she thought. "I'm listening," she said warily.

"You are not to be seen in the field with Detective Mezini. I don't care what your personal relationship is with him—"

"Wait a minute—"

"Really, it's immaterial," he added quickly, speaking over her. "You can do whatever you want, just be discreet."

"We certainly don't want it to appear that the great *Observer* is brought to heel by some sleazy story in *The Sun*," she said spitefully.

He agreed they'd send out a press release announcing her return. It was his way of convincing the staff that he still cared about hard-hitting investigative journalism. To savor the moment, Ollie walked across the newsroom back to the old I-Desk office, which she would now have to herself. She had to admit she felt odd looking at the two empty desks which held memories of her old boss Jan Watkins and the researcher Pat Cole. Their ghosts hovered over the place.

Ollie shrugged off the macabre thoughts and got back to work.

Meanwhile, there were no more leads on the murders. For her part, Ollie told me she went door-to-door again in the neighborhoods where the killings took place and found nothing out of the ordinary. *The Great God of Stories has its own laws of motion*, she thought.

30

WORKING THE SOURCES

I WAS THINKING ABOUT the greedy private equity guys and their partners in the short selling scheme. I know that people of that ilk often leave a trail of blood behind, metaphorically speaking, and I was wondering once again if they just might be capable of real bloodshed, as in premeditated murder.

That got me thinking about Brent Garner, my go-to finance expert and old pal. He had been my classmate at the police academy. He worked the streets for many years until he got tired of the chaos and put his badge away. He went to law school and joined the office of the SEC as an attorney.

We arranged to meet at the Union Oyster House in Boston, one of our favorite places. Men in aprons stood behind the semicircular bar and shucked oysters by the dozen as waitresses brought plate after plate to the tables. We sat at a quiet booth in the back, where we had some semblance of privacy. His rimless glasses and pink skin made him looke like an academic, but that was misleading. He always came in first in the physical tests at the police academy. He could bang out 15 pull-ups and run a five-minute mile with little visible effort.

Brent was a dogged investigator with a cop's instincts and a gift for numbers. Those skills came in handy at the SEC, where he was often called upon to sift through reams of data.

He and I bonded in many ways, partly because we discovered that we both have synesthesia. He has the arithmetical or mathematical variety, which means that he sees numbers as a ladder extending forwards and backwards in space. Maybe that's why he's so quick with mental arithmetic.

"Is this meal on me, or you?" he asked.

"Since I might be handing you a case, I think the Feds can afford this one."

"Deal. What's up?"

I told him about Fast Accurate Clear Truth, AKA FACT Investors, and their scathing report about Bay State Media, *The Observer*'s parent company—setting the stage for the short selling. And I explained how the Persephone private equity fund had exploited the murders to buy the paper at a bargain price, only to decimate the staff.

"You realize that what Persephone did probably isn't illegal," Brent said.

"I know. It's sleazy as hell, though," I said.

"Yeah, waaah-waaah, Sleazy is permissible. By the way, you're buying half a dozen cannolis after this. Heaven on a plate, pal. We're gonna walk over to Modern Bakery in the North End when we're done here. This is going to be complicated and you need to pay extra for the privilege of tapping my skull."

"All right, all right. Hear me out: What if either FACT or Persephone were somehow connected with the murders?"

"Slow down, slow down. Give me the chronology here," Brent said.

I knew I had his full attention now.

"I think I'm gonna need a dozen cannolis. Janice loves 'em. Especially from Modern Bakery."

"I have to say, it's a low move to bring your lovely wife to the table as an absent party into the negotiation. This is getting expensive."

"Cheap bastard. You want my help or not?" He smiled.

"A dozen it is. The scenario may have gone down like this: Let's say the first murder is just one of those things that happens. Then comes the second, and the third, which may have been part of a larger plan. The newspaper is on the edge to begin with, like all other publications these days. The murders just drive down the value of the company further, until the hedge fund guys swoop in."

"You think finance guys may have pulled the triggers, or hired people to do it for them?" Brent asked skeptically.

"I'm saying it's *possible*."

"What about insiders at the paper?"

"I was getting to that. Can you help me find out if any of them were involved?"

"Off the record? Get me a list of the paper's employees."

"That I can do."

"Yeah, I understand you have some, uh, shall we say connections there, pal."

• • •

Two days later I was in my car when my cell phone rang.

"You got a pencil?" Brent asked.

"Let me pull over. Where are you?"

"On a secure line, outside the office. You know I'm not supposed to do this without a warrant. You owe me big time for this."

"Yeah, yeah, don't go all Boy Scout on me," I said. "Okay, I'm at the side of the road. Tell me."

Brent gave me three names.

"You think these jokers were in on the scam?" I asked.

"All I know is that they shorted the stock," he said.

• • •

Ollie and I decided to celebrate our four-month "anniversary" at a restaurant called Il Casale in Belmont. She especially liked the place because their Manhattans are made with whiskey aged in oak barrels, imparting notes of vanilla and caramel. Not to mention that Belmont Center, all of one block long, was cozy. "If I ever have children, I'd want to raise them in the town," she said.

Deadline on Arrival

Belmont has a touch of Norman Rockwell, as if you might spot a smiling policeman comforting a would-be runaway kid sitting on a stool at a deli counter. The town center boasts an ice cream parlor, a sporting goods store, even a bookstore—all independently owned. There once was a Macy's, but it had long since closed. "Still, I wonder if I could ever be happy in the burbs," Ollie said. "Too quiet at night."

I was uncharacteristically mute as I sipped my drink. The silence wasn't uncomfortable, though Ollie could tell I was distracted.

"Mez, are you there?" she said.

The waiter interrupted us to explain the specials. He had an extravagant manner and an Italian accent. He described the burrata appetizer, with pistachios, Mediterranean honey, Sicilian oregano, extra virgin olive oil, smoked sea salt, and grilled piadina. "And then," he said, "there's Nonna's meatballs."

"Hold on, sir," I said. "What is piadina?"

"Piadina, Dio mio," the waiter said. "Italian flatbread."

"I'll have the burrata," Ollie said. "You had me when you mentioned pistachios."

"And add the meatballs, please," I said.

"Excellent choices," the waiter said with a bow.

"Bring us two more Manhattans, if you would," Ollie said.

"With pleasure," the waiter said as he ambled away anikafully.

"So, what's up, Z?" Ollie asked.

"I learned from a source at the SEC that three people from *The Observer* sold the stock short," I said.

"Who?" Ollie asked in a millisecond.

"Any guesses?"

"Don't tease me, Z. I—"

"All right, Nico Lyons ..."

"That figures," Ollie said. "He's the business editor. Resident brain. He'd know an opportunity when he saw one. Who else?"

"Oscar Sosa."

"No way. He isn't exactly a Wall Street type. A beer and bowling kind of guy."

"He was on the list, believe me," I said.

"Who else?"

"You'll love this ... *Paul Green*. El Capitan himself."

"He may be an asshole, but I never thought he'd be a *traitor*," she said. "I can't believe it. You know this for a fact?"

"Absolutely."

I was amazed that she was so surprised. Then again, press people, like cops, always close ranks and find it hard to think ill of any of their colleagues.

"It's a business, just like any other," I said.

"Maybe, but journalists aren't usually that greedy."

"Maybe Paul is the exception."

The waiter brought the appetizers and their drinks.

"You make a bella coppia, a beautiful couple," he said.

"Yeah, I like them big and dumb," she said.

"Women always say the opposite of what they mean when they are in love, Signorina," the waiter said.

I nodded as he walked away.

"Sexism. In the newsrooms, in the restaurants ..." Ollie said.

"He's harmless."

"Bucking for a big tip,"

I think she wanted me to say something romantic. I've never been particularly good at sappy stuff, though. I changed the subject to avoid my discomfort. "Tell me about these characters," I said.

"Nico Lyons is a walking financial encyclopedia," she said. "I could see him taking a short position in the stock as an experiment or as an intellectual exercise. He's probably more curious than greedy."

"And Sosa?" I asked.

"He's a real conservative," she said. "Stands by the president, no matter what. Always spewing political opinions, mainly to bust the newsroom liberals. My guess is he didn't put in much money because he's always broke.

"Paul is the wild card, though. Never thought of him as a financial wizard, that's for sure. But hey, an opportunity's an opportunity."

After taking a drink, Ollie said, "I seriously doubt these guys are killers."

"Agree, but Paul seems suspicious. I'll bet he made a fair amount of dough on this. I still think the perp is some sort of maladjusted loser, probably living in his mother's basement and amusing himself with video games and porn."

"But remember what Grimes told us," Ollie said.

"I know, I know, don't rule anyone out. But I envision the sort of guy who couldn't get a date even if he drove a Porsche."

"You're saying women respond to fancy cars?"

"No, I mean—"

"Relax, Z, I'm teasing. I'm not so sure that this is a guy who spends all day enjoying the view from his basement windows, though. I hope we're not going to talk business all night."

"You're right. Tonight, we celebrate."

• • •

The next evening, I rang Oscar Sosa's bell. He came to the door with a can of Budweiser in his hand. His considerable belly pushed out against a stained white T-shirt.

He invited me in right away. I guess he didn't mind cops. I suppose everyone in the newsroom knew who I was by now.

"I assume you're not here to ask me about the Red Sox, Detective. Or should I say, Badge?" Sosa said. He was referring to *The Sun*'s column about the "Babe and the Badge." Despite myself, I winced.

"Mind if I sit down?" I asked.

"Sure, go for it." Sosa pushed a pile of magazines off the sofa onto the floor, which was already cluttered. Clearly a bachelor's apartment. Dirty dishes on the coffee table, crumbs on the carpet.

"So, what's up?" Oscar asked.

A cool cat, I thought. "Let me jump right in. Did you short *The Observer*'s stock?"

He laughed uproariously. "Is that what this is about? How much do you know about my finances?"

"I know you've been divorced twice and that you're paying out a lot of alimony and child support," I said.

"Yeah, and I pay religiously, even if I don't live that way. Right now, I'm on unemployment and I still send my exes—plural—the money."

I couldn't help laughing myself. Oscar was very likeable.

"I have to ask you again, though. Did you short the stock?"

"Yeah, I did," he said. "I invested $500 bucks after Nico told me that the shorts were circling. Hell, it was public by the time I jumped in. Reuters even did a story about it. I waited a while, then did the trade on a lark, on a day off. And you know what happened? I was late to the party. Story of my life. The freaking stock went up, not down. I ended up losing half the money. Guess I should stick to betting on the ponies. Or are you gonna bust me for that too?"

I laughed again.

"You want a beer, Detective? All I got is Bud. In cans."

"You wouldn't report me, would you?"

"Hell no, bro," he said.

"Why not? As long as you don't think you can bribe me with one beer."

"By the way, it's none of my business, but—" Oscar said.

"Yes …" I knew exactly where he was going.

"Ollie is one of my favorites. You're a lucky man, Detective. Don't fuck it up, okay?"

"I'll try, Oscar. I wish you better luck on your next investment."

We clinked cans. *There are times when the badge has to stop acting like the badge*, I said to myself.

• • •

Next came Nico Lyons, the business editor. Unlike Oscar, Lyons had survived the bloodbath at *The Observer*. Ollie told me to wait for him about 7PM in the parking lot because he was regular in his habits and tended to leave the building at that time every day. I had never met him, though she described him as a skinny guy with black hair, aviator-style glasses, and a shuffling gait. He was hard to miss when he came out.

I saw his eyes open wide in recognition for an instant, just before he tried to look like he didn't care.

"Got a news tip, Detective?"

I chuckled. "Nope, I'm clueless."

"Now you know how we feel every day," Nico said.

"I wonder if you're selling yourself short, though."

He lost his cool for a second, then laughed. I knew I had his attention. I figured he'd play it directly.

"I'll bet you wonder how I knew," I said.

"Wasn't that a line from a song?"

"You mean 'Heard it on the Grapevine?'"

I instinctively disliked this guy. He looked at me over his glasses as if he were studying a rare specimen, some inferior form of homo sapiens. I was sure he tended to view cops as fools—all guns and no brains.

"I heard that you made some interesting plays in the company's stock."

"I'm not saying I did, but even if it happened, would that be illegal?"

"Should it be?" I asked. "There is such a thing as insider trading. If you had access to secret information and used that to your advantage, that could get you in a lot of trouble."

"That's right. Except no one in management told *me* anything secret."

"You're a libertarian, I hear," I said. It was fun toying with this bastard.

"Correct."

"What exactly does that mean? That you don't believe in drivers' licenses or required training for lawyers and doctors? Let the market sort it out."

"Milton Friedman, I'm not, Detective," Nico said. "I do believe that the government that governs least, governs best, though."

"I guess you think short selling is permissible then."

"Tell me why we should always root for a stock to rise. If it's falling, so be it. Making money on it is simply taking advantage of gravity, if you will."

"Does it bother you that you're profiteering because your own paper was ruined when innocent people were murdered?"

"I guess that depends on how you define innocent. I was raised Catholic, Detective. Ever heard of original sin?"

"That argument is beneath you," I said. I couldn't believe he was going into catechism mode. Then again, this is Boston, where the Catholic church reigns supreme.

"Maybe. But I believe that markets should be left to their own devices and that opinions should be expressed freely. If I say that the CEO of a given business is incompetent, that's protected speech. If an investment firm makes a value judgment about a stock, that's equally equally legal under the First Amendment."

"Even if the opinion is based on lies, or if someone is taking advantage of violent crimes?"

"I don't think morality should play a role in business. If I make money on the stock, I spend it at the grocery store, the movie theater, or at the First Draft. Every dollar circulates."

"The multiplier effect. But evil can multiply too."

"Assuming I did short the stock, what if I gave the money to charity to benefit the victims of the crimes? Would that exonerate me in your eyes?" Nico asked.

"I don't judge, I just enforce the law," I said. "How much did you make on the deal?"

"If you're any kind of a detective, you'll find out for yourself."

• • •

I took that as a challenge. First, I called the Attorney General's Charitable Trust division to find out if there were any non-profits established to benefit the victims of the Headline Hunter. There were already two in existence. Then I asked a contact at the AG's office if the list of donors was publicly available and found out that charities are not required to post them.

I was able to wrangle a quick warrant to investigate Nico's bank accounts, though. Sure enough, he had written a check for $11,500 just two weeks ago, to the Family Victims Fund. That matched a deposit he received from a brokerage firm for the same amount. I also discovered that he had made his trade after the news about FACT's report was published in Reuters. Like Oscar, he apparently had no advance warning.

Time to erase a haughty libertarian from the list of suspects.

• • •

I went to Ollie's home for dinner that night. I always made fun of her kitchen, which would have been current in 1975. The stove was flanked by avocado green counters that had deep scratches. Pale yellow linoleum, what was left of it, completed the look.

"O, we need to have a date sometime, at Home Depot," I said. "I'm sure I would have loved your Aunt Jessie, and I know she took care of you, but I don't think she was exactly Martha Stewart."

"Watch it now, Z," she said abruptly. "Maybe it is time for an upgrade. I just can't bring myself to do it. This is the way she left it. Her heart may have been weak, but it was huge. I feel as if it's still beating here somehow. She was the one person I could count on after my dad died. Every time I walk into this kitchen it makes me feel safe."

"Sorry," I said sheepishly. "What's for dinner?" I changed the subject to dodge an uncomfortable moment.

"Frozen pizza."

"My favorite," I said. "I'll make the drinks."

As we ate, we got down to business. I told her what had happened with Oscar Sosa and Nico Lyons.

"Sosa is harmless. Acts on impulse. But what do you make of Nico Lyons?" I asked.

"He's probably frustrated," she said. "He has spent his career writing about business, instead of doing it. Sometimes reporters feel like they're just bystanders rather than participants. That can be really discouraging for super smart guys like Nico. Shorting gave him a chance to feel like a player, I suppose."

"Then there's your Mr. Green. How do you think we should approach him?"

"As if we're trying to pick up a porcupine."

Brent called at that moment.

"Mez, I would say I found a smoking gun, but it's more like a smoldering howitzer," he said. "Paul Green was communicating regularly with FACT and Persephone."

"Did you get a warrant for this?" I asked.

"I didn't yet, but I will later so we can get the full story. I do know that he was giving them specific information about the financials at the company."

"Why would they care about the exact numbers?" I asked. "Everybody knew the paper was in bad shape. Especially after the murders."

"Yes," Brent said, "but the finance bros didn't know just how bad things were. Bay State Media is a public company, and they don't break out the paper revenues and profits separately in their financial reports. They also own some tiny TV stations and a couple of smaller publications, so it was hard to determine exactly what was happening in each division.

FACT and Persephone knew the company was hemorrhaging, but it was unclear just how much blood they were losing. The more specifics they had in the exaggerated reports they filed, the more authoritative it seemed. That meant the markets took them more seriously and—"

"The stock dropped even further," I said.

"You got it, Mez."

31

TOUGH DAY AT THE BEACH

ON THE WAY DOWN to Cape Cod, Ollie was glad that we were out of the public eye. No one to notice that we were working together again. That meant that Will Cabot would never know that she was violating her agreement to be discreet. But this was one encounter she didn't want to miss. Especially with the new information about Paul that I had shared with her.

I sensed her discomfort about her role and told her that she'd be able to produce a great story about the murders. If we ever solved the case, that is. Might even be a magazine piece. Maybe *The New York Times* or *The New Yorker* would bite.

"Practically impossible to get into those pages, Z."

"Yeah, but this could be a once-in-a-lifetime story."

"I hope it's just once," she said and went back to watching the scenery.

She said she always thought Cape Cod was beautiful, especially around Provincetown where the light is so magical that photographers come from near and far to experience it. Bay meets open ocean as the peninsula narrows to a point. Joel Meyerowitz's *Cape Cod Light* was one of her favorite books.

"Yeah, I think he picked up where Edward Hopper left off, capturing the alienation in the faces of the people he photographs," I said.

"You do have an eye, Z," she said.

"For what?"

"For intelligent women."

"I was always told that intelligence and erudition are the ultimate aphrodisiacs."

"I'll let you know if I really get turned on."

"Something to look forward to, I guess."

"If we're still together," she said. *Was she kidding?*

"Why do you like the Cape so much? To me, it's too crowded." I guess I was trying to deflect a potentially difficult dialog.

"It's only overrun in the summer."

She explained that she had happy memories of her college days when a guy and girl she knew had dropped out and moved from Providence up to the Cape in the winter. They were scraping by on odd jobs—cleaning a laundromat once a week, pumping gas, counting traffic for the state, anything to get by. She'd often visit them and walk the snow-covered beaches. It was soothing to have an entire stretch of sand to herself, especially on moonless nights when the white lines of the breakers stood out against the black water.

When she went away on vacation in July or August, she had to leave the state, otherwise it didn't feel like a break. But on this October day, she was relishing the serene solitude of the place. As we neared Green's home in Wellfleet, she began to envy him. Life would be superb in a solitary house on a bluff far above the waves. It was far from luxurious, but it was comfortable and that's all that counted.

Though she had been there before, she didn't take in the details the first time. As we got closer, she noticed that the house had weather-beaten cedar shingles and white trim on the windows. The front yard was mostly sand, with a few blades of browned-out grass poking up here and there.

To our surprise, we came upon a crime scene. Three cars from the Wellfleet Police Department were parked on the street with lights flashing. At first, we weren't sure the commotion had anything to do with Paul. Then we saw an ambulance in his driveway. As we walked up to the front door EMTs were taking him out on a stretcher. He waved a quick hello with his right arm as they lifted him into the back of the ambulance. His left was bandaged.

I flashed my badge to the Wellfleet cops and we headed indoors, where we found a distraught Jan Watkins. She was wearing sweatpants, a wrinkled T-shirt, and sneakers. Her hair was disheveled. When she saw Ollie, she collapsed into her arms and sobbed. Every time she exhaled, a strong smell of alcohol wafted out like the long tail of a sad comet.

Ollie tried to comfort her as I made my way back outside, where I huddled quietly with the local police. Ollie could hear the bass undertones of our conversation but couldn't make out the words.

"Can you tell me what happened, Jan?" Ollie asked gently. She always hated asking that question, a standard item in a reporter's repertoire.

"Not entirely s-s-sure," Jan said. "He was, he, shot."

"Did you see it happen?" Ollie asked.

"No, heard it. Outshide. Near the beach." She was slurring her words.

I came back inside to find Caleb Baird, the book reviewer, entering through the back door. Ollie and I looked at each other but hid our surprise.

"I guess I picked the, uh, wrong day to visit," Caleb said sheepishly. He walked over to Jan and put his arm on her shoulder in his usual awkward manner. He looked over at us and muttered something about a gunman.

Ignoring him, I said, "The Wellfleet cops said Paul's going to Cape Cod Hospital. Jan, do you want to ride with us?" I looked at Ollie as much as to say, I don't think she's in a condition to drive. Ollie's look showed that she agreed.

"Should I come too?" Caleb asked.

"No, why don't you stay. We don't want too many people there," Ollie said. He seemed to be happy to remain at the house.

"Were you here when the shooting occurred?" I asked.

"Uh, y-yes," he said. He was clearly nervous. "I already told the Wellfleet cops what happened."

"Which was what?"

"H-, he was on the beach and said someone shot him."

"Where were you at the time?"

"On the porch, drinking coffee."

"Did you see who it was?"

"No. Paul ran up to me, and, and, his arm was bleeding."

"We'll get back to you later," I said. "We need to get to the hospital now."

Caleb looked scared as we drove away.

• • •

On the way Jan told a rambling, incoherent story. She had moved in with Paul, she said, because she wanted to live a quiet life on the Cape. Since there were few opportunities for journalists at her level, she thought she might toy with writing a book. Or do some painting.

Living with Green was hard. He kept saying that he had unfinished business. Always talking about the murders. He said that the cops (no offense, she told me) were too stupid to catch the killer and that he could have done so on his own if he were still running the paper. He thought of the staff as a private police force.

"What about the shooting?" I asked. I was growing impatient with her disjointed monologue.

She took a battered flask out of her pocketbook and took a long drink.

"What is that?" Ollie asked.

"Rum with honey and shinnamon," Jan said, again slurring her words. "'Stunts the brain, but blunts the pain,' as my dad used to shay."

"You were saying," I prompted.

"Paul kept ranting that he had it figured out." Jan said. "Thought he'd take the story to *The Sun*. Then stormed out of the house onto the beach. About five minutesh later, heard a shot," she said.

She paused to take another drink, then burped, as delicately as she could, with her hand on her mouth.

"Excush me," she said.

"No problem," I said irritably.

"I went outshide and saw Paul h-holding his arm," Jan continued. "He said shomebody was walking up the beach, pointed a gun at him. Said he backed away, toward the house but got shot before he got inside. He was sitting on the porch schteps, blood coming out between his fingers."

"Was he shot in the hand too?" I asked.

"No, he was holding his arm, like I said," Jan said. "Bleeding onto his fingers."

By the time we arrived at the hospital, we had fallen silent. The emergency room receptionist told us Paul was in surgery, so we went to the waiting room. Jan kept excusing herself every ten minutes to go to the bathroom, no doubt for more nips. After three or four hours we were invited to go to the recovery area. Paul was sitting up in bed and munching on crackers. Jan greeted him and they kissed in a perfunctory way.

"Ah, the investigators," Paul said with quotes in his voice when he spotted Ollie and me. "Got shot. No idea." He was still in a stupor.

"I hope the pain isn't too bad," Ollie said.

"Ask me again when the drugs wear off," Paul said.

"We'll give you some privacy," I said. "I'm sure you want to rest." I motioned to Ollie to leave the room with me.

She followed me out. As we were rounding the corner she stopped abruptly.

"Mez, I remembered something. When I visited Paul there was a book on his coffee table about conceptual artists," she said.

"And?"

"He had tagged the part referring to a guy named Chris Burden, who did a lot of crazy stuff."

"Like what?"

"He had someone shoot him and called it art."

"Do you think Green staged this?"

"Could be. Burden was shot in the arm. Green might be crazy enough to do something like that."

"To deflect suspicion?"

"Maybe," Ollie replied.

As we headed down the hallway, we saw a Wellfleet cop, who was following up on the case. He was speaking with a doctor. I recognized him as one of the officers who had been on the scene. I introduced myself to the cop, Tony Castro, and the doctor, June Walls.

"Dr. Walls was just telling me—" Castro said.

"The bullet entered Mr. Green's upper arm on the inside and narrowly missed the humerus, which would have been shattered otherwise," she said. "It tore through the bicipital tendon. Minor wound, luckily for him. We fixed everything in surgery."

"Any evidence of gunpowder residue?" I asked.

"We took a swipe of the wound at the house," Castro said. "We're waiting for the results." I think Castro thought I was a bit condescending, as if I thought that the Cape Cod cops didn't know what they were doing.

"We should check Paul's hands," I said.

"Already done."

"We should also check out that guy who was at the scene. Can you find out if he's still there?"

"Let me see." He called one of the cops in Wellfleet. "He's gone. Went home."

"Too bad," I said.

A while later we walked back into the room, where Jan was sitting on the edge of the bed and holding Paul's hand.

"Are you awake enough to talk now?" I asked.

"Questions, questions," Paul said.

"How are you feeling?"

"Okay, I guess. Not every day I take a bullet."

"I guess not."

"Jan said you told her you knew who the serial killer was. Care to share your ideas?" Ollie asked.

"Why is she here?" Paul asked, pointing to Ollie.

"Because she has been following me around," I said. "I think you're familiar with this arrangement."

"I have nothing more to say now."

"While we're at it, why were you giving the private equity guys confidential information about the paper's finances?" I asked.

Paul waved me away.

"He needs to resht now," Jan said, coming to his rescue. Paul closed his eyes. I'm sure he was pretending to be groggier than he was.

"We'll be back to you," I said. Paul opened his eyes and I could tell he saw my determination.

We headed back to Boston. I figured the feds would take over the financial investigation from that point on.

The next morning Tony Castro called and told me the tests came back negative for gunpower residue, both on Green's hands and on the wound. Ollie was sitting across the table from me in her bathrobe.

"Does that prove he didn't fire a gun?" she asked, after I filled her in on the conversation.

"Maybe. Or he could have done it with gloves on. There was no gunpowder residue on his arm either, which means that the gunshot didn't come from extremely close range."

"What's next?"

"First, I'm going to visit Caleb. Wanna come? We'll talk to him about Chris Burden."

• • •

On the way to Caleb's house in Watertown, Ollie asked me a question that had long been on her mind for some time. "Z, why do you want me to tag along?"

"Because you keep me from making a fool of myself with the weirdos."

"I'm serious."

"You have insights into these media types. They're foreigners to me. And you're a good sounding board. Plus, I like looking at your legs."

"You're a dog. Just for that, I'm going to screw up your interview."

Caleb was visibly nervous when we arrived. I gathered that he tended to fall back on literary conversation in moments of stress or uncertainty.

"You're like Mr. Porfiry in *Crime and Punishment*," Caleb said.

"I guess that makes you Raskolnikov, Caleb," I countered. My familiarity with Dostoyevsky was like an uppercut to his jaw. *Point one for me*, I said to myself. "I take it you like detective fiction, Caleb."

"Not really. I don't care who killed Roger Ackroyd."

"That was Christie's best, if you ask me. You might want to read it. Are you familiar with Chris Burden, by the way?"

"Should I be?" Caleb said nervously.

"Maybe. You reenacted his performance piece." I paused for a moment to let that sink in. "We know that Green didn't shoot himself. And no one bought that story about a random guy showing up on the beach."

"I think you just played along with the experiment," Ollie said. "You finally had a chance to do something *really* creative, even if it was twisted."

He felt cornered, and it showed.

"You always hated the bottom-line types who pulled the news business down. And you exploded," she said. "You decided to help Paul get back at the financial guys."

"N-, No," he insisted. "If you want to arrest me, Detective, go ahead."

"Caleb, we can have a frank conversation here," I said, "or we can bring you to my office and talk in a more formal setting. Is that what you want? I don't think you're a killer…"

"But you did shoot Paul," Ollie said. "Hell, I wanted to shoot him myself hundreds of times, along with everyone else in the newsroom."

"I meant no harm," Caleb said. "I mean, he begged me to do it. He didn't have guts enough to shoot himself. Plus, it was only a .22."

"He knew it would let him off the hook, because he couldn't be the murderer if he got shot himself," I added, as if to be helpful.

"Are you going to arrest me?"

"No, Caleb," I said softly. "We *could* charge you with conspiracy to commit the Headline Hunter murders." He gave a start.

"But you're exempted, under the case of Ignazio Vs. Silone, where the Supreme Judicial Court of Massachusetts exonerated an assistant who harmed an artist in a performance piece. It established a new doctrine called Conceptual License. Relax, for now. Just let us know if Paul shares anything incriminating. That's the price you pay for us to leave you alone. Don't disappear."

Caleb nodded vigorously. His relief was apparent.

Once we were in the car Ollie said, "Ignazio vs. Silone? That's bullshit, isn't it?"

"Yeah, I made it up. Ignazio Silone was an Italian writer."

"You're outrageous."

"Thanks for the compliment," he said. "You weren't so bad yourself."

"Do you really think Paul is the killer?"

"Not sure," I said quickly. "I have more questions than answers at this point."

32

SHORT SALES, TALL PROFITS

JAN LATER TOLD US that she sobered up enough to drive Paul home safely when he was discharged, though she wasn't sure if her reflexes were up to the task.

On the way back to Wellfleet he was in a good mood, for him, though he continually criticized her driving. She had known him for so long that she was used to his tyrannical ways. Every time she tried to fight back, he reminded her that she was a broken-down drunk who was lucky to have him. She wondered why she stayed.

She knew how to maintain a "working high" when she was at the paper. She made of point of renting an apartment within walking distance of *The Observer* so she wouldn't have to drive to work. She had lost her license once and was terrified about hurting someone. In fact, she was terrified about everything.

When she lost her job, she had no savings (all those bars were expensive, and rents were high in Boston) and she was about to be evicted from her apartment. When Paul offered her shelter, she simply caved. He never missed a chance to remind her that she was living off his charity.

When they got home from the hospital, she pretended everything was normal. She fussed over him, tucked him into bed, and made sure he took his antibiotics.

"I love it when you go all Florence Nightingale on me," he said. "Come and give me a kiss." (In case you're wondering, she gave us all these details.)

Sometimes he can truly be nice, she thought. After he fell asleep, she sat in an easy chair with a book about the American presidency on her lap and a bottle of wine on the drum table next to her. She poured the Chardonnay into her favorite oversized goblet, which looked more like a vase. It held an entire bottle. That helped her maintain the illusion that she was drinking just one glass. *It was going to be a pleasant evening, as long as she didn't get too drunk to read*, she thought.

• • •

"Too complicated to discuss on the phone," Brent Garner told me, alluding to some new information.

He arranged to meet me at The Summer Shack in Cambridge where the food was good, the atmosphere casual, and the privacy ample. Every time I walked past the huge tank with live lobsters there on the way to the tables, I was tempted to order one, but eating it would be too much work and too messy. I prefer food I can consume with a knife and fork, especially when I want to concentrate on the conversation. I ordered scallops, and Brent opted for fish and chips.

"You come to a restaurant noted for its cuisine, and you go for fish and chips?" I said.

"Have you ever tried it here?" Brent said.

"No, but—"

"I'll let you taste it, and you won't be so high and mighty. It's prime, believe me."

"Okay, forget I said it," I said. "I'll bet you'd order a hamburger at a steak house."

"I would if it was good. Keep this up and I won't tell you what I found out."

"I guess I better shut up then."

"It's all incredible. Where do you want me to start?"

"Jeez, will you quit teasing me and deliver already?" This sort of joshing had been going on ever since our days in the academy.

"I'm tired of helping you flatfooted cops. You can't believe how hard to was to figure this all out. I had to pull out all the stops."

"Boo-whooo."

Ignoring me, Brent continued. "It's a rogue's gallery. Let me put it in language that even a dumb ass like you can comprehend. We found out that Mr. Paul Green contacted FACT on—." He checked his notes, "… June 12, after the four murders. By the way, do you know what that dirtball's salary was at the paper?"

"No idea," I said.

"One hundred twenty-five K. Not exactly a fortune for the man in charge," Brent said.

"He smelled a lot more money, I guess."

"Let me finish," Brent said. "Judging from emails we collected, and it never ceases to amaze me how many of these white-collar morons leave paper trails, I swear their IQs drop whenever they sit down in front of a computer—"

"Will you quit editorializing and tell me what you found out?"

"Okay," Brent said. "Guess when Paul shorted the stock?"

"*Before* the report came out …"

"Right, and it gets worse. He did it with money he *borrowed* from FACT," Brent added.

"How much?"

"One million, two hundred and fifty thousand bucks."

"Sweet deal for him."

"Considering that stock dropped by forty percent, he probably walked away with five hundred K after taxes."

"Can you prove this?"

"Yeah, with bank records. These guys think they're never going to get caught, so they don't hide the proceeds in the Caymans or wherever. Really stupid."

"How much did the FACT guys make?"

"Probably three million. We'll have those numbers soon. You haven't asked me about Persephone and your boy Aldous Denby."

"I was getting to that," I said.

"I hate country-club pricks like him," Brent said. "They pretend to be legit and they're just gangsters on yachts. That guy bought the whole operation for a song when the price of the stock plummeted. Then he'll gut the paper—"

"He's already done that."

"Yeah, I know, but what he's done so far is only the beginning. He'll bleed out the cash and sell it off for parts. Maybe he'll sell the land to some condo developer."

"I know. What can we get him for?"

"We, nothing. This isn't going to be a police department bust where you happen to acknowledge the invaluable assistance of the SEC."

"I don't give a fuck who gets the credit."

"Hey, relax, pal. Don't you know when I'm busting you?" We both smiled.

"Is it legal if Persephone took advantage of the low share price and swooped in?" I asked.

"Ordinarily, yes, but they misused inside knowledge," Brent said. "Remember, insider trading involves the breach of a *fiduciary* duty, that means an obligation of trust and confidence, while in possession of material, nonpublic information."

"But they had no fiduciary responsibility to the paper and Bay State Media."

"Good point, Mez, but Paul Green did," Brent said. "He certainly broke the law by revealing confidential information, for his own benefit, to the tune of half a million bucks. FACT and Persephone are co-conspirators. And we can get them all of them for wire fraud, because they sent information over email. We have all their communications, the trading records, and so on."

"Did you find anything to connect them with the murders?" I asked.

"That's your department, Mez. We handle the financial stuff and you deal with the blood and guts. I wouldn't be surprised if they were involved, though. Guys like Aldous Denby and Liam Terrell, that FACT asshole, sometimes have underworld connections. They might have been just crazy enough to kill people to get control of a paper. If that's true, one of them will turn. If not, Paul will, trust me."

33

CONSEQUENCES
November

JUST BEFORE THANKSGIVING, the office of Boston's US Attorney Nora Hayden announced that major indictments would be forthcoming in the so-called Headline Hunter case. Even though her news conference was announced at the last minute, twenty local and national print reporters and half a dozen TV crews showed up.

Hayden read a statement outlining federal charges against Paul Green, Liam Terrell of FACT, and Aldous Denby of Persephone for securities fraud, mail fraud, and insider trading. She cited the efforts of the SEC's Brent Garner and Detective Ronan Mezini. Bail was set at five-hundred K for each defendant.

Hayden spoke quickly and decisively. "This spate of murders has created a reign of fear in the city we all love. No longer are we able to enjoy the free flow of information and rarely can we savor a spontaneous exchange of ideas in the press. These indictments represent an important first step in restoring honor and dignity to a paper which has been a Boston institution for 150 years."

Ignoring the raised hands of reporters, Hayden continued: "We know that the killer is still at large, and we hope to bring him to justice so that the horror that has pervaded media circles will disappear. We pray that the city can return to some semblance of normalcy."

"Do you have any suspects for the murders?" a TV reporter shouted out.

"At this time, we do not," Hayden said. "But Detective Mezini and his team are working diligently on the cases. We ask anyone with any information to come forward."

"Do you think the defendants were involved in the murders?" a network TV reporter asked.

"We cannot speculate on that," Hayden replied.

"Is the FBI involved?" Amy Stout asked.

"Yes, they are," Hayden answered. "Working in conjunction with the Cambridge Police Department."

"Do you think that the local authorities have been flatfooted?" Amy Stout asked.

"On the contrary, they have followed up every lead. Indeed, Detective Mezini worked hand in glove with the SEC in this matter," Hayden said.

I bet Brent was happy about that last comment.

• • •

To celebrate the indictments, I insisted on taking Ollie to Charlie's Kitchen, one of the holdovers from the old days in Harvard Square before it became a bundle of bistros and boutiques. I remember the bar fondly as the "Home of the Double Cheeseburger" when my buddies from the Police Academy and I would eat there late at night to soak up the booze and laugh at the college kids. Charlie's made just one concession to yuppiedom, with its new garden area in the back, but it was still an unpretentious pub with decent food.

"I love this place," Ollie said as we sat down.

"Really?" I asked. "You're not just indulging me?"

"Are you kidding me, Z? I grew up in Jamaica Plain, rememb-ah?" she said, mimicking the endangered R in the Massachusetts accent. "This reminds me of Doyle's somehow. I was heartbroken when that place closed."

She was referring to the ultimate Irish pub with pictures of martyred hero Michael Collins on the walls—walls which had witnessed the rough conversations of working men and the false promises of politicians who frequented the place. There are pubs with character, then there are Boston bars, which bring personality of place to a whole new level of idiosyncrasy and blarney.

Once our meals arrived—both of us ordered double cheeseburgers and fries, of course—we clinked beer mugs.

"Congrats, Z. You deserve this," Ollie said.

"Thanks, O. Brent Garner is amazing. Let's hope the indictments stick."

"The Feds know what they're doing."

"Yeah, but the dirtball defendants will have really sophisticated lawyers who can make this seem like a dispute over the cake budget for a PTA meeting. And meanwhile, we have no leads on the murders."

"I don't know how to say this—" Ollie said.

I'm sure I looked worried. "Is this gonna hurt?"

"In a way," she said. "It's not about you. I found another suspect."

"Who?"

"I'll get to that," she said. "I wasn't sure at first. I talked to the kids at the frat house again, and the neighbors of *both* of the Alec Moores, and the people who live near 2.0's apartment."

"And..."

"I showed as many people as I could find a picture of a certain man. Several said they had seen him on the scenes at the time of the murders. I questioned them closely, believe me."

"Who—"

"I'll tell you in a minute, I promise," she said brusquely. "I went and looked back at visitor's logs at a place you know."

"What place?" I asked.

"The Mountain Refuge mental hospital. The paperwork showed that Johnny had walked out at the times of the murders," she said. "I hate to say it, Mez, but it's true."

I was crestfallen. "That's crazy," I said.

"Maybe. But the logs don't lie, Mez." With that, she handed me copies of the crude handwritten documents and pointed out the entries showing Johnny's movements on all the dates of the killings.

"You know he was free to come and go," she said calmly.

"How would he get from way up there in New Hampshire down to the city? Impossible. He doesn't have a car." My voice was rising.

"No, Mez, improbable, but not impossible."

I took a long drink from my beer in a vain attempt to douse my anxiety. I was seeing undulating circles of clashing pink and brown colors around her head. I wasn't sure what that meant. Altogether, though, the effect was unpleasant.

"Think about it. He's unstable. Violent. And he has a major grudge against the paper. Plus all the bullets came from a .38. Many cops used those guns."

"Yeah, but his was confiscated."

"C'mon, Mez, it's easy to get a gun in Boston."

"How did you get these logs?"

"I'm a reporter, remember? I used a little bit of charm, and I lied a little."

"Let me look into this," I said, grabbing the logs.

"I'm sorry, Z. I had a hunch, and I followed it." she said, as she grabbed my hand.

Ollie took a bite out of her cheeseburger, wiped her mouth, and took a sip of beer. I hadn't even touched my food.

"You drop this bombshell, and you can still eat?" I said, in disbelief.

"Sorry, I guess I'm nervous."

"*You're* nervous? I'm about to throw up."

"I'm here for you no matter what."

"You're here for me and you investigate my best friend? What about Johnny's phony confession? He didn't know *anything* about the crimes."

"He could have easily faked that, pretending that he was garbled."

My cell phone rang.

"Bad timing, but I should take this," I said. "Right," I said into the phone. "Where? I'm on my way." I hung up. "Another murder," I threw two twenties down on the table.

"I'm coming with you," Ollie said.

I wasn't entirely happy about her tagging along. I guess that duo routine was getting more and more uncomfortable.

• • •

Yellow tape already surrounded the house in East Cambridge when I arrived in my car. Ollie took a taxi by herself, to avoid linking us together.

At the scene, I put on my cop face and was about to walk right by her without speaking. I thought better of it, stopped quickly, and said, "Gotta go in. You'll have to stay here."

"Pleeze," Ollie said. "This isn't my first crime scene." She suddenly went into a serious mode too.

I ducked under the tape and walked into the house. No doubt Ollie was thinking I was treating her like a child, as if she didn't know how to behave. She probably figured I was upset because she threw the evidence about Johnny at me.

A few minutes later I texted her and told her who the dead person was. This feature story about the victim had appeared in *The Observer* a week prior:

TEACH YOUR CHILDREN WELL

By Alice Weeks
Education Reporter

You might say Edna Juniper is old school. She insists on perfect attendance, neat penmanship, good grammar, and exquisite manners. That's why all the children in her eighth-grade class in Cambridge are terrified of her. Yet she stays friends with most of her former students forever.

One of them is Cambridge City Councilor John Almis. "Ms. J?" he said with a laugh. "She once humiliated me because I said 'Me and my friend Joey played ball yesterday. Would you say *me* played ball she asked? No, it's Joey and *I* played.' I never forgot that."

Another former student, Audra Brennan, is now an attorney at an intellectual property law firm in the Seaport. She said Ms. Juniper's nickname was "The Terrorist" because she would write examples of bad grammar on the board, then wipe them away aggressively, wielding the eraser as if it were a weapon. "'Get this stuff out of my classroom, out of your writing, and out of your life,'" she would say.

Stories like these show why the governor's office named Edna Juniper Teacher of the Year.

Alice Weeks, the education reporter who wrote the story, showed up at the crime scene.

"I thought we were done with all this," Alice said, visibly shaken. Ollie tried to comfort her. She could tell that Alice had never covered a homicide before. Murder was rare on the education beat.

Alice was petite and had a penchant for floral dresses that made her look older than her 35 years. In fact, her demeanor was redolent of a schoolmarm, perfect for her specialty.

A crowd of other journalists were gathering on the street. Ollie noticed that Amy was there too. A TV reporter was already doing a tease on camera for the news. "Another person profiled in *The Observer* is killed. Is the Headline Hunter at it again?" he said.

Ollie rolled her eyes at Alice, who sadly shook her head.

I walked out a minute later and approached Ollie. She introduced me to Alice, who was now crying openly.

I pulled a crumpled tissue out of a pocket and handed it to her. "Don't worry, it's clean," I said.

She wiped her eyes. "Sorry," she said. "Not used to this, I guess."

"It's never easy. Do you mind if I ask you a few questions?" By this time six or seven reporters were clustered around us.

"I guess, if I can help."

I pulled her aside for more privacy. "C'mon, guys, give us some room," I said to the crowd. They complied, reluctantly.

"When did you last talk to her?" I asked.

"Last week. She was really, really sweet," Alice said. "Everyone loved her. Parents, principals, everybody. She was one of the nicest people I ever met."

"Was she married?" I asked.

"No," Alice said, "but she had lots of kids, as she said. Thousands of them. Her students, of course. She remembered all their names. They were like her family."

Amy Stout barged in and asked me how she was killed.

"A gunshot wound in the back of her head," I said abruptly. "She was found in her back yard."

"Another Headline Hunter victim?" Amy asked.

"I don't know," I said. "Officer Keegan will have more information for you shortly." I almost spat out Keegan's name.

• • •

My team and I went door to door to door in the neighborhood to no avail. As expected with this string of murders, the crime scene was clean. No signs of forced entry. No fingerprints, other than the victim's and Alice's. By the time I got home it was one in the morning and I was bushed.

I FaceTimed Ollie to say goodnight.

"You look like you just went 10 rounds with Mike Tyson, Mez," she said.

"Yeah, I'm licked."

"How did it go?"

"Not too well. Not much to go on."

"You want to come over?" she asked. *There was lust in her voice, I felt.*

"I'm going straight to the mattress. I'll be out by the time my head hits the pillow," I said, hoping I didn't sound too distant though I was starting to feel that way. I was probably still smarting about the accusations against Johnny.

"Did you follow up on the situation with Johnny?" she asked, as if reading my mind.

"Yeah, let's talk tomorrow. I can barely stay awake," I yawned.

"Want to meet for lunch?"

"Sure. Why don't you come over? Tomorrow's Saturday. I'll make my patented Bloody Marys."

"Do I have to wait that long?"

"I gotta sleep. My brain feels like it's full of cotton." *I could tell she was upset that I wanted to be alone. Maybe she was too proud to show it.*

"See you around noon. Good night, babe."

"No, I'm the badge, remember? You're the babe."

"Not funny," she said. "Sleep tight."

• • •

The next day she knocked on the backdoor and I yelled, "It's open." She seemed buoyant when she came in.

I was busy shaking the cocktails so I couldn't kiss her properly. She gave me a peck on the cheek during a pause in my work.

"This is the closest thing to a liquid meal imaginable. Taste," I said as I handed her a Bloody Mary.

"Mmmm," she said as she took a sip. "It's like a cross between tomato soup and gazpacho."

"With a kick."

"What's in it?"

"First, Tito's Vodka. Straight from Austin, Texas, and smooth as a baby's skin. Tomato juice, of course. Horseradish, tabasco, black pepper, and—"

"A lot of spices!" she said.

"As I always say, life without coffee and hot sauce has no meaning. Now where was I? Oh yeah, you have to add dill, for that distinctive zing, a squeeze of lime, and a dash of celery salt. You shake it over ice like your life depends on it. Insert a celery stalk. That gives you something to stir it with and to munch on. You like?"

"I like," she said.

"I've been swamped. Not sure where to start. First, we eat." I was hesitant to start the conversation.

The timer went off on my phone—telling me that the tuna shish kebob on the grill in the backyard was done. I brought the steaming plate of fish to the dining room table, which was already set. My dinnerware was simple, white dishes with a blue circle around the rim, cloth placemats with a checkerboard pattern, and paper napkins. Nothing fancy, but Ollie was impressed.

For maybe the fiftieth time in our relationship, we clinked glasses. "To justice," I said, and we ate heartily.

"Z, are you going to bring me up to date?" Ollie asked.

"Like I said, I don't know where to start."

"Hold that thought, I have to go to the bathroom," she said.

"You want another one of these Bloodys?" I asked when she returned a few minutes later.

"No thanks, I'm good."

I took a gulp of my drink. "Let me tell you what's been happening. As you know, all arrows pointed toward Aldous Denby from Persephone, Liam Terrell from FACT, and your boss Paul Green. The question that we have asked ourselves remains: are they killers? It's one thing to manipulate stocks, and another altogether to murder people. That BS stunt that Green pulled with the shot in his arm never fooled anybody. By the way, I did some digging in the newspaper archives and found some, uh, fascinating articles that he had written back in his reporting days."

"About what?" Ollie asked.

"He profiled a murderer for hire. Got an interview with him in state prison. His name was Phil Dawson. In for life with no parole. A stone-cold psycho. Interesting that Paul was so fascinated with him. His story described the bastard's MO."

"What was it?" Ollie asked. *I could tell that she wasn't sure why I was telling her all this.*

"He drilled a small hole in the trunk of his car. Folded down the back seats and lay down on his stomach. The barrel of his rifle would stick out only a few inches, so it was almost completely hidden. He'd shoot the victims from a distance. That made it difficult to figure out where the bullets came from."

"Didn't John Muhammed do that?"

"Yeah, maybe he copied Dawson. They called Muhammed the ..."

"DC Sniper," she said.

"Right. Except that guy killed seventeen people. Dawson wasn't quite so, uh, prolific. He only killed ten. Dawson told Paul Green he'd park his car diagonally across the street from the victims. Sometimes he'd even put a for sale sign on it, to make it look less suspicious."

"An old trick."

"Get this: Paul visited the guy in prison six times *after* the story ran."

"How do you know that?"

"Concord Prison keeps track of the visitors," I said. "And it's all digitized, not like the antiquated stuff at Johnny's mental hospital. Easy to search."

"Do you think Paul got ideas from this guy?"

"Maybe. At first, I thought there's no way he could be a killer. You can't learn the technique just by talking to someone who's done it. It's hard to aim at another human being and pull the trigger for real. Then things got weird. We rechecked the evidence from the crime scenes and found his DNA at every one of them."

"How did you get a sample from him?" Ollie asked.

"From the IV at the hospital. The Wellfleet cops were on the ball."

"Did they have a warrant?"

"I assume so, but I'm not even sure they needed one."

"You never told me any of this."

"Everything has gone down so fast that I have been playing catch up myself."

"Did you confront Paul?"

"The Wellfleet cops did, and he denied everything," I said. "He even offered to take lie detector tests. He said that Dawson—the guy he profiled—simply fascinated him, and that's why he went back so many times."

"Is Paul out on bail?"

"Yeah. I think he used his house as collateral."

"How come this story never got out?"

"The Wellfleet cops wanted to keep it quiet. I was impressed with them. They're pros. Especially that guy Tony Castro."

Ollie's expression was deadpan. As a seasoned reporter, she had long since learned how not to react quickly to new information.

"What about the DNA?" she asked. "That seems pretty incriminating, to say the least."

"You would think so," I said. "But the material was actually his mucus. Very strange. It was comingled with fibers that seemed to come from Kleenex and Q-tips, along with remnants of plastic."

"Plastic?"

"Yeah, from a baggie," I said.

"I don't get it," Ollie said.

"It's well known that Green is severely allergic and that he's always sneezing and wiping his nose. Somebody probably took used tissues out of his wastebasket, stored them in a Ziploc bag, then smeared the gunk on the victims' bodies with a Q-tip."

"Who would do that? Wouldn't that person have left some of his own DNA behind too?"

"I'll get to that. I forgot to mention that the GPS on Paul's cell phone shows that he was never anywhere near the crime scenes."

"Z, you're burying the lead, as we say in the news biz. Delaying the main point."

"I know. This may sound random, but do you by chance remember the unsolved murder of a Brown grad student in Providence about eight years ago? I think you were there at the time."

"Yeah," Ollie said, "he was an art history guy, as I recall."

"Bad actor. Harassing female students. Even raped one of them."

"What does he have to do with all this?"

"He was shot in the back of the head, just like the Headline Hunter's victims, and found outside. Could be the same perp. Many so-called serial killers take a long break between murders."

"Absolutely. Serial doesn't mean constant."

"Bear with me. As you know, the Hunter's first four victims were cruel to their partners. Both Alec Moores, V 2.0, Wilhelm Stafford."

"You're saying the Hunter started in Providence years ago?" she asked.

"Maybe. I began to think about this case in a different light when you told me that the 'real' Alec Moore's mistress complained about the way he treated her."

"Yeah, that was pretty good reporting, I thought."

I let that comment pass, for now.

"Being a reporter is frustrating, isn't it? So passive. You've said so yourself. You just write about bad things that people do. The stories attract attention, then the evil comes back. Like crabgrass. So much better to be a novelist, so you can control the characters. But you couldn't get that going, could you?"

"Why are you bringing this up?"

"To highlight a few things.'

"Like what? You want to remind me that I'm a failed novelist? I think you're a member of that club too." She suddenly turned harsh.

I ignored her comment and continued with my explanation. "Wouldn't it be better to take it all into your own hands and just do away with the bad guys?"

"Meaning exactly what, Z?" Her face registered little emotion.

"I first became suspicious when one of my pals in the records department told me that you had been checking the domestic violence rap sheets for weeks," I said. "He told me you looked at the files for each of the four victims one month *before* the murders started occurred. Why?"

"I was looking for patterns in domestic violence cases," she said in a flat tone. "What about the logs showing that your buddy Johnny Garlowe left the hospital on the nights of the murders? How do you explain that?"

"Fakes," I said. "I checked the originals. You dummied them up."

"Bullshit. That guy is crazy enough to—"

"Unlikely. He's too far gone. You almost had me when you told me those lies about the neighbors seeing someone that fit his description at the scenes."

"What about the bullets? All 38 caliber, pointing to a common police gun."

"Right, but a type of gun that most cops today don't use any more. A gun that *had* been standard issue for Boston cops when your dad started on the force. He probably kept using it because it was comfortable. Like a glove that fits. A Smith and Wesson six-shot .38 revolver. The gun you kept for sentimental reasons."

"Yeah, and it's pointed at you under the table," Ollie said in a surprisingly straightforward way. "The bullets travel at about 750 feet per second, and they can do a lot of damage. My dad drilled that into me."

"A bit tricky to fit it with a silencer, but you managed," I said. My voice broke. I didn't flinch, but I was clearly upset. "You must have swiped a few tissues from Green's wastebasket at the office when no one was looking and smeared some of the stuff at the crime scenes. *Your* DNA was co-mingled with Green's at the scenes."

"How do you know that?"

"I took a sample from a glass you had used," I said. "When I got the results, I was sick. I realized who I had been sleeping with."

"*Whom* you had been sleeping with, you mean," she said sarcastically.

I put my hand into my shirt pocket and pulled out six bullets. "I took these out of the gun when you went to the bathroom. You shouldn't have left it in your purse."

Ollie's shoulders sagged. She lifted the gun, unlocked the cartridge, and spun it. Empty. She started laughing, in a forced way.

"Z, tell me this is an elaborate joke."

"The joke's on me, because I fell for you and it's going to be hard to put that away," I said.

"Don't you think I felt something special too?" she asked. "I've always had a hard time with intimacy."

"Save it for the psychiatrist who examines you for the pre-trial report." *I'm sure my face was as hard as diamonds. She had never seen me look that way. I have black eyes that no doubt projected dark fire and I'm sure that my shoulder muscles flexed under my shirt. She could see I was serious. Dead serious.*

Ollie was growing desperate. "What about Edna Juniper?" she asked. "You think I killed an innocent teacher too?"

"Yeah, to throw everybody off the trail. Smart move. You broke the pattern. She never hurt anyone in her short life. I have to admit, it took me a while to make sense of the business with the two Alec Moores. I assume you weren't stupid enough to kill the wrong guy. But you managed to get two for the price of one, so to speak.

"Maybe you found out about the real Moore's domestic situation after researching the story about him spreading TB, then you looked far and wide to find another guy with the same name who was also an abuser. Killing both of them was another way to sow confusion. By the way, that story about Moore the salesman doing S&M with his mistress was all BS. You made that story up. No wonder you said the woman wouldn't give you her name. That's because she didn't exist."

"There were so many lies, including that fabricated tale you told me about the car that tried to run you down in *The Observer*'s parking lot. Were you trying to get my sympathy?"

Ollie just stared at me, with no expression.

"One more thing," I said. "Throwing that brick into Alec Moore's house was stupid. That was clumsy."

I paused to collect myself. "The financial clowns played right into your hands, didn't they? They saw an opportunity, but they weren't killers themselves. Their greed was a fringe benefit for you. I do want to know one thing, though. Why did you shoot the victims in the back of the head? Is it because you couldn't face them?"

She ignored the question. "Can you still face me, Z?" she asked. Her tone was forlorn.

"I'm going to miss you. But—"

"You're a cop first. Is that what you were going to say?" She paused and blinked back tears. "You're such a hypocrite. You covered for Johnny but you're turning on me."

"There is a slight difference, Ollie. Johnny didn't kill anyone. And for the record, I never, ever covered for him. Besides, I couldn't exactly trust you after this."

"I'm pregnant, Z. Does that change anything?"

I took in a deep, involuntary breath. At first, I didn't believe her because I thought she was playing for pity, once again. But one look at her eyes convinced me that she was telling the truth. I knew her well enough to determine that quickly.

I finally figured out what the smell was that I had detected around her when I first saw her. Handcuffs, predicting her future. She was soon to wear them. I first sniffed them back in the police academy and the olfactory memory never evaporated. I should have recognized the scent earlier. My synesthesia was trying to tell me something about her, but I was too obtuse, or too much in love, to pay attention. From now on I should pay attention to the signals.

Oddly, I never could bring myself to tell Ollie about my synesthesia. I was being protective, I guess. It's strange how we sometimes withhold key secrets from those we love.

There was a knock on the door. I knew who it was. "Come in, guys," I said, trying as hard as possible to sound normal. Two cops in uniform stood at the back door. "Olivia Burns, meet Officers Amin Bashar and Jasmine Shelton."

"You're under arrest for murder, Ms. Burns," Shelton said as Bashar handcuffed her. As they were reading Ollie her rights, I stared hard at her. She didn't look back when they led her away.

Brent Garner appeared at the back door a moment after the police left. He was carrying a bottle of Jameson.

"Sit down, amigo," Brent said.

Aunt Eleanor came through the back door not a minute later.

"How did you know?" I asked. I looked at Brent and saw the answer. He had asked her to come.

Without saying a word, he poured three ample shots of the whiskey and sat down.

"I hereby cancel all cannoli debts," he said. I knew he was just trying to make me smile, which I did. Then I choked back a sob and downed my shot.

We drank in silence.

34

RESOLUTION?

Two Months Later, January

I HAD TAKEN A LEAVE of absence from the police force. Reporters swirled around me at first. Every time I'd leave the house at least one of them would be out front waiting for me. The questions were all predictable: "When did you find out Ollie was the killer?" "Were you in love with her?" "Are you going back on duty?" "Will you write a book?"

Speaking of books, a couple of agents approached me and asked if I'd be interested in telling my story. They offered to find ghostwriters. A Hollywood producer even called. I dismissed them all. Eventually, the press and the agents stopped badgering me.

True to form, Melissa Pugh from *The Sun* did a column with the headline "The Badge Minus the Babe," and it brought a smirk to my face.

While Ollie was awaiting trial, she was held at the South Bay House of Correction in Boston, near the so-called Methadone Mile, close to the Barnes Hospital where Moore was poisoned. She looked pale and drawn the day I visited.

Her face was expressionless except for a strange glint in her eyes that the dirty plexiglass barrier between us could not fully conceal. As she sat down, we picked up the phones at the same time.

"What do you want?" she asked, with more than a hint of hostility.

"Just wanted to see how you were doing," I said.

"You worried about me, or the kid?"

"Both."

"Well, the crêpes suzette could be better. I wish they had them with Nutella."

I couldn't help but laugh.

"O, I—"

"I know, Mez, don't say anything." Her stare was fierce. "I'd rather not talk, because I don't want us to exchange any angry words. You picked an awkward time for a conversation."

She stood up and turned sideways so I could see her in profile. "Check it out." The baby bump was showing, even under the ill-fitting orange jump suit.

"Looking good," I said gratuitously because I wasn't sure what else to add.

"Ever charming, Detective."

"I still—"

"Care?"

"Something like that. I'm surprised you're keeping the baby."

"I'm Catholic, remember. We don't believe in abortion, though I do think it's a matter of individual choice." I thought she was kidding, but I wasn't sure. The irony of a murderer assuming a pro-life position wasn't lost on me, and my expression probably indicated my thoughts.

"Yeah, I know," she said. "Hypocrisy, right? It won't surprise you that I don't believe in capital punishment either."

"Do you need anything?" I asked awkwardly.

"Nah. They give me plenty of pre-natal vitamins and decent medical care. The state doesn't want the guilty to suffer," she said with a smirk. "I know all about pregnancy in prison. I did my senior thesis on it. I think I told you that. In fact, you get much better treatment if you're carrying a kid."

"I'd like to read your thesis sometime."

"It's packed away somewhere. I guess they impounded my stuff."

"There's something I have to ask you."

Reading my mind, she said, "It's your kid. I'm many things, Mez, but I'm not a cheater."

"Thanks, I guess," I said. "You sure you don't need anything?"

"Yeah, I could use a file, or maybe a gun."

With that, she hung up the phone and told the guard she wanted to leave. I didn't stand up until the door closed behind them.

• • •

Amy sat in the former I-Desk office by herself. Will Cabot had promoted her to Ollie's position as the Investigative Editor. She felt strange to be away from the relentless pressure of the police beat but now she had a chance to take her time and do in-depth journalism. Will asked her to write an article about Ollie, from the "insider's perspective." The headline he crafted, "The Killer Among Us," embarrassed her, especially because most readers assume that reporters write their own headlines. That just isn't the case. Amy wondered how Ollie would react to the article. When the phone rang, she had her answer.

"Hey," the familiar voice said.

"Ollie, I was just thinking about you."

"Good or bad?"

"I wish you I could have interviewed you for the story instead of that fool Keegan. I had to fill in a lot of blanks."

"So it goes. You got it mostly right, I suppose," Ollie said.

"Hey, I should thank you."

"For what?"

"For sending me those pix of Troy and that, uh, bimbo."

"I cannot confirm or deny that."

"You just did."

"Can we go off the record?"

"Sure, whatever."

"I thought about killing him. But he was never violent, as far as I know," Ollie said. Amy shuddered at this admission, but recovered quickly.

"The *only* good thing I can say about him is that he never hit me. Do you mind if I ask you something, again off the record?"

"Go."

"Are you going to plead out?

"No comment," Ollie said. "Incidentally, I know the Persephone deal was canceled after the arrests and that a new private equity firm took over. How are they?"

"Not bad. They reinstated some of the people who were laid off. We may be able to cover the town again. Why do you ask?"

"I was going to pitch you some stories," Ollie said, with a smile evident in her voice.

Amy laughed. "I'm sure you have lots of leads in there."

"You have no idea, sweetheart. I want to ask for a favor."

"Tell me."

"Look after Mezini for me, please."

"Will do. He's a good guy."

A voice on the line said, "You are almost out of time."

"Thanks, kid," Ollie said and abruptly hung up.

• • •

By June, five months later, I had gone back to work. The department took me off the homicide unit to minimize the stress and reassigned me temporarily to white collar crime. No blood spilled, just money stolen. For the time being that suited me. I had no further contact with Ollie. She never reached out to me, nor did I to her.

One Saturday I slept late. When my cell woke me up I heard news that made me speed to the prison with lights flashing. The staff was expecting me, and they led me into the infirmary where a nurse handed me a baby boy.

I learned that Ollie had swaddled him in a blanket and left him on her bed—tucked behind a pillow against the wall, far away from the edge. Then she slit her throat with a shank she made from a loose piece of the bedframe. The nurse gave me a note as I cradled the baby in my arms.

I looked down at my son and tried to see if he looked like his mom. Something about the shape of his chin reminded me of Ollie. His eyelashes were really long, just like hers. *Otherwise, I felt as though I was face to face with a miniature version of myself. I had never experienced such a concentrated rush of love, tinged with regret that the boy would never know his mother.*

I unfolded the note and held it in one hand as I gripped the baby with the other arm. I didn't want to read it but felt I had to. Ollie's handwriting was neat and precise:

Dear Z,

I tried to write to you many times to explain why I went astray. I'm not sure I understand it myself. I suppose I wanted to make some sort of a statement, albeit with an exclamation point. I'm not trying to be glib. There is so much madness in the world that some of it, maybe a lot of it, crept into my soul. Though you read my college essay about my dad's death, you still don't know everything. I left out something that I never shared with anyone, not even Aunt Jessie. That lowlife "Baby G" actually raped me that day.

The first murder down in Providence seemed, how can I say it, correct. The guy was a creepy grad student and teaching assistant who threatened to give bad grades to nubile young women unless they came across.

As for the Moores, Stafford, and V 2.0, they were just abusers, pure and simple. I didn't set out to be an avenging angel. I just wanted to even the scales. Plus "the media" had been so high and mighty, at least in their own minds, I wanted to knock them down too. Once I started killing, I couldn't stop.

In here, I'm more bored than anything else. I've memorized every crack in the walls. I try to read, but my mind goes haywire.

I leave our son to you. If you want to give him up for adoption, I'll understand. If you keep him, I'm sure you'll worry that he might have his mom's crazy genes. That's doubtful though. A propensity to kill is not necessarily inherited. And with you as a dad, he'll have a chance for a normal life.

I won't blame you if you have a paternity test. I would do the same thing if I were you. That'll prove that he's your kid.

I'll let you name him, in any case. I made a will and left my house to our son. I suggest you sell it and put the money away for his education.

By the time you read this, I'll be gone. I would say that I love you, after my fashion, but I don't think you'd accept that.

O

She was right about one thing. I did get a paternity test. The police department's chemist put a rush on it. As expected, it confirmed I was the father.

I brought the baby home and named him Renato, Italian for reborn. Somehow that seemed appropriate. My hours were more regular in white collar crime and that made it easier to take care of him.

On the third day of my paternity leave my door opened. It was Aunt Eleanor.

"You can't knock?"

"Don't get sassy with me, boy. I changed—Ah, you know the rest. And now it's time to do the same for your son. I can't imagine you handling this by yourself."

"Aunt Eleanor, I—"

"Go take a nap and give me that kid right now, before I spank you." With that, she took over.

I was fragile, and I knew it. I thought of going to a therapist but then it occurred to me that there was one person whom I already knew who could help me sort this all out: Dr. Jack Grimes.

He made a special trip back to Boston to see me. We sat in my living room while Renato slept. I explained the broad outlines of Ollie's life, that her mom had died from cancer when she was four, that she was raped when she was a freshman in high school, that she watched her father and the assailant kill one another at the home she could never bear to leave, and that her beloved Aunt Jessie, arguably her best friend, died just after her freshman year at college.

"A lot of earthquakes, and many aftershocks, I'm sure," Grimes said.

"I suppose so," I said. "When you told us not to rule anybody out, I never thought it would come to this."

"Neither did I, to tell you the truth."

"I'm trying to make sense of all this, Dr. Grimes."

"Jack, you mean." I always thought he was arrogant, but he was quite warm after all.

"Thanks. It was nice of you to come." I was on the brink of crying. "Why would she do all this?"

"People in her situation know how to separate different parts of their lives. On one level, she was your girlfriend and a reporter, and on another …" He paused for a few seconds.

"Do you think she was flawed from birth?"

"That's the big question, Ronan. There are a hundred billion neurons in the brain, and each one is linked with ten thousand others in a complicated web of networks. One misconnection there, a misfire over here, and things can go askew. Then there's the rape. If that doesn't mess up a kid, what would? Victims of sexual assault often feel powerless afterwards. Especially since she was what, 14 when it happened?"

I nodded.

"That would have caused PTSD, for sure. Plus, big problems with relationships. And with trust. People in that situation often become manipulative, cunning, or secretive."

"She sure fooled me, until the end."

"Her looks helped, didn't they?" he asked with a slight smile. I answered with a sad smile of my own.

"Having her dad and aunt as decent role models helped stabilize her, I suppose, at least on the outside," he said. "But part of her would always be that defenseless teenage girl who needed comfort. Maybe that made her want to strike first before she got hurt again."

"But why take it out on strangers?"

"In her mind they weren't strangers. They were all related to the rapist. It was a reckoning, of sorts. Anyone who mistreated a partner deserved to pay. The killings made her feel powerful. In a twisted way she may have gotten the same sort of rush that Ted Bundy experienced when he strangled his victims and watched the life fade from their eyes."

I shuddered. "I understand why she killed herself. She couldn't have withstood jail."

"Agreed. Many of the serial killers I've encountered hate boredom more than anything else. The numbing routine of prison, the same lousy food. No excitement of any sort."

• • •

After Grimes left, I stood over Renato and watched him sleep. If it weren't for him, I thought, I probably would go to some remote island and live out my life in solitary contemplation. Maybe even join a monastery as a helper. Preferably a place that made brandy so I could sample the merchandise when the monks weren't looking, I joked to myself.

Eventually I'll need to get back to the world. My son will take his place in it before too long.

Acknowledgments

THIS IS THE SECOND MYSTERY I have published with Paper Angel Press. Once again, I want to thank Managing Editor Steven Radecki for his continued faith in me. He is supportive and flexible beyond words. Then comes Lisa Jacob, Senior Acquisitions Editor, who went through the copy with a surgeon's care. Her suggestions *greatly* improved and sharpened the story. She caught many mistakes and inconsistencies.

I can say with no exaggeration that this book would not exist without the countless inputs from my oldest pal, Jack Stilwell, a retired CFO with the mind of a literary critic. He is generous to a fault.

Greg Bauer, another old friend and retired finance guy, also has a deep sense for literature. He, too, was immensely helpful.

I am grateful for the insights gained from many other readers. In no particular order, I thank my son Jack, my cousin Tammy Brayshaw, Robin Platt, Frank Flaherty, Leslie Sciandra, Elizabeth Saltonstall, Rusty Stieff, Tony Castro (my brother-in-law and a Homicide Counsel in the Bronx District Attorney's office), Elisabetta DiCagno, Gabby Lombardo, Phil Landa, Susan Shelby, Lynda Snyder, and Ian Todreas (a lovingly exacting critic).

Thanks, of course, to Lawrence Hopkins (who owns the famous Daedalus Restaurant in Harvard Square). He appears here as his genial self.

A special homage to John Strahinich, my lifetime "consigliere."

As always, all my love to my wife Mary, my daughter Lauren, and my son Jack—the trio to whom this book is dedicated. I promise never to portray any of you in my mysteries.

About the Author

Before starting his communications company, Greg Stone spent a decade as a journalist in New York, Minneapolis, and Boston. In addition to the two Ronan Mezini mysteries, he has published three business books. Greg lives just outside Boston with his family and the world's cutest rescue dog.

Also by the Author

DANGEROUS INSPIRATION

Book Two in the Ronan Mezini Mysteries series
by Greg Stone

Synesthesia alters detective-turned-novelist Ronan Mezini's perceptions. But can it help him find the killer?

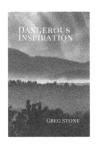

YOU MIGHT ALSO ENJOY

THE STORK
A Shelby McDougall Mystery
by Nancy Wood

Shelby McDougall's past is behind her. Almost.

FRUIT OF THE DEVIL
by Mary Flodin

Ms. Aurora Bourne would do anything to protect her students from harm ... even if that means going up against the most powerful corporation on the planet.

PIOUS REBEL
by Jory Post

After her partner dies suddenly, Lisa Hardrock realizes how little she knows about the life she's been living—and starts exploring her questions in a blog that unexpectedly goes viral.

Available from Paper Angel Press in
hardcover, trade paperback, digital, and audio editions
paperangelpress.com

Milton Keynes UK
Ingram Content Group UK Ltd.
UKHW052054300624
444882UK00001B/102